F

King of Swords

†

Book I in the Assassin series

Russell Blake

First Edition

ISBN: 978-1480170537

Published by

Reprobatio Limited

FOREWORD

King of Swords is a work of fiction. Any resemblance between the characters and real people, living or dead, is coincidental. Having said that, the backdrop and historical context of the novel is based in fact. The drug war in Mexico has been an ongoing confrontation between government forces and the ever-strengthening cartels – now the largest illegal drug trafficking network in the world, whose primary target market is the United States.

Thousands of police and soldiers have been killed over the last ten years, as the war has intensified due to a crackdown by pro-U.S. administrations. Cartel members slaughter one another by the thousands each year, as well as huge numbers of innocent bystanders. The brutality of the turf wars that are a constant and ongoing facet of the trade is stunning; well over a thousand children have been butchered during the last decade, as have countless family members of traffickers, killed in retribution or as a deterrent.

The last two Secretaries of the Interior for Mexico died in suspicious air crashes.

The Sinaloa cartel is real. The Knights Templar cartel is also real, as is the Gulf cartel, the Tijuana cartel, and Los Zetas cartel. New cartels pop up when the heads of the old groups die, and the names change with some frequency. The only constant is the bloodshed; the natural consequence of the economics of trafficking in an illegal substance that generates in excess of fifty billion dollars a year, wholesale, for the cartels in Mexico: a country where the average person makes a hundred and sixty dollars a month.

A DESCRIPTION of the TAROT CARD:

The King of Swords

In full regalia, the King of Swords sits proudly on his throne – with a long, upward-pointing, double-edged sword clutched in his right hand, and his left hand resting lightly on his lap. A ring adorns his left Saturn finger – representing power and commitment to responsibility. The King's blue tunic symbolizes a desire for spiritual enlightenment; his purple cape symbolizes empathy, compassion and intellect. The backrest of his throne is embellished with butterflies, signifying transformation, and crescent moons orbit around an angel situated by his left ear, positioned, perhaps, to lend a delicate guidance. The backdrop of the sky has very few clouds, signifying pragmatic mental clarity. The trees dotting the landscape stand still, with not a rustle – reflecting the King of Swords' stern judgment.

The King of Swords Reversed

The reversed King of Swords depicts a man who is ruthless or excessively judgmental; when reversed, the King of Swords suggests the misuse of mental power, authority and drive. The reversed King of Swords can represent manipulation and persuasion in order to achieve selfish ends. He is a very intelligent character who likes to demonstrate to others his superiority, either verbally or through actions. It is best to be wary of this type of person because, although he may be charming and intelligent, he is remorseless and can do only harm. He has only his personal interests in mind and will do whatever necessary to achieve those interests, even if it means destroying others.

INTRODUCTION

Three years ago, Pacific coast, Mexico

Armed men lined the perimeter of the large contemporary home on the secluded stretch of seashore just north of Punta Mita, twenty-three miles north of Puerto Vallarta. The stunning single-level example of modern Mexican architecture sat overlooking a cove, where the heavy surf from the Pacific Ocean flattened out over the shallow offshore reef a hundred yards from the beach. Nine-foot-high concrete walls ringed the compound, protecting the occupants from prying eyes and would-be intruders. Not that any were in evidence. The property and the coastline for a quarter mile in each direction belonged to the house's secretive owner – Julio Guzman Salazar, the Jalisco cartel's chief and the eighth richest man in Mexico, although his name didn't appear on any roster other than the government's most wanted list.

The building's Ricardo Legorreta design boasted thirty-eight thousand feet of interior space, with nine bedrooms in the main house, separate servants' quarters adjacent to the twelve car air-conditioned garage, a full sized movie theater with a floating floor, its own solar and wind power generation system, and a full time domestic staff of eleven. An Olympic-sized swimming pool with an infinity edge finished in indigo mirrored glass tile created the illusion of water spilling into the deep blue ocean.

The white cantera stone pool-area deck took on a pale cosmic glow as the last sliver of sun sank into the watery horizon, making way for the dark of a late-November night. The armed men encircling the house were hardened and efficient, exuding a palpable air of menace as they roamed the grounds, alert for threats. The security detail, which traveled with Salazar everywhere he went, consisted of eighteen seasoned mercenaries who were proficient with the assault rifles they held with nonchalant ease.

Motion detectors provided an early warning system outside of the walls, where infrared beams crisscrossed the expanse between the beach and the house, ensuring that nothing could penetrate the elaborate defenses undetected. Salazar could afford the best security money could buy, and his private army comprised not only Mexicans and Nicaraguans and Colombians, but also two South Africans and a Croatian. All had seen more than their share of combat, either of the civilian variety in the ongoing drug skirmishes between rival cartels, or in full-scale armed conflict in the Balkans or Africa.

At seven p.m. precisely, the bright halogen headlights of expensive vehicles began making their way down the long road from the coastal highway that connected Puerto Vallarta with Mazatlan, and through the enormous gates of the opulent home. Each car was allowed inside to drop off its passengers after undergoing scrutiny from the guards charged with Salazar's protection, who inspected the SUVs inside and out. During the next hour, seven Humvees and Escalades discharged their loads before pulling back out of the compound and parking in a brightly lit area designated for the purpose. Two armed gunmen patrolled the flat expanse, weapons cocked and loaded.

In the constant drug battles that were the norm on mainland Mexico, every minute held the possibility of instant death for those in the trade, and so the men on the security team were in a constant state of readiness for attack. Their vigilance had paid off many times over the past decade, when rival factions had attempted to challenge Salazar's stranglehold on the Jalisco trafficking corridor. He'd emerged victorious from that series of ever-escalating brutal engagements, the last of which had culminated in nineteen corpses beheaded or shot execution-style in Culiacan over a three month period.

The Sinaloa cartel was one of the most powerful in the world, and for some time had nurtured aspirations of expanding its lethal tentacles into Jalisco, the neighboring state to the south – Salazar's home turf. The Sinaloa cartel controlled much of the marijuana produced in Mexico and had grown to be the largest cocaine and heroin trafficking entity in the world, handling over seventy percent of all Colombian product that made it into the U.S. Salazar's operation was considerably smaller, but the brutality of his tactics made him a difficult adversary to encroach upon; after ten years of unsuccessful attempts to execute him, an uneasy truce now held sway.

The lush, planted areas of the compound were lavishly appointed. The beachside pool deck's verdant landscaping was circled with the flicker of tiki torches – placed there for the big event that was just getting underway. An eighteen-piece mariachi band in full regalia had assembled by the massive *palapa* over the hotel-sized outdoor pool bar. The musicians aired their traditional music for the guests, who were almost exclusively children and their mothers. It was Salazar's oldest son's seventh birthday; the party was an important event. Attendees had come from as far as Mexico City to honor Julio junior's big day. There was a giddy sense of privilege and wealth in the festivities – the boy had been presented with a pony, along with every imaginable video game and technological miracle a young man could wish for.

Clowns and acrobats japed and tumbled around the sidelines, performing astounding feats of dexterity and contortionism amid long bursts of yellow flame from a troupe of fire-breathers. Peals of adolescent laughter punctuated the melody of strumming guitars and blaring horns and violins, while the women circled the children's area clutching piña coladas and daiquiris in their lavishly bejeweled hands. All the guests knew one another – Salazar's social circle was small and exclusive.

Off to the side, Salazar and a handful of his closest male friends and associates stood beside a fifteen-foot-diameter fire pit, smoking Cuban cigars and drinking five-hundred dollar tequila from brandy snifters as they discussed business in hushed tones, occasionally glancing a watchful eye over their wives and offspring. Salazar was easily distinguished from the group due to his height and distinctive facial hair – he was barely five four, and sported a Lincolnic beard in the fashion that his father had affected until he'd died in a car crash when Salazar was nine years old.

Two female dancers in traditional folk garb approached the specially erected stage with a male dancer in the classic Mexican vaquero outfit, who executed a series of exhibition tricks with a lasso, dancing with the whirling rope to the delight of the assembled children. When he was finished, the trio remained on the stage. A spotlight flicked on. From a newly pitched tent adjacent to the pool, a man in a black suit emerged, flamboyantly brandishing a large sombrero. He bowed to the arc of enraptured kids before finally placing it onto the head of the birthday boy.

The crowd laughed and clapped in mutual surprise – this was one of Mexico's most beloved singers, popular for two decades before Salazar's son had been born. He swiveled and moved onto the performance area with a practiced ease and began singing one of his most famous ballads, a perennial favorite with young and old alike. The adults sang along and clapped, as did the children, who were captivated by the theatrical production numbers and the pomp of the event.

A small prop plane meandered along the coastline at an altitude of nine thousand feet, its lights extinguished, its radar off and its radio silent. The pilot held up a hand with two fingers extended, and then watching his digital timer, made a curt gesture, signaling to the man in the rear that it was time. The passenger, dressed head to toe in black and with a balaclava covering his face, nodded and gripped the lever of the sliding door on the fuselage's side, twisting it and forcing it open. He was instantly buffeted by a blast of warm air which tore at his clothes and burned his eyes, until he pulled a pair of night vision goggles into place and hurled himself into the dark, rushing void. The wind clawed at him as he tumbled through the night sky, the plane's droning engine inaudible over the howl of the wind. After counting to twenty, he pulled the handle of his specially configured parachute harness and whumped to a near halt, the straps straining at the arrest of his descent.

A black rectangular glider-parachute billowed above him as he manipulated it with two handles, until he quickly got his fall under control and directed himself at the glowing patch of coastline where the party would now be in full swing. He glanced at the luminous hands of his oversized military-blackened Panerai watch and smiled under the woolen mask. So far everything was going according to plan.

A few minutes later he could make out the flat roof of the main house, where three armed sentries watched the proceedings by the pool and scanned the beach for threats. He was now barely fifteen hundred feet above the compound. Even at that altitude, he could hear the music and singing, and make out the shrieks of glee from the children as they chased each other around the party tables to the bouncing melody of the band. As he'd hoped, the volume of the musicians drowned out any hint of flapping from his chute. The rooftop security men were engrossed with the show, so were unlikely to look up.

He connected the right control cable handle to a clasp on the harness, which made steering more difficult but was essential to momentarily freeing his hand. From a strap on his chest, he grappled with the grip of an MTAR-21 compact assault rifle: a small, evil-looking weapon with a silencer and flash suppressor. The gun was affixed to the harness with a three-foot nylon rope to prevent an inadvertent loss during the nocturnal descent. He groped until he felt the familiar pistol grip and trigger guard, and flipped the safety off. He was now two hundred feet above the roof at the far end of the house – the three sentries were still on the beach side of the roof, watching the entertainment and scanning the surf line.

When he was twenty yards above the men, his weapon belched three short bursts, catching all three guards unawares and ending their lives before they could register any surprise. His feet alighted on the waterproofed concrete surface next to them, and he immediately reeled in the chute, securing it in place with one of the guard's guns after shrugging out of the harness.

Eighty feet away, on the far end of the roof, a gathering of gulls stood with a black bird – a raven or crow – in their midst, silently observing the new arrival from the sky. A sound from below startled them, and the gulls scattered into the evening sky. The black bird remained, as if undecided, and then with a squawk also flung itself into the night.

The assassin stole his way, catlike, to the corner of the house nearest the beach and carefully unpacked the contents of his backpack, extracting two spare 32-round magazines for the gun, a black nylon rope with a grappling-hook, three grenades and four smoke grenades, a fiber optic scope on the end of a black aluminum telescoping rod, a heavily modified sniper rifle with a collapsible stock, a silencer and ten-round magazine for it, and a waterproof camera. He slipped one of the magazines into a pocket on the side of his pants, along with the camera, and turned his attention to the sniper weapon.

Inspecting the rifle and confirming it was intact, he drew several deep breaths, preparing himself for what was to come. He carefully threaded the silencer onto the barrel and unfolded the carbon-fiber stock, then inserted the magazine and silently eased back the precision-machined bolt, chambering a round. Ready now, he flipped the night vision headgear up and out of his line of sight and peered through the telescoping fiber optic lens at the festivities below. He quickly located the group of male guests and confirmed Salazar was among them. Satisfied that his quarry was in his kill zone, he surveyed the rest of the deck and spotted three security guards unobtrusively standing in the shadows at the base of the portable lighting towers that illuminated the party. Returning his attention to Salazar, he calculated the distance and the strength of the light breeze – not that it would make much difference on a shot that was no more than sixty yards; it was force of habit.

One of the fallen sentries' radios crackled as a coarse voice intruded, demanding a status report. He reached over and turned the volume down, then returned his focus to the celebration, this time peering over the edge of the roof through the scope of the rifle.

Salazar was gesturing at the famous singer like an orchestra conductor, singing along with him, obviously well on the road to inebriation, when the top of his head blew apart, speckling his entourage with bloody shards of bone and brains. He crumpled soundlessly, his limbs slack, dead before his brutalized head slammed against the ground. A second ticked by as the shocked group registered what had happened, even as the band continued playing, unaware that the party had just come to an abrupt end.

The farthest security guard lurched backwards, dropping his gun as he died, and then the screaming from the crowd began. The other two sentries swiveled around with weapons in hand, searching for assailants. A slug tore the second guard's throat out as it sheared through his spine, and the third guard's chest erupted blood even as he wheeled around to his fallen associate. Pandemonium reigned as the women ran crying towards the house with their terrified children in tow. The band fell silent and hurriedly made for cover behind the concrete pool bar, instruments clattering against the deck stone as they took flight.

A large exhibition light on the periphery exploded in a shower of sparks, then the other three quickly followed suit, and finally the spotlight shattered, leaving only the torch flames and a few indirect wall sconces on the house. Salazar's friends had rushed to their families and were herding them to safety inside, leaving the expansive pool deck empty save for the band and the trembling entertainers.

On the roof, the uninvited guest tossed the rifle onto a dead guard's chest and methodically lobbed the grenades over the front of the house, not looking to see where they landed, their detonations ample evidence they'd found a mark where the rest of the guards had been stationed. He raced back to the beach side of the roof, pulled the pins on the smoke grenades and threw them onto the right side of the pool deck, allowing the breeze to waft a dense fog over the area. Satisfied with the effect, he wedged the steel hook into the concrete roof lip and tossed the line down to the ground. He scanned the walkway that ran along the wall's edge to confirm there were no armed assailants immediately proximate, and swung his legs over the side, sliding down the rope to a flagstone, where he landed in a crouch.

From the plants at the side of the deck, the dead guards' radios crackled with panicked orders as he moved through the smoke to the fire pit, where Salazar's corpse lay sprawled face down on the white cantera in a pool of blood. He hauled on a shoulder and flipped the body onto its back, then fished in his pants for the tarot card that was his signature. Carefully balancing the image of a crowned man holding a sword on the cartel kingpin's mangled face, he took two pictures with the little camera before returning it to his pants pocket, then reached down and stuck the card in Salazar's gaping mouth so that he could be sure it wouldn't blow away during the ensuing action. Peering through the billowing clouds that largely obscured the house, he pulled the tab on his last smoke grenade and tossed it onto the sand, enveloping the beach with an impenetrable haze.

A hail of bullets tore a chunk of stone from the deck a few feet from him; he swiveled in a crouch and fired a few short bursts from his silenced assault rifle in the direction of the barking male voices. Another bullet ricocheted off the fire pit, signaling that it was time to make his departure. The surviving guards from the front of the house were closing in, and even he was reluctant to take on over a dozen armed men in a wide-open gunfight.

He unclipped a final grenade from his backpack chest strap and pulled the pin, flipping it roughly thirty feet towards the house, and then unclipped the MTAR-21, emptied the magazine in the direction of the approaching guards and tossed it aside, satisfied with the screams of pain from their direction. He wrenched the night vision goggles off his head and threw them as far as he could before turning to run for the beach. The grenade's concussion delivered yet another delay for his pursuers – the shrapnel from the explosion would stop any chase long enough for him to get a thirty second lead, which was all he needed. He sprinted to the water line across the luminescent sand and without hesitation dived into the mild surf, swimming energetically as he strained towards the mouth of the cove.

A beam of light played across the water from the beach, and he sensed bullets shredding through the waves around him as he plowed further from shore. Counting to himself, he swam submerged for twenty seconds at a time, coming up for gulps of air before plunging into the safety of the deep.

Once he was past the partially-submerged spit of land at the mouth of the cove he angled to the right, and within a few moments reached a slimy outcropping of rocks a hundred yards from the angry killers on the shore. He fumbled around in the dark until he found the smooth fiberglass side of the black jet ski he'd secured there the night before and hurriedly tore the camouflage fabric from its sleek hull and freed it from the barnacle-covered stones. The tide had risen to the point where the small watercraft slid easily onto the waves, and within seconds the engine fired and he tore off into the sea, jumping easily over the surf that roiled atop the reef line.

A few bursts of distant rifle fire chattered across the water but he was already out of range – the shooting was little more than a lament from the thwarted security. Savoring the adrenaline rush as he flew over the small swells at fifty miles per hour, he reached beneath his chin and pulled the soaking balaclava over his face, jettisoning it into the Pacific as he plotted a course south, where a vehicle waited on a lonely stretch of beach for his nocturnal arrival.

Tonight would be the stuff of legends, he knew. In a business where money flowed like water, he'd just pulled off the impossible in a spectacular and flamboyant manner. After this, he'd be able to command whatever fee he wanted, and there would be an international waiting list of eager clients. He'd left the card in Salazar's maw to seal the deal and continue to build his reputation. It had started years ago, as an idea he'd gotten from an article he'd read about the American war in the Middle East, where the kill squads assigned playing cards to each target they were hunting. He'd liked the idea, but had taken it one step further with a unique flourish. When he'd begun his career as contract killer, he'd made a point of leaving a tarot card with a depiction of the King of Swords on it – the significance of which was known only to him – and he'd adopted a nickname that now struck fear into the hearts of those he targeted.

King of Swords. *El Rey de Espadas*. Or as the press had taken to calling him, *El Rey*.

It might have been a little melodramatic, but nobody was laughing now that his legacy of impossible kills was the stuff of front page headlines. Not since the exploits of Carlos the Jackal had an assassin gained such notoriety, and he'd carefully selected the contracts he'd taken for maximum publicity value, in addition to the money. He'd quickly developed a reputation as a phantom, an invisible man – a contract arranged with him was as good as putting a bullet in the target's brain at the time the deal was negotiated.

El Rey was a star, a legend, and even his clients approached him with a certain trepidation when they required his services. These were generally men who butchered whole communities to make a point, but who deferred to *El Rey* out of respect.

He'd earned it the hard way, by taking the sanctions that were considered impossible and then delivering. In his circles, respect was won at the edge of a knife blade or the barrel of a gun. It was blood currency. And now, he could name his price. Tonight's logistics had cost him just under a hundred thousand dollars – the contract price had been two and a half million. Not a bad evening's work. But after this, his rate would start at four million and quickly increase from there, depending on the level of difficulty.

Off to his left, the lights of Punta Mita's expansive coastline sparkled in the overcast night. Some of the homes along that stretch of beach cost well over five million dollars, he knew. Rich *Gringos* and successful *narcotraficantes* were the only ones who could afford them, and with a little luck, soon he would be part of the elite that called the area home. But he'd need to do a few more jobs before he could hang up his tail and horns and call it quits, and he was in no hurry to retire. *El Rey* loved the adrenaline rush of the kill; the more planning involved and the greater the level of challenge, the better.

He glanced down at the dimly illuminated compass he'd mounted beneath the handles and made a small adjustment to his course, musing at the direction his life had taken as he sliced through the inky water, effortlessly making his escape into the warm tropical night.

PROLOGUE

Two years ago, Puebla, Mexico

The central square in downtown Puebla was typical of larger Mexican towns; a cultural hub for the community as well as a gathering place. Tourists from all over the country traveled to visit the cathedral adjacent to the square; the area was one of the most picturesque in the region. A steady procession of cars cruised around the city center, although traffic was kind in the early afternoon. A light breeze rustled through the trees that sheltered picnickers from the harsh sunlight as they languished on the freshly trimmed grass, the faint aroma of delectables from the nearby restaurants wafting across the common like a gastronomic siren song.

Rosa sat at one of the quaint cafés with her daughter, Cassandra, eating fresh fruit sorbet. It was summer, so school was out, and they were visiting Rosa's parents for a week – a refreshing break from the press of humanity in Mexico City, which was among the largest cities in the world, and the place she reluctantly called home.

The weather was hot, but not punishingly so, and free from the oppressive pollution that hung like a blanket over the valley where Mexico City resided. Some of the air quality problems were a function of geography, and some were due to the virtual absence of any emission control on cars until recently. The capital of Mexico was surrounded by hills, which prevented the thermal layer of un-breathable toxins from dispersing. It was one of nature's cruel tricks that so many people lived in an area where breathing the air was the equivalent of smoking a pack of cigarettes a day.

She wished that they could move, maybe to Guadalajara, where the weather was usually nice and the verdant region of Lake Chapala was little more than an hour away, but her husband's job wouldn't allow for that. She hated that they were locked into living in their little three bedroom row house in Toluca, near the airport, in a neighborhood that seemed chronically victimized by crime; but life wasn't always fair or easy and they were doing the best they could.

Rosa had a decent career as an insurance agent for her own small agency, and between her income and her husband's they did as well as they could expect, but sometimes she was affected by a sense of melancholy, especially as she watched her eight-year-old daughter growing up in less than ideal conditions. Cassandra had been a kind of miracle; Rosa's doctor had convinced her that she would never be able to carry a baby to term due to a host of chronic immuno-deficiencies, but a strong faith in God and skilled care at the hospital had brought Cassandra howling into the world, where she'd been Rosa's pride and joy ever since.

Glancing at her daughter, Rosa brushed Cassandra's hair out of her eyes, and using a corner of her napkin, wiped away a smudge of strawberry from the little girl's upturned lips. Cassandra – Cass – gave Rosa a look of embarrassment and hastily rubbed her forearm across her face. Rosa smiled at the gesture. That was another way to do it, she supposed.

A policeman on patrol tipped his cap to the pair as he strolled by; she returned his smile out of courtesy. A striking example of classical Mexican beauty, with flashing eyes the color of espresso and black hair that shimmered like silk against her *café-au-lait*-complexioned skin, she was accustomed to admiring attention from men, even though she'd long ago pledged her heart and soul to her husband – the love of her life.

Cass had inherited her stunning features, but with an unexpected twist of dirty blond hair – a testament to her father's partial German lineage several generations back. Even now, barely an adolescent, she was a gorgeous child, and Rosa knew she was destined to break hearts when she blossomed. It was not out of the question that she could be a model once she hit her teens; a few of Rosa's friends had already said as much.

As they watched the cars go by and the kids playing on the square, both mother and daughter felt happy to be relaxed in a place that was safe and relatively unspoiled. They'd just finished lunch at a small restaurant at the base of one of the old hotels facing the church, enjoying the best chicken Mole Poblano Rosa had tasted in years. Mole sauce was more of an art than a recipe, and each region had its own take on the dish. In Puebla, the sauce was nearly black, as thick as liquid tar, redolent of chocolate and clove and thirty-something other spices and ingredients. It was a rich and heady dish, and few restaurants could pull it off as well as the one they'd dined at. Puebla was one of the Meccas of Mexican culinary accomplishment, and Mole Poblano was a signature Pueblan specialty.

Cass had busied herself naming the pigeons that paraded and strutted across the street in the square, and one particularly unctuous example of male avian belligerence had captured her attention. She'd announced to Rosa that his name was *El Guero* – the pale one. The bird was almost blindingly white and had a remarkable presence; a swagger in each step and with chest puffed out, he fanned his wings and tail feathers in a display of mating finery. The smaller gray females were clearly impressed with his moves, as was Cass. Back and forth he swooped, cooing loudly as he pranced, the bird king of the Puebla park holding court for his admiring subjects.

Finished with their post-prandial treat, mother and daughter left the vicinity of the square and made their way to the parking lot where they'd left their car – a Peugeot that had never seemed to run correctly since the day they'd bought it new, on payments that amounted to twenty percent annual interest. Rosa hated the little blue beast, and was counting the days until it was paid for so they could sell it and get something more reliable.

Two blocks from the square, an ivory Ford Expedition pulled to the curb beside them, and two men who had been following a few yards behind abruptly grabbed the pair and forced them towards the rear door. Rosa screamed, as did Cassandra, who also kicked and tried to bite her assailant's arm. One of the men punched Rosa hard enough to break her nose in an effort to stop the yelling, before he manhandled her to the vehicle. There was sparse pedestrian traffic on the sidewalk, but the few people who saw the altercation stopped walking, frozen in place. Kidnappings were an unfortunate and all too regular feature of some larger Mexican cities, and the armed gangs that specialized in it were not to be trifled with. Shootouts were not uncommon, because those drawn to the profession were typically violent and desperate, with nothing much to lose.

The man who had punched Rosa pinned her on the rear seat while the other man lifted the struggling, screaming Cassandra and stuffed her next to her mother. One kidnapper got in back with the pair; the other climbed into the front passenger seat. The truck roared off down the street in a cloud of exhaust and a squealing of tires. It had no license plate, a not particularly rare occurrence for those who didn't want to pay registration fees, so there were no immediately identifying marks other than a description of a large white Ford SUV.

The man in the rear seat slapped duct tape over Cassandra's mouth, then reached over and did the same with Rosa. The abductor in the passenger seat trained a pistol on Rosa's head, convincing her quickly that creating further havoc could be a fatal miscalculation. Cassandra sobbed into the tape, terrified of what was happening and what was likely to come.

Twenty-five minutes after being snatched off the street in broad daylight, their assailants threw Rosa and Cassandra down a flight of stairs into a basement with a filthy mattress and a broken sewer line evacuating into one of the corners. The stink was overpowering, and once the tape had been torn from their mouths, Cassandra vomited all over herself, infuriating the four men who descended the stone stairs a few minutes later. The largest of them slammed her against the far wall and issued angry instructions to one of his subordinates, who quickly returned with a hose from the garden immediately outside the basement entrance.

Rosa attempted to shield her daughter, but the large man grabbed her by the hair and punched Rosa in the stomach, knocking the wind out of her and crippling her with pain. She collapsed on the floor, helpless, and two of the men alternated kicking her with their pointy-toed cowboy boots. After a few blows, she mercifully slipped into unconsciousness. Even so, the men continued to rain kicks on her until they tired of the sport and turned their attention to the young girl.

A stream of cold water struck Cassandra in the face. The men laughed as she screamed in fear and rage at the shock, as well as the vision of her mother's inert form in the filth on the dank basement floor. Once the vomit had rinsed clean, the large man approached her huddled shape as she shivered, soaked and terrified, and tore her dress off, ripping the thin fabric as though it was tissue. Grunting, he lifted her like a rag doll and threw her onto the stained mattress. Stunned, she cried in panicked horror as the men circled her in preparation for the afternoon's diversion. The large man fumbled with his belt, and the others smiled in anticipation as Cassandra's unholy shrieks reverberated off the uncaring walls of her private hell.

Two days later, a package arrived at Rosa's husband's work with his name written carefully on the label in black felt pen, with a return address in Puebla – that of Rosa's parents. A local courier brought the box in and the receptionist signed for it, then instructed the mail boy to take it to his office, where he was preparing for a staff meeting with his immediate subordinates.

No one working that day would ever forget the screams of horror and grief that emanated from his office when he opened the special delivery. Inside, wrapped in plastic and surrounded by crushed newspaper, were Cassandra's and Rosa's heads, neatly severed at the third cervical vertebra, with their eyes crudely sewn shut. Each had the brand of a scorpion seared into their foreheads, and the tail of a scorpion protruded from their mouths, where the predatory arthropods had been lodged as calling cards.

෨෴

Four months ago, Durango, Mexico

The crowd broke into a rousing cheer as Hector De La Silva took the podium at the rally. Long one of the more popular governors in Mexican history, his term had passed without him seeking re-election – his aspirations for the presidency as the likely successor to Mexico's highest office quite obvious. He'd already begun the convoluted and colorful campaigning that made Mexican elections something of a spectacle – the fiery rhetoric and accusations vivid and damning, the promises lofty and inspiring. Nobody actually believed anything the candidates said – history had shown that no matter who was in power, the campaign promises were immediately forgotten as soon as the voting was over, but the process was celebrated for the showmanship and sense of theater.

Hector, or *'El Gallo'* as he was known – the rooster – was in his element; a consummate performer from decades of holding political office, he knew how to play to a crowd like a virtuoso. He was famous for slamming his forehead into the podium when his speech reached its climax, underscoring the sacrifice he was prepared to make on behalf of his constituency – the head-banging routine was now as popular and expected as the flip off the top rope in the Mexican wrestling matches: the *Lucha Libre*, where masked wrestlers-cum-gymnasts performed amazing feats of physical dexterity as they pretended to fight each other. Nobody believed that was real, either, and yet it was hugely popular, trailing only soccer for entertainment value.

The assembled spectators waited in quivering anticipation as *El Gallo* mounted the stage, clad in an everyman rancher's shirt and sporting a cowboy hat. This was a man of the people, a member of the masses, he assured them, even as his four hundred dollar ostrich-skin boots gleamed in the sunlight. Never mind that his brothers were among the wealthiest landowners in the region, or that his father had been a household name in building low-income housing. Forget all that, his demeanor seemed to demand. Here was a humble, simple man, who reluctantly would shoulder the considerable burden of steering the nation back onto the path of righteousness, having somewhat lost its way – though certainly not because of the actions of his political party, which was also the current president's. No, the country was in mortal peril because of a crisis in morality, exemplified by the surge in popularity and power of the drug cartels.

He cleared his throat and began to speak, a deep baritone long bent to the artifice of holding an audience's attention, well modulated, passion and intensity obvious in every syllable without any evidence of stridency. This was a man's man, a visionary, a leader capable of finally, after centuries of oppression, delivering to the Mexican people the promise of their legacy.

"Look at the prosperity Mexico has enjoyed over the last few years. Under the party's leadership, a new, burgeoning middle class has been created, and poverty has been eradicated in many of its most pervasive forms. Our economy is the eleventh largest in the world, strong and resilient, like the Mexican people, who have triumphed in the face of adversity and built a better future for our children!" *El Gallo* proclaimed, emphasizing points by stabbing at the air with his hat.

The crowd burst into well-choreographed spontaneous applause, led by party agitators who were in attendance to galvanize cheering at the appropriate points. The television cameras tracked over the thronged celebrants – one could hardly watch the outpouring of enthusiasm without being moved.

"I love my children, and I have taught them to love God, and Mexico. I like to think I've shown them the difference between right and wrong, between good and evil, between a road with promise and one that leads to purgatory. Children are the country's future, and so we must do everything in our power to build a safe environment where they can excel. They shouldn't have to worry about drug cartels shooting up the streets, or pushing their poison in our schools. We cannot give in to their terrorism.

Not because it's the right thing to do. Not because it's the easy thing to do. But because of the children. We must do what it takes, for the children, for Mexico's bountiful harvest of talent and hope!"

A hunched figure adjusted the tripod of the high velocity rifle, watching as the oration hit full stride and the gathering of citizens applauded again. The actual words were lost on him because he was behind the speakers, in the tower of the church five hundred yards from the optimistic assembly. He was invisible to the security forces in place around the rally, the rifle recessed in one of the small rectangular openings of the tower's pinnacle.

The gunman watched the red balloons that framed the stage for clues as to the amount and direction of any wind. He was in luck. The late spring gusts were nowhere in evidence. It would be an easy shot.

He was startled by a car backfiring on the road below. Several security men ran in the direction of the percussive blast, accompanied by six soldiers. They watched as an ancient farm truck rolled down the street, straining under its load of hay. At the next intersection, the engine backfired again; the group of gunmen exchanged relieved looks, laughing with merriment at their defense of *El Gallo* from a poorly tuned V8. The sentries returned to their positions as the great man continued to paint his verbose vision of a bright new future.

A crow landed on the balustrade of the tower and fixed the man with its beady stare. For a reason he couldn't define, he was momentary chilled; the hair on his arms standing erect. He wasn't a believer in omens or symbols, but lurking somewhere in his schooldays the crow was deemed a foreteller of bad luck. An impression from his past nagged at him, tried to surface, but he shrugged it off – he didn't have time to waste on being spooked by a bird. The man grinned at his own imagination – allowing a crow to throw him. It would be a day of bad luck, all right, but not for him.

The crow bobbed its head several times, then pecked at the stone it was standing on before giving up on its project and flying away.

He reached into his pants pocket and extracted a pair of dense foam earplugs before setting them in front of him, along with a digital watch displaying the time. He had thirty seconds. Checking to ensure that everything was in place, he compressed the plugs and inserted one into each ear before returning his attention to the florid man pontificating on the stage. He seemed to be reaching a crescendo, and the gunman couldn't help but smile again. This was going to be a funny one, if there ever had been. He couldn't wait to see the papers tomorrow.

El Gallo was building his intensity, railing against the cartels as the embodiment of Satan crawling over the planet in human form. The words were powerful, and the emotions high as his voice increased in volume.

"These scum are a cancer on the body of the state; they are toxic purveyors of poison and suffering. They accommodate the demands of the rich *Gringos*, who buy their products even as their own country collapses from the weight of its own excesses. They have turned Mexico into their whore, and its children into their slaves. We suffer so that pimps and rich socialites can snort the devil's dandruff during their orgies. I would send a message to these traitors who suckle at the tit of the false god to the north. I would send a telegram. The message is, no longer will we be your burros or your lapdogs. No more will you use our blood to lubricate your war machine. We are Mexican, and we are tired of being the back yard where you dump your problems, where you come to turn our daughters into prostitutes and our sons into groveling peasants. Your time is over, and we will now reclaim the bounty that is our birthright! We are strong and proud. And most of all, we are Mexican. We are family – and we will be free!"

The bells of the church began ringing, announcing the arrival of the noon hour, and *El Gallo*, in fever pitch, slammed his head forward onto the podium in his now-famous trademark move. The crowd burst into a spirited and hearty applause.

It was only when he slumped to the floor with blood spreading over the back of his hand-stitched white silk cowboy shirt that the screaming began.

The young novitiate moved with easy determination to the doors of the church as the pealing of the bells trumpeted God's grace and presence in everyday life. An ancient woman crossed herself as he passed, her weathered face momentarily glowing with a devoted smile. He turned when he reached the door and genuflected, his cassock brushing the ground as he crossed himself before the vision of an unfortunate savior crucified so that humanity could be saved, movingly depicted in the statue that dominated the wall above the altar. The sun streaked through the elaborate stained glass windows over the door, bathing the interior in a dazzling multicolored glow; the nearly empty chamber radiated a tranquility that was regrettably absent from the cruel world just outside the doors.

With bible in hand, and fingering his rosary, he exited the house of worship and crossed the street; a pious man on a mission to save the world.

Twenty minutes later, the bodyguards and soldiers crept up the stairs to the tower top, guns at the ready as they strained their ears for any hint of threat. The huge bells had fallen silent, and the only sound besides the scream of the sirens from the square across the wide boulevard was the cooing of amorous doves taking refuge in the tower rafters.

The leader of the team held up a hand in warning when he spotted the rifle, still on the tripod, a single spent shell casing lying by its side. He grudgingly inched towards it; the blood drained from his face as he saw the item held in place by the votive candle.

The stern countenance of the highly-stylized rendering of the royal presence seemed to sneer at the intruders, the brandished sword proclaiming to one and all the regal superiority of the seated man.

He approached the card as if in a trance, then reached down and retrieved the tattered rectangle, holding it up for his men to see.

The King of Swords had struck again.

CHAPTER 1

April 18 – 6:15 a.m., Mexico City, Mexico

The concrete walls of the industrial building on the outskirts of the city were painted a garish orange, the roll-up steel doors clashing navy blue with a coat of high-gloss enamel. The large parking area was empty except for three Cadillac Escalades – an unusual sight in the neighborhood, which ran more to dirt roads and twenty-year-old Dodge trucks. The surrounding buildings were the dingy gray of unpainted cinder block, with rusting rebar sticking out of the roofs where the builders hadn't bothered cutting off the steel from the support beams. Graffiti covered almost every area; the raw odor of garbage and filth pervaded the run-down outpost.

The Mexico City skyline shimmered in the distance; tall buildings thrusting angrily to the heavens, into the perennial layer of brown pollution that hung over the valley. A rooster crowed its welcome to the first rays of dawn. Two scavenging dogs trotted from building to building, their emaciated forms a testament to the pickings to be had. In the near distance, a shanty town of rough tarpaper walls with tarps or corrugated steel roofs emitted a sour stench, while here and there the sorry structures belched smoke into the air from early morning wood fires stoked up to cook the day's sustenance.

A small mirror on the end of a rod eased out from around the corner of one of the neighboring buildings, enabling the Federal Police officer manipulating it to watch the orange structure without having to duck his head into view. Seeing nothing, he made a series of short hand movements to the group of thirty heavily armed commandos behind him. This was the armed conflict team that consisted of the most battle-hardened members of the Federal Police force, who specialized in urban assaults, usually with backup from the army or the navy. All the officers had been marines, and

19

all had been in numerous armed engagements with the *narcotraficante* armies that were the scourge of mainland Mexico.

The men ran towards their orange objective, crouched low so as to present less of a target. The commander's radio crackled with confirmation that another group of similarly equipped police commandos had the rear of the building covered, as well as the flanks. He checked his watch, then pushed the button that would start the stopwatch function before making another series of hand signals to indicate they were going in.

Three of the officers carried a heavy steel battering ram with handles on it to knock down the front door in seconds; each of the windows had two officers framing the glass, ready to fire through it or take out anyone who tried shooting from inside. The commander made a fist, and the iron projectile drove the steel door into the building, knocking it off its hinges. Eight of the men entered, with more ready to follow. The distinctive popping-chatter of Kalashnikov assault rifles began echoing around the large warehouse, quickly answered by the more sonorous burst-firing of the M16 assault rifles the police favored.

Even though the *Federales* had the overwhelming majority odds due to sheer numbers, their adversaries inside the building continued the firefight until they'd exhausted their ammunition. When the shooting eventually petered out, the surviving drug dealer tossed his pistol away and raised his arms over his head, having already jettisoned his empty assault rifle.

The final tally was four civilians killed and five police, with three more officers seriously wounded – in spite of their body armor and precautions. The leader of the team moved to the surrendering shooter and slammed him across the face with his rifle butt, then, reaching around his equipment belt, retrieved a set of blackened steel handcuffs. He ordered the bleeding man to lie on his stomach and slapped them around his wrists. Two other officers dragged him to his feet, past the fallen bodies of his entourage, out to the waiting police van.

A tall, athletically proportioned man in his early forties, wearing the distinctive blue uniform of the Mexican Federal Police, ran a hand through his thick, slightly graying hair and let forth an exasperated sigh. Captain Romero Cruz circled the object of his attention, a seated man shackled to a metal chair bolted to the floor in the center of the room. A solitary hundred watt incandescent bulb hung from the ceiling, providing meager but adequate illumination for the interrogation cell. The captive was a high-ranking member of the Knights Templar cartel – close allies with the Sinaloa cartel. This man, Jorge Rodriguez Santiago, was rumored to be a confidante of the Sinaloans, which made him doubly valuable to Captain Cruz. Santiago had been the sole survivor of that morning's bloody firefight; a surprise capture who normally would have been holed up in Michoacan, where his brutal gang ruled with an iron fist.

Santiago glared at Captain Cruz, blinking away the sweat and blood that trickled from his hairline into his eyes. The look conveyed an almost demonic hatred, and an arrogance born by the knowledge that no prison in Mexico would be able to hold him for long. Cartel chieftains tended to escape with astounding frequency, no doubt due to the abundance of money at their disposal to lubricate the system.

This was not the first time Santiago had been arrested under serious circumstances, so for him, it was merely an annoying interruption to his lucrative criminal career. The last time the case hadn't even gone to trial; the judge miraculously ruling that the prosecution had failed to make an adequate case. That had been a blow for the *Federales*, and was among the judge's last decisions before he retired to a hilltop compound in Costa Rica, to live out his days with a nineteen-year-old soul-mate who had a nose for stimulants, as well as an apparent affinity with vastly older men.

Santiago began spewing vitriol about what would happen to every member of the force who had participated in his arrest. Cruz stepped forward with surprising speed and backhanded him – a dismissive slap – more an insult than a rebuke.

"You're going to regret this, you bitch–" Santiago spat.

Since the slap hadn't gotten the message across, Cruz punched him in the jaw – it was he who would do the talking, and Santiago would answer the questions put to him, only speaking when told to.

Cruz blew on his reddened knuckles, the skin abraded by the prisoner's coarse stubble. He motioned to the other man in the room, his lieutenant, Fernando Briones, to bring him the nightstick that lay on a table in a corner of the room. Briones, a compact pit bull with skin the color of brandy, obliged.

Santiago spat a bloody lump onto the floor, then grinned at the captain, displaying a mouthful of gold-capped teeth, with an incisor now conspicuously missing.

"You hit like a pussy, you *marecon*," Santiago sneered.

Cruz slammed the wooden club into the side of the captive's head; his ear began streaming blood as it swelled from the blow. Santiago appeared momentarily dazed, and for once didn't have an insulting comeback.

That was more like it.

Captain Cruz glanced at Lieutenant Briones and made a gesture with two fingers. Briones fumbled in his uniform shirt's pocket and fished out a packet of cigarettes, offering one to Cruz. He took it, and Briones lit it for him with a disposable butane lighter. He inhaled the smoke with evident satisfaction, and then blew a stream of nicotine into Santiago's tearing eyes.

"These are good. What are they? Cuban?" Cruz asked.

"Argentine," Briones told him, holding up the pack so Cruz could see it. "*Parisienne*. They're made with black tobacco – they don't have all the impurities the American brands do. They're supposedly better for you. They taste better to me, so who knows…"

"Imagine that. Cigarettes that are good for you. What will they think of next?" Cruz sighed mild bemusement, and then approached Santiago. "So, you shit-bird, do you like cigarettes? Is that something you like to put in your mouth when you don't have a burro cock in it?" He puffed a few times, ensuring that the cigarette tip was glowing red, then held the ember against Santiago's neck. The sickeningly sweet smell of searing flesh was a small price to pay for the shriek of blind pain and fury that burst from the warlord. Now they were getting somewhere.

"You see, you piece of shit, you're not so tough. You're a big man when you have a bunch of your boyfriends around with guns, but alone, you're nothing. Listen to you, blubbering like a baby. I bet you'd give me a blowjob right now for a piece of ice to cool the burn, am I right?" Cruz asked conversationally.

Santiago struggled against the restraints holding his wrists, tearing flesh in the process. Blood dripped deep crimson from the black metal cuffs.

"So now you're starting to figure this out." Cruz paced around Santiago while he talked. "I can do anything I want to you. Anything. You have no power here. I am judgment day for you – I'm God and the devil rolled into one, and you *will* tell me what I want to know. I actually hope you hold out and this takes a while, *puta*. I'm going to enjoy inflicting every morsel of misery I can on your worthless carcass." Cruz paused, blowing a few lazy smoke rings. "Two of the men who died this morning were my friends. I'm sure they experienced considerable pain before they passed on, so I look at this as payback on their behalf. If I have my way, before this is done you'll be begging me to kill you. You'll cry, and you'll tell me things I didn't even ask about just to get me to stop. And I'll savor every minute of it. In fact, I'll think up new and creative ways to cause you so much pain that you'd stab your mother to death with a crucifix to make it stop. Part of me really hopes you make me do this the hard way."

Santiago glared at Cruz, his fury palpable. "I want to see my lawyer," he hissed.

Cruz nonchalantly swatted him on the other side of the head with the nightstick, the impact making a dull *thunk* against his skull. He struck him on the upper arms a few times, for good measure.

"I'm your lawyer. And I say case closed, you lose. Now I'm going to ask a few questions, and then you're going to answer them, or I'm going to make you wish you'd never been born. You want to try me on that? What's that line from the Clint Eastwood movie? Do you feel lucky?"

"I'm not saying anything."

Cruz took a final puff on his cigarette and then applied it to Santiago's neck again, generating a bloodcurdling howl of agony.

"Well, I don't believe that. I think you will. In fact, I'm betting on it. So here's my first, simple question. Where's Carlos Aranas hiding these days?" Cruz asked.

Aranas, or '*El Lobo*', was the absolute boss of the Sinaloa cartel, and the object of Cruz's investigation into the latest string of grisly drug-related slayings in Mexico City. Cruz was a special type of cop, the Mexican equivalent of the top echelon of Homeland Security in the United States, and he'd been given virtually unlimited latitude by the president himself to do whatever it took to bring the cartels, whose violence was terrorizing the country, under control. Cruz headed up an autonomous task force that was working its way up the food chain until it got to the chiefs of the various cartels – the Knights Templar cartel, the Tijuana cartel, the Gulf cartel, a host of others; and the most powerful and dangerous – the Sinaloa cartel.

Cruz had earned his role by being tough, extremely smart, relentless, and incorruptible. A combination that was rare anywhere in the world, but in Mexico, virtually unheard of. For Cruz, bringing down the cartels wasn't so much an occupation as a religious cause, and his life's exclusive focus.

And the biggest fish in that particular polluted pond was Aranas, whose savagery was legendary; a fact Cruz knew firsthand.

"Come on, Santiago. Where's *El Lobo* hanging his hat?" Cruz asked again.

"You must be crazy if you think I'm going to talk to you. Give up *El Lobo?* You're insane," Santiago said.

"That's right. I am. And if you don't give me what I want, you're going to find out exactly how dangerous a crazy man can be, especially when he has your testicles in his hand, like I do yours. So talk," Cruz insisted.

"Fuck you."

Cruz sighed again and nodded at Lieutenant Briones, who burrowed around in a rucksack before extracting a two-foot-long tube with a pair of electrodes on one end and a handle on the other. A cable ran from the evil-looking implement to a metal box with a dial, which Briones dutifully plugged into the wall. Cruz held up the wand and inspected the electrodes with a grim smile.

"Do you know what this is? We got this from some Guatemalans who were operating a kidnapping and torture ring. This is a *picana* – or as you'll soon think of it, your worst living nightmare. It delivers a high voltage electric shock, but with low current. Since you probably didn't pay much attention in school, that means it's excruciatingly painful, but won't leave a mark, so it can be used for hours without leaving any trace. I've heard about these, but never actually used one." Cruz brandished it like an épée. "I've been saving it for when I captured one of the Sinaloa cartel captains, but you know what? I'll make an exception today, seeing as I'm in a good mood, and you'll be the first I use it on. Now the question is, do we start with the genitals, or maybe go with the less tender areas as a warm-up? I don't want to see your miserable tiny prick if I don't have to, so I'm thinking we start on your neck, and work down," Cruz explained dispassionately.

Santiago's eyes flared wide with terror.

"Oh, I see you might be familiar with it? Why am I not surprised? I'll bet you never thought you'd have one used on you, though, huh, tough guy? Today's just full of surprises, isn't it?"

Cruz walked over to the table, picked up a bottle and returned to Santiago. He poured a few drops of water onto the prisoner's neck, just above the blistering from the cigarette burns. Santiago shook his head, trying in vain to avoid the stream, further tearing his wrist skin.

"The water increases the conductivity, for maximum effect. Now, one more time, and then this gets uglier than you can imagine. Where is *El Lobo*?"

"Cornholing your mother."

Cruz looked at his lieutenant and laughed, a dry sound devoid of amusement. "We have a comedian. That's very funny stuff. Hold that thought for a minute." He glanced at Briones. "Lieutenant, give me about half the maximum voltage to start, and let's see how the funny man reacts," Cruz instructed. "Bring that rag over here and help me stuff it in his mouth. We don't want our esteemed guest biting his tongue off and spoiling the party."

Briones tossed the rag to Cruz and approached Santiago from behind. He clamped his hands on either side of Santiago's head, grinding his thumb into a pressure point just below the ear to force his jaw open. Cruz jammed the rag in and hurriedly pulled his hand away lest Santiago bite him. He stepped back, regarding the result with professional satisfaction.

Briones stationed himself by the rheostat and waited for a signal. Cruz nodded.

The lieutenant hunched over the box and turned the dial halfway up. The rod emitted a faint hum.

"You might want to plug your ears, Lieutenant. I have a feeling our boy here is going to be crying like a bitch kitty in a second," Cruz said. He applied the rod tip to Santiago's neck.

The reaction was immediate. Santiago's entire body stiffened, his eyes bugged out, and his face turned beet red as his stifled shrieks penetrated the rag. Cruz studied Santiago impassively as he flayed and convulsed for ten seconds, then he disengaged the *picana*.

Cruz made a gesture with the device, and Briones pulled the rag from Santiago's mouth, who greedily gulped air as though he'd been drowning.

"Give me something, Santiago. Or I can do this all day. In fact, you know what? I bet I could charge admission to the families of the cops you killed this morning; make money allowing them to use it on you, if I get tired. Remember, I'm authorized by the president to do whatever it takes to get information, so there's no way out of this for you."

"You…you are so screwed," Santiago hissed through swollen lips. "You don't even know it. And your president? He's a dead man."

Cruz shrugged, and Briones returned the rag to Santiago's mouth and then cranked the knob again. Cruz held the wand to Santiago's neck, this time for twenty seconds.

Briones cut the current and removed the rag.

"Oh, look, what a shame. The big brave drug lord pissed his pants like a little schoolgirl. Hey, pissy pants, are we having fun yet?" Cruz taunted.

"Your brat pissed hers before I did her," Santiago growled, spitting blood at him.

"What did you say?" Cruz's eyes narrowed to slits.

"You heard me. She was pretty good for a five year old, or whatever she was. I think she kind of liked it when I had my boys go at her, too. Shame she lost her head. I could have trained her to be really—"

Cruz dropped the *picana* and pummeled Santiago's face with his fists. Briones grabbed his arms from behind and dragged him away, but not before he'd inflicted considerable damage. Santiago was now bleeding freely from cuts on his cheek and a newly broken nose; a bloodshot eye was swollen half closed. Cruz stood panting his anger out until he regained enough control for Briones to release him.

Santiago raised his head.

"Tell the president I had a hand in having him killed, will you?" he spat.

"What are you talking about? You're nothing. An insect. You have nothing, and you'll rot in prison until you die. You, kill the president? You're a urine-soaked piece of shit, nothing more," Cruz growled, barely containing his rage.

"You remember that when *El Rey* takes him and his American master out. I'll be watching it on TV. That's a day people will remember for a lifetime."

"You think these puny lies will buy you bargaining power? You're mistaken. It's pure bullshit. And it's not going to work."

"Remember you said that when your ass-licking president is lying dead with the *Gringo* dog. Remember how smart you were." Santiago fixed Cruz with his good eye. "And remember when your little baby was on her hands and knees, begging for me to give it to her, like your stinking whore wife did, and I—"

Cruz cranked the control box to maximum and took two steps towards Santiago, jamming the prod into his soaking crotch.

Santiago convulsed and screamed so horrifically that Briones was momentarily frozen in place. As Santiago convulsed, smoke began to rise from where the prod was in contact with his wet pants. Briones raced to shut off the current, and Santiago slumped over, unconscious.

Cruz spat on Santiago, and then handed the *picana* back to Briones, who averted his gaze.

"Let's take a break for an hour and let this fecal speck stew in his filth. Maybe he'll get more talkative now that he sees what I'm capable of," Cruz said, checking his watch and straightening his uniform before moving to the door. "I'll see you back here at five. Grab something to eat. This could be a long night."

Briones' eyes stayed glued to the floor, and he didn't respond.

"Hey. Lieutenant. These are the bad guys. They killed a bunch of cops this morning, and this one claims he raped and killed my wife and daughter. This is an animal. Nothing but an animal...," Cruz said.

Briones slowly raised his head and met his stare. "He's probably lying about your daughter, sir. The story is well known. He used it to bait you, to get a reaction—"

"It worked then, huh? I'll bet he thinks twice about doing it again. Go get something to eat. We need to keep at him until he breaks. And he will break. Make no mistake about that," Cruz assured him.

"Yes, sir."

Cruz knocked twice on the door in a distinctive pattern; it swung open, unlocked from the exterior. Two beefy police officers stood outside, guarding the room. These were men fiercely loyal to Cruz – men he trusted with his life. One of them handed Cruz back his service pistol, which he holstered.

Cruz instructed them not to allow anyone into the cell while he was gone, then marched down the dank yellow hall, past two more armed federal police officers, to the scarred double doors of the industrial steel elevator. He punched the button and stood waiting as Briones joined him.

"I'm sorry if I seemed to lose it, Lieutenant. It was momentary. It's been a long day, and I think I'm tired from the assault this morning." Cruz stabbed at the button again, impatiently. "You were right. I gave the prick exactly what he wanted – a reaction. Learn from that. Always keep your emotions out of the job," Cruz softly advised the younger man.

"I think I would have shot him," Briones admitted.

"That's why we don't allow guns in the room." Cruz turned his head and studied the lieutenant's profile. "Are you sure you're up for this? I can arrange a replacement if you'd rather sit it out. I won't think any less of you – this is a tough assignment, and this part isn't for everyone."

"No, sir. I was also friends with several of the men who were killed today. I would want the same if one of these scumbags killed me. It's the least I can do…to help you with this."

"Good man. I'll see you in an hour. I'm going to my office to start a report."

"Do you…sir, no disrespect, but do you think there's any truth in what he was saying about the president – and the U.S. president? He sounded pretty cocky for a man in his position," Briones ventured.

"That's why I want to write it up. I don't know what to think right now, but these bastards have turned the country into a killing field wherever they go, so I wouldn't put anything past them. I want to capture exactly what he said while it's fresh in my mind. We can investigate later. But yes, I'm taking it seriously. I agree he seemed sure of himself, and that's troubling."

"And he mentioned *El Rey*," Briones underscored.

"I know. Then again, that's like mentioning the boogieman. So it may mean something, or nothing. But either way, I'll record it, and once we're done with him, add it to the pile of things to do," Cruz concluded.

The elevator finally arrived, and the two men stepped aboard. They rode up two floors to the ground level in stony silence, each lost in his own thoughts. Briones exited and proceeded purposefully to the security area that led to the outside world, while Cruz continued to the fifth, where his task force occupied the entire floor.

His mind flitted back to the day, two years prior, when he'd opened the container and seen his life crumble around him, his beloved family brutally butchered to send him a message. He pursed his lips and forced the images and emotions back into the ugly little box where he kept them hidden away and closed the door on that line of thought. He would extract revenge and make the bastards pay the ultimate price for their crimes, but he couldn't do it by wallowing in despair. There had already been more than enough of that after the slaying, when he'd taken a two month leave of absence and stayed drunk for most of it in Los Barriles, over on the Baja peninsula – an area that was uniquely free of the drug battles prevalent on the mainland. The southern part of Baja wasn't a good trafficking choice, because there was only one road north, and it had military checkpoints every seventy-five miles, making it the hardest route imaginable for drug smuggling. Whereas northern Baja, by the border, was a battle zone much of the time – the Tijuana cartel had been at war with the Sinaloa cartel, leaving hundreds dead during the last year.

He'd crawled into a tequila bottle and stayed in a haze for six weeks, gradually emerging from the funk with a purpose. He would go back to work, and he would make those who'd destroyed his dreams of happiness pay for their savagery. He would avenge Rosa and Cass, and he would be merciless.

El Rey? Fuck *El Rey*. *Cruz* would be the bloody sword of fury descending upon his enemies, cutting them out of life like a cancer. And he didn't need some tarot card voodoo to do it. They would pay. And he would be the mechanism of their destruction.

Romero Cruz was far more committed to scorching the earth, hunting down and annihilating enemies than some fairytale ninja assassin. Cruz had nothing to lose; he was already dead inside, which made him far, far more dangerous. The man who didn't fear anything was the worst enemy you could have, and that was what Cruz had become. His was the wrath of the righteous, and he would extract his pound of flesh from the wicked, and they would pay with their lifeblood.

That was his mantra every day.

That was why he still woke up.

To be an angel of vengeance.

CHAPTER 2

General Alejandro Ortega studied the features of the man sitting across from him, wondering what he needed to say to make him happy. Because the last thing he wanted was for the attorney who represented the Sinaloa cartel to be unhappy with him. That could be a quick trip to an unmarked grave, even for an army officer of his rank. It had happened before.

Ortega didn't intend to test the man's patience. Carlos Zapata was one of the wealthiest lawyers in the country, and a visit from him was never a good thing.

"I wasn't aware that Santiago had been captured. That must have been a *Federal* exclusive operation. I can assure you that the army was never notified. If it had been, well, it's unlikely he would have been apprehended, obviously," Ortega stated in the formal-and-polite tense of Spanish.

"Jorge Santiago is a trusted ally of my clients," Zapata said crisply. "His incarceration is an affront to their authority, and calls into question their ability to protect those who rely upon them. I won't bore you with how delicate the balance of trust is on handshake deals. There's a bond, and friends look out for friends. So my question is, how can something like this happen, and how can you make it right?"

"I can assure you I started making inquiries the moment you called and informed me of the issue. It's not public yet. None of the television stations or newspapers have reported anything," Ortega observed, nervously smoothing his gray moustache.

"We need to know where he's being held, so I can get someone on filing motions with the court for immediate consultation with him. I know how this works, and we cannot afford for him to disappear for two weeks to be 'interrogated' in a back room somewhere."

"Of course. You'll know everything, as soon as I find out. This is deeply disturbing to me as well," Ortega assured him.

Zapata leaned forward. "My clients are bound to start asking what value they're receiving for their money if friends can be attacked by government forces with no warning. And I'll remind you that it's not in anyone's best interests for precarious power structures to be disrupted by the absence of a strong leader. That will lead to instability – younger rivals challenging one another for position, which inevitably leads to unfortunate outcomes."

"I understand. Please convey to your clients that this was an unfortunate and unforeseen result of action by forces not within my purview. And even though I had no part in today's events, I'll still work diligently to ensure everything that can be done, will be," Ortega promised.

"Start by finding out where he's being kept. Then you can stand back and stay out of the way." Zapata rose from his chair and fixed Ortega with a frigid glare. "You're lucky you don't have to go report on the bad news to my clients yourself. They don't take these sorts of setbacks lightly."

"No, I wouldn't imagine that they do. I'll call as soon as I know something."

"Do that."

Cruz was waiting patiently in the hall, chatting with the two guards, when Briones emerged from the elevator and strode hurriedly towards them.

"Sorry, sir. I got stuck in traffic on the way back from my house. There was an accident…," Briones offered.

"Forget it. We've all been there. Let's get back to our shit-bag and see what we can shake out of him. You okay? Ready for this?" Cruz asked.

"Perfect. Let's get to it."

The guard unlocked the door, and Cruz and Briones entered the cell. Santiago was slumped over in his chair, still unconscious. Cruz paced over to him and jerked back his head by the hair, looking for any trace of fakery, but didn't see any. He quickly took a pulse, which was faint and uneven.

"Get medical down here immediately," Cruz told Briones, who hurried to the door and alerted the guards. One of them murmured into his radio for help. Briones came back to help Cruz with Santiago.

They un-cuffed him and laid him on the floor. Cruz walked over to the *picana* and gave Briones a hard look. The lieutenant hastily gathered up the cord and the wand, stuffed it back into the rucksack, and carried it from the cell. The two sentries stood impassively by. Cruz knew he could count on them to have seen and heard nothing. Loyalty was a precious currency in the force, and you watched your peers' backs if you wanted to go very far. It could be your own ass on the line at any point, so it was always better to be discreet.

After a few minutes, Cruz heard the distinctive sound of a gurney being wheeled down the corridor to the interrogation room. Two paramedics ran a quick check on Santiago's vital signs, then heaved him onto the gurney like a sack of cement. Cruz ordered the two officers by the door to accompany Santiago to the hospital and stand guard in whatever room he was in – if he needed surgery, they were to take up a station outside of the operating room. He wanted to take absolutely no chances that Santiago could escape, or be broken out of captivity by his mob.

Cruz took the elevator up to his office, accompanied by Briones, and they got their stories straight for the inevitable investigation should Santiago die. It would be a cursory formality, to be sure, given that the captive had participated in gunning down a group of police that morning, but it was better to be prepared in advance. Both men had been with the department long enough to know how the drill worked, so they agreed that it was best not to mention the *picana* or the battering during questioning. Any injuries could be attributed to the assault and gunfight. Nobody was going to look too closely at the rights of a violent, psychopathic drug peddler; as long as they remained on the same page, there wouldn't be any issues.

Cruz showed the lieutenant his interrogation summary, on the off chance he'd omitted some key element or gotten something wrong or remembered it differently. Briones read it slowly and placed it on the desk between them when he was done.

"Really, the only thing we got from him was that he claims to have been involved in your family's execution, which is unverifiable, and he also claims to be involved in a plan to assassinate the president, as well as the American president. Which is also unverifiable. Where does that leave us?" Briones asked.

"I think we have to assume, given the circumstances of the interrogation and when and how he blurted it out, that there may be some truth to his claim. Santiago isn't smart enough to invent a story like that while in extreme pain. Besides, it doesn't come across on the report, but the way he said it…you heard him – it was like he was bragging. Like he wanted me to know what he'd done, so when it happened, I'd understand the power he wields," Cruz concluded.

"I know. I got that, too. It's what makes me nervous about all this. He seemed almost…I don't know, almost happy with himself. And if he actually did hire *El Rey*, we have a real problem."

"That's the understatement of the year. The fucking media has made *El Rey*'s exploits more popular than reality TV, and it will result in an uncontrollable circus if even a hint of this leaks. It has to be just you and I that know about this until I'm able to nose around and see if we can find any corroboration," Cruz warned the lieutenant.

"The cartels certainly have the money to hire him…," Briones mused.

"I know. That's what scares me. We've all seen the twisted schemes these lunatics can cook up." Cruz stopped and stared out the window. "But why kill the president? He's only going to be in office till the end of the year, so why bother?"

"Some kind of a power statement? To show the population who really runs the country?"

"Could be. But I don't buy Santiago would spend a fortune to prove a point. And it could backfire on him. I don't know. Who the hell knows what these animals dream up while they're high?" Cruz groused.

"What do you think it costs to hire *El Rey* to do something like this?"

"*El Rey*? Probably, oh, I don't know, five million U.S.? He's got to be the most expensive killer in the world by now. I'll say one thing, he knows how to market – now that he's a celebrity in the press, he can command a lot more. These cartel bosses are just like everyone else. They read the papers, too, and money is no object to them…" Cruz trailed off, considering his last statement. Santiago could easily afford five million – just as easily as he could fifty. The take on trafficking Mexican cocaine was estimated to be more than thirty billion dollars per year at wholesale prices. That was almost the national budget of North Korea. So money was certainly not an issue.

"So how do we proceed from here?" Briones asked.

Cruz surfaced from his ruminations. "We wait to see what's wrong with Santiago. And then we try to follow up on any leads, and root around to see if anyone on the street has heard any rumors. A loudmouth like Santiago would never be able to keep quiet about something this big, especially if he was behind it."

The desk phone rang, and a terse conversation ensued before Cruz slammed the receiver down.

"They took him to Hospital Angeles, in Pedregal." Cruz let out a sigh. "We'd better get over there and see what the damage is. Santiago would be the best place to start if we're going to get to the bottom of this."

"Traffic will be hell. It's going to take hours to get there."

"Nobody said that police work was all glamour and fun, young man." Cruz, who was only five years older than Briones, often called the lieutenant 'young man' as a subtle reminder of the power structure. "Hope you don't have any plans for tonight," he added.

"Not anymore."

Even with the emergency lights on, it took them fifty minutes to get to the hospital. Dusk had set in as they pulled into the lot by the emergency room. Traffic congestion in Mexico City was infamous, especially during rush hour, and it could take close to forever to cross the city during peak periods.

The pair approached the marble-floored lobby of the pristine edifice and took the elevator down one floor to the operating rooms. Cruz had spoken with one of the officers sent to guard the prisoner, and he'd reported that the doctors had rushed Santiago into surgery after a hurried evaluation. The officer had called for backup, and there were now eight heavily armed tactical squad members lining the hallway to the surgical theater. Cruz walked purposefully to the officers guarding the polished steel operating room doors.

"What are they doing in there?" he demanded.

"Some kind of procedure for his brain," the officer replied.

"His brain? What's wrong with it? Did they tell you anything?" Cruz asked.

"No, they just said that his pupils had a problem, so something was wrong with his brain. He never regained consciousness; that's all we know right now."

34

Cruz stalked the hallway, mind racing. A few minutes later, a green-gowned doctor emerged from surgery, blood splattered down his front, and removed his mask to speak with Cruz.

"I'm Dr. Consera. I presume you're running this show?" he asked Cruz.

"Captain Cruz. Yes, this is my prisoner. He shot four of my men this morning and was taken after a considerable struggle," Cruz informed him, for the record.

"Well, that explains the contusions and bruising…"

"Why are you operating on him? Was he hurt by the blows he sustained?" Cruz asked.

"Not really. We did a CT and an MRI, and this man has an abnormal heart. An area is enlarged, which is typical of victims of chronic atrial fibrillation." The doctor flexed his hand, trying to get the muscles to relax. "No, what happened is that something, probably the morning's events, caused a bout of fibrillation, and a clot formed in his heart and then traveled to his brain. Your man had a massive stroke. We went in through his leg and removed as much of it as we could so blood flow could return to the affected area of the brain, but it's anyone's guess how much permanent damage he's experienced. In these cases, you just don't know," Dr. Consera explained.

"So he's in a coma?"

"Precisely. His brain has been deprived of blood for at least an hour and a half, maybe more. Blood carries oxygen. Human tissue requires oxygen to live. If it was totally deprived of blood for that long, or longer, it doesn't look good for him."

"Then what's the prognosis?" Cruz asked.

"Poor. It would be a miracle if he ever regained consciousness. But in the end, we'll just have to wait and see. I'd normally do a positron emission tomography scan of his brain to see what level of activity the area the clot-affected portion retains, if any, but it would be a waste of time at present. Maybe in a few days, but right now, he's in God's hands," the doctor concluded.

"Or the devil's. The man is a major *narcotraficante*, Doctor, and probably snorts kilos of cocaine every week."

"That would make the chronic heart condition much worse, of course. It would explain a lot."

"One thing I don't understand. How does the clot form – from his heart beating, what, faster?" Cruz asked, genuinely curious.

"Atrial fibrillation isn't necessarily tachycardia – a racing heartbeat. It can also be where the heart skips a beat, sometimes a lot of beats, which has a tendency to allow blood to pool in the enlarged heart chamber instead of pumping through. A little sticks to the valve, and then a little more, and pretty soon you have a clot the size of a pencil eraser headed for your brain, and, bam, game over. Once it lodges, more blood begins to clot behind and in front of it, so it's a downward spiral from there. We went in through the femoral artery into the brain and sucked out as much as we could get, and pumped blood thinners through him to get the remaining clotting to dissolve, but the damage already done after such a long period without oxygen…well…" The doctor held out his hands in a show of helplessness.

"Then there's nothing that could have prevented this?" Cruz asked, seeking to clarify how the stroke would be reported by the doctor.

"Not really. If he was on medication, and he didn't take it, that could have caused problems as his blood thickened over time. Of course, the shock of being in a gun battle and being captured and, er, questioned…my official position is that this was just an unfortunate occurrence that was the result of an underlying medical condition, and couldn't have been realistically prevented." The doctor assessed Cruz frankly. "Although you might want to avoid putting cigarettes out on prisoners, or bludgeoning them," the doctor said quietly, glancing at the guards to ensure they hadn't heard him.

"Thank you for all your help and explanation. What happens to him now?"

"We'll transfer him to a private room in the intensive care wing, and watch and wait. That's all we can do."

Cruz joined Briones, who stood talking quietly with several of the other officers.

"He's in a coma. Probably forever. But I still want a guard on him in case there's some kind of divine intervention and he comes to. I do not want this asshole having a miracle escape on our watch, do you read me?" Cruz ordered.

"Loud and clear, sir." Briones stepped away from his companions, and they wandered a few feet down the hall. "Do they know what caused it?"

"He's got a bad heart, and it shot a blood clot to his brain. He stroked out. Nothing we could have done about it, the doctor tells me," Cruz said, holding Briones' gaze.

"He seems awfully young to have a bad heart," Briones observed.

"Santiago's two years older than I am. But this was a congenital condition. So it's not the same as a heart attack, or coronary artery disease. It's a combination of Hoovering coke, and God knows what else, and inheriting lousy genetic material."

"So yo – we're in the clear."

"Yes. But I want him guarded twenty-four-seven for the duration. He's too high profile, and he's got nine lives. I don't want him strolling out because he beat the odds yet again."

"I'll schedule a detail. What are his chances?" Briones asked.

"About the same as Shakira being at my house when I get home."

"So don't hold my breath," Briones concluded.

"I think we'll be okay if we station four men at the hospital in eight hour shifts. I want one outside his door, and another at the entry to ICU, and then two more downstairs outside the lobby doors. The last thing we need is his gang trying to break him out. We know he's a vegetable, but they don't, so I could see one of their bright young bulls thinking it would be a great idea to come into the hospital shooting. These pricks have no fear, and even less sense, so anything could happen," Cruz warned him.

The stainless steel double doors of the OR opened, and two nurses wheeled Santiago down the hall, an IV drip attached to his inert arm. Cruz motioned to them to stop.

He approached Santiago's bruised and battered face, now deathly pale.

Cruz leaned over his head and whispered into his blood-caked ear, "Looks like you didn't win this one, did you, you piece of shit? I hope you come out of the coma, and live a very long life in excruciating pain. Consider it my promise to you that I will make that happen. Now, get well soon…" He straightened, smiled at the nurses, and allowed the gurney to continue its journey along the antiseptic halls.

CHAPTER 3

Cruz remained at the hospital for another hour, ensuring that the security provisions were adequate and that everyone was aware of the importance of their captive. His command was filled with men he had handpicked himself, so he was confident that they wouldn't let him down – and perhaps more importantly, that they wouldn't talk to the press. That was always a consideration when a powerful cartel member was arrested. It was big news, but coverage brought with it a set of headaches he'd just as soon do without.

Once he was satisfied that there was nothing more to be done, he retrieved his vehicle and headed for the freeway, exhausted from the challenges of the drawn-out day and longing for the solitary comfort of home. It would be at least another seventy minutes before he rolled into Toluca, so he resigned himself to joining the indolent swarm of bumper-to-bumper cars that were still clogging the roads even at nine at night.

His late model unmarked Dodge Charger was one of the perks of running the anti-drug taskforce for Mexico City and the rest of the country. It was an important position that he'd been awarded by his superior after his predecessor had been killed in a brutal series of slayings around the time the Mexican crackdown on drugs had begun, under the auspices of a newly elected president. That had been almost six years ago, and Romero Cruz had aged noticeably during his tenure – the most obvious toll having been levied during the last two years, following the savage murders of his wife and daughter.

He ran his hands over his weary face, unconsciously tracing the fine line of the knife scar that ran from his hairline down the right side to his jaw, and felt older than his forty-one years. The job was a twelve hour a day, six day a week obligation, and since he'd lost Rosa and Cassandra, it had become more of a seven-day grind. Now that there was nobody waiting for him at home, he spent most of his time in the office or the field, battling adversaries who had infinitely greater resources; all on behalf of a regime that was riddled with corruption.

It was easy to be demoralized at times like this, but Cruz wouldn't allow himself to entertain thoughts of failure. The job was the only thing he had now, the only thing that kept him trudging forward instead of eating his pistol and ending his misery. It enabled him to cling to the hope that he would find the men who had been responsible for the death of his family and drag them to justice, or barring that, put a bullet between their eyes – the latter being his preference, because Mexico didn't have the death penalty and the prisons were notoriously luxurious for drug lords. It wasn't unheard of for imprisoned kingpins to have private chefs, hot and cold running prostitutes, all the alcohol and drugs they could consume, air conditioning, plush mattresses, satellite TV, cell phones, bodyguards, even beloved pets. The list went on and on.

Cruz contrasted that to his home – a simple three bed, two bath, two story affair with department store furniture, a small enclosed yard, and bars on all the windows and doors. There was no question that the cartel leaders had infinitely richer lives, but at a steep price – their existences were ones of non-stop violence. Besides the drug trade, they all engaged in kidnapping, murder for hire, extortion, assault, rape, prostitution, slavery, torture…every imaginable depravity, and some that were beyond imagination. It was a short, brutal existence where you burned bright then faded fast. Few of them made it to Cruz's age – less than a few, at that.

He stabbed the button of the car stereo, and Juanes' distinctive brand of Latin rock boomed out of the speakers. Cruz wasn't big on music, but it made the long crawl home seem shorter somehow. He tapped his fingers on the wheel as he hummed along, momentarily transported out of his head to a place where melodies lingered.

The CD was beginning its second rendition by the time he pulled off the freeway and weaved his way through the quieter streets that led to his little *colonia*. In the last year, the community developer had finally honored his promise and installed an electric security gate to keep unwelcome cars out, and they now had a grizzled security man who sat in the small concrete bunker to the side of the gate, watching a portable black and white television round the clock. His doppelganger counterpart appeared at seven every evening, relieving him until seven the next morning. Cruz gave a two fingered wave at the night man, who inevitably peered at his car like he'd never seen him before, then dim recognition struck, and he activated the opener with a salute: an inebriated sentry with nothing to do.

As Cruz swung his car into the carport that substituted for a garage on the homes in his tract, he noted that the usual Ford Lobo truck, the Mexican version of the F-150, was stationed a few yards away. The vehicle, or one much like it, sat in front of his modest home night and day, with two uniformed police on constant rotation. This was a requirement given that every cartel in Mexico viewed Cruz as its mortal enemy – it was not unknown for even higher-ranking police personnel to be slain in their sleep.

Of course, that hadn't helped Rosa and Cass; they'd been over a hundred miles away.

He shook off the thought. Recriminations wouldn't bring them back, nor would they help him sleep, which he desperately needed to do at some point. Cruz's nights weren't easy, even two years after opening the special delivery box, and no matter what his doctor prescribed for him he rarely got more than four hours of continuous rest. The therapist he'd been forced to see had ventured it might take years for him to be able to sleep normally and exorcise the nightmares of his family's final moments, especially if he continued his stressful vocation.

Quitting the federal police force wasn't an option for him, for a host of reasons. He'd be a dead man within weeks of going into the private sector – payback for his years of hounding the cartels and making their lives as miserable as he could. And his job afforded the potential of avenging Cass and Rosa's death.

But most importantly, all Romero Cruz had ever wanted to be, since a little boy, was a policeman. The uniform and the job were as integral a part of his personality as the color of his hazel eyes, or the shape of his nose. Being a *Federal* was not just his day job – it defined who Cruz was.

Inside the house, he flicked on the lights and climbed the stairs to his bedroom before sluggishly changing into sweats. He hung up his uniform, next to three others exactly like it, and placed his Heckler and Koch pistol on the bedside night table before going back downstairs to the kitchen to root around for something edible.

Dinner would be another sandwich, his weeknight staple, unvaryingly filled with turkey, salami, chorizo and cheese, then melted in the microwave and consumed at the breakfast bar or on his shabby couch, in front of the television. He allowed himself two beers per night, no more, and savored the rich taste of the cold Bohemia he favored as he watched the vapid crap that passed for programming. It wasn't much of an existence, but it occupied the time between leaving and returning to the office, so he was fine with it, such as it was. He recognized that this was no way to live, but since he'd been on his own it was all he could bring himself to do. Taking another pull on his beer, he reached for the remote and turned up the volume to drown out the emptiness that now sequestered the house, then waited for the ghosts of his dead family to visit him once again.

General Ortega swirled his José Cuervo *Reserva de la Familia* tequila in a brandy snifter, enjoying the aromatics of the smoky oak mingling with the distinctive scent of the agave distillation. He'd just arrived at Zapata's offices; late for a social visit, but not unheard of. The general's presence was auspicious; he had progress to report, something far too sensitive to discuss over the phone – progress of the kind the attorney would want to hear as soon as possible.

"Carlos, I'm glad you could see me on such short notice," Ortega began.

"Always a pleasure," Zapata said. "You made it sound urgent, so how could my response have been anything other?"

"I have unfortunate tidings, but also some good news, I think. Which would you prefer first?" Ortega asked.

"Give me the bad. Always the bad; save the best for last."

"Santiago is gravely injured, and his associates are all dead. At least, the group he was meeting with today," Ortega reported.

"How seriously hurt is he?" Zapata was already trying to calculate what impact Santiago's absence would have on the ongoing operations of the cartel. The last thing they needed was yet another bloody power struggle among one of his client's allies.

"It's hard to know for sure, but my sources tell me he's in a coma," Ortega said.

"A coma, eh? That's bad. Very bad." Zapata appeared to consider it, then waved in the air with a limp hand. "But, fine – what's the good news?"

"We know where he's being held," Ortega offered.

"Well, spit it out. Where is he?" Zapata demanded.

Ortega sipped his drink and chose his words carefully. "I want you to know that discovering this was difficult. I had to go to considerable trouble to find someone who would talk." He wanted to ensure that Zapata and his clients understood that he'd gone an extra distance for them. Hopefully, that would appease any anger over his being caught unawares about the morning's attack. He wanted to drive home the idea that he was irreplaceable and of continuing value to them. Worth keeping alive.

"Yes, yes. All right. I'm sure it was. Now, where is he being held?" Zapata repeated.

"Hospital Angeles, in room eleven of the intensive care ward. He was transferred there this evening, and chances are that's where he'll stay for the duration."

"I know the facility. What else were you able to find out?"

"There are armed *Federales* all over the place. Two on the floor with him, and more outside the building. In my opinion, any rescue operation would be ill advised, because they're completely ready for one. They're expecting it," Ortega warned him.

Zapata swirled his drink, lost in thought. After several minutes like this, he stood and toasted Ortega, signaling that their meeting was concluded.

Ortega finished his tequila and placed the snifter on Zapata's desk. "I hope your clients find this of value."

"Oh, I think I can promise they will. Thank you for coming by. I'm sure that their expression of gratitude will be unmistakable," Zapata assured him as they walked to the lobby area of his opulent offices. The general grasped his hand and shook it warmly before walking out to the street, where his chauffeured car waited to take him to his mistress' apartment for a spell, before heading dutifully home to his wife.

Zapata placed a call to one of ten cell numbers he'd been given for use this month. Each phone would be used once, and then discarded. To reach his client quickly, he opted to dial the next number down the list. Even though all cell numbers had to be registered in Mexico, in an effort to curtail kidnapping calls from blind numbers, there were any number of domestic staff who would gladly sign for a line, and then give it to their employer in exchange for twenty dollars. Everyone won in that transaction – the client, who got a sanitized communication channel, the phone company, who sold a phone, the manufacturer, whose phone was purchased, and the unfortunate who pocketed the twenty dollars. It was a win-win for all except the police.

When the phone was answered, Zapata relayed everything he'd learned. The conversation was short and to the point, taking less than sixty seconds from start to finish. There was absolutely no way in the world this method of communication could be traced, so it was the preferred option, other than 'in person' meetings.

When you printed money in your back room, the inconveniences of contriving work-arounds to government surveillance were miniscule compared to the rewards.

The hospital was quiet at five a.m., as the night shift finished its chores and prepared to hand over responsibilities to the fresh shift arriving at seven. The corridors were largely empty other than by the emergency room and intensive care. In the operating rooms, orderlies were busy preparing the chambers, sanitizing every surface in anticipation of the impending early morning surgeries. It was all part of the daily syllabus, and there was a rhythm to the activity that was startlingly efficient for Mexico, where things tended to be chaotic and unstructured.

On the ICU floor, a complement of nurses made rounds at all hours of day and night. They'd quickly grown accustomed to the armed *Federal* stationed outside the coma patient's room. After some initial unease, they now hardly noticed him. He sat quietly across from the door of room eleven, his M16 laid across his lap, watching the comings and goings in the busy ward. It was tedious duty – the only thing more boring was sitting outside the ward door, like his partner was doing, where very little went on. The biggest challenge for the officers was staying awake.

Every two hours, a nurse would come and check on the patient, taking his temperature and verifying that all the equipment was still hooked up correctly and that the IV bag hadn't run dry. Vital signs were monitored at the main nursing station that occupied the entirety of the central area of the ward, where a number of screens showed blood pressure, pulse and respiration readings for all occupied rooms.

Several of the pretty young nurses stopped to chat with the handsome policeman in their midst, but for the most part he could have been asleep with his eyes open. He'd asked one of the doctors what the chances were of the patient coming to; could he be playing possum? She'd laughed and told him there was more chance he'd grow wings and fly. The nurse pointed out the monitoring equipment to him and explained how it worked; they'd see substantial changes to his pulse and blood pressure if he ever came out of the coma.

At six a.m., a new nurse sauntered past the groggy officer, smiling at him flirtatiously and pausing for a few moments to inquire how he was holding up, and would he like her to bring him a cup of coffee on her next round. He accepted the offer graciously as she entered room eleven, clipboard and thermometer in hand.

Once inside, she expertly wedged a chair to hold the door closed, and moved hurriedly to the patient's side. After a quick scan of the room for any cameras, she took a pen from her blouse and carefully unhooked the IV bag. With steady hands, she unscrewed the pen and extracted a small syringe concealed in its fully-functional shaft. She glanced at the door, pulled the orange safety cap off the needle tip with her teeth and inserted it into the catheter, then drove the little needle home and depressed the plunger. Satisfied that the vital signs on the monitor were still reading normal, she reconnected the IV, slid the spent syringe back into the pen shaft and returned it to her blouse pocket, where it rested innocuously with two other pens.

The entire episode had taken less than ninety seconds. After stepping back to the door and removing the chair, she smoothed her blouse and adjusted her bra so her breasts were nearly bursting out of the snug top. She breezed, smiling, out of the room and waved at the officer, promising to be back in a few minutes with some hot, strong coffee. He admired the fit of her tight white pants as she walked down the hall, and reminded himself there were worse gigs he could have drawn than this. If only something interesting would happen. The boredom was a killer.

Six minutes later, the monitor alarm sounded in room eleven, signaling that the heart rate had dropped to zero, as had blood pressure. A different nurse came running from the far end of the ward, and after taking a brief look inside, called for help. A minute later, a team arrived at a jog pushing a crash cart. A harried doctor brushed past them to get to the patient's side.

For hours, the *Federal* had fought a drowsy battle against sleep, but now the area around him was a crisis zone, with personnel running to and fro with grim expressions. So captivated was he with the unfolding life or death drama, it took more than thirty minutes for him to realize the nurse hadn't returned with his coffee.

CHAPTER 4

At six-thirty a.m., Cruz's day began with a call at home from the dispatch desk, who sought to patch him in to the ranking officer in charge at Angeles hospital. He pawed the sleep from his eyes and fumbled on the nightstand for the phone, almost knocking his pistol onto the floor in the process. He lifted the handset to his ear and croaked a greeting.

Two minutes later he was wide awake, shivering in his shower as he took a hurried rinsing before heading into the office. There was little point in driving all the way to the hospital to confirm that Santiago had drawn his last breath. He had no reason to doubt that was the case. People died in ICU every day, and Santiago's trauma had been severe. His bad heart had done the Mexican people a favor, sparing them the expense of trying the bastard and housing him, in luxury, no doubt, for the rest of his life. Cruz felt a fleeting spike of guilt; maybe the interrogation with the *picana* had been a little overzealous and had triggered the stroke, but a darker part of his heart actually hoped that was the case. Whatever, he'd sleep better after helping take out one of the most savage cartel bosses in the country.

The law worked differently in Mexico than in the U.S., and Cruz couldn't see how his counterparts there ever got anything accomplished. Mexico used Napoleonic law as its basis, where the accused was assumed to be guilty until proven otherwise. It was usually a safe bet they were. In Cruz's experience it was rare to meet an innocent man, especially in his area of specialty. How the American authorities could hope to be effective when they were constantly hamstrung by inquiries and hearings and attorneys was beyond him.

As he donned his uniform, he thought about the history of the drug racket in Mexico. It had all changed when the established marijuana traffickers, who also moved small amounts of Mexican heroin into the U.S., hooked up with the Colombian cartels and became their shipping arm. This relationship solidified in the 1980s, and soon the cartels were getting paid in product rather than cash. That created a substantial incentive for them to expand and move from transporting to full-scale distribution.

There had long been drug trafficking in Mexico on a regional basis, but once the cartels began getting huge sums of money from their cocaine distribution, the cottage industry developed into a national network. It hadn't helped that, for many years, before it was absorbed into the current CISEN group, the head of the Mexican intelligence organization, the DFS, had sold DFS badges to the top cartel bosses, giving the traffickers an effective free pass to do as they liked. But the real power came to Mexico's cartels once the Colombian syndicates imploded, leaving a vacuum that was filled by their Mexican partners. In a matter of a few decades, a small smuggling scheme in Mexico became a mega-billion-dollar enterprise, and the violence had escalated in proportion to the wages of sin.

Now the country was in crisis as the government battled the cartels, which had a propensity for butchery. The war against them had begun in earnest under President Fox, in 2000, but escalated to the current fever pitch when Calderon became president in 2006. Both presidents had been very sympathetic to U.S. policy, and had cooperated with the U.S. initiative to quash the drug traffickers, which had only resulted in driving the violence levels through the roof.

Cruz clumped down the stairs and hit the button on his coffeemaker, impatient to get out the door. With Santiago dead, there was sure to be a bloody turf war. That would have been fine by Cruz, but innocents tended to get slaughtered at an alarming rate whenever one of these skirmishes flared up.

He gulped down a cup of scalding coffee and raced to his car, anxious to be in the office to brief his team on the likely outcome of Santiago's passing. He also wanted to establish a game plan to deal with information-gathering, to establish whether there was any hint of a contract out on the president.

The journey to the office was excruciatingly slow due to an accident, and even with his detachable emergency roof light it took him forty-five minutes to make it through the security gates of his building.

A few of his staff were already there, having anticipated that it would be a big day. Two of them were reading the newspaper featuring a banner headline and an old photo of Santiago. The story proclaimed that the top Templar chief was dead after having been apprehended in a gun battle. The article was short on facts and long on conjecture and hyperbole, which was to be expected. Mexicans were under no illusions that their media existed to tell them the truth about anything. It was more a form of entertainment, and the national pastime was figuring out who was lying more, the papers or the government.

Cruz figured there must have been a leak at the hospital. His team knew better than to talk to reporters; there was no way anyone was less than a hundred percent in his group. These men worked as diligently as Cruz did, having followed his example and committed to treating their job as a crusade. Those who had found the pace too demanding were long gone, which was just as well. Cruz believed that he was fighting a war for the very soul and future of Mexico, and these men were his soldiers. Everyone shared that perspective and felt the same way. If the cartels won, Mexico lost. It was a battle between the productive and the predators. And predators couldn't run a country or operate schools or build roads. Predators could only destroy and steal and abuse. They couldn't be allowed to prevail, or the nation would be plunged into chaos, just as Colombia had been for two decades, before slowly pulling out of the tailspin.

He had Briones call a staff meeting for his immediate subordinates, who would brief their squads later, and went over the ramifications of Santiago's death. They would be closely monitoring the situation in Michoacan from their *Federal* brethren there and would send resources, including soldiers and weapons, as the situation demanded. There was very little upside from Santiago's death – although a major parasite had been removed from the game, the fear and expectation was that the younger, hotter heads would start a bloodbath in their bids for eminence in the region. It was almost a given that the bodies would start appearing, sans heads, at an increasing rate. Cruz only hoped they wouldn't see any more daylight shopping mall shooting battles or grenade attacks on densely populated areas, as they had just a few years previous, before Santiago had ascended to the throne.

After the meeting broke up, Cruz motioned for Briones to sit.

"I thought about the whole assassination problem and concluded we need to gather more intelligence before we bring anyone else in on it. Nobody's going to take this seriously if we don't have something more that Santiago's wild claims."

Briones nodded. "One of the things we can do is see what events will be taking place that will bring the president in contact with the American president. There can't be many."

"Agreed. But we'll need to get our feelers out into the streets and see if there's any buzz. Santiago was a blowhard, so he'd have been unable to keep his mouth shut. We need to nose around and find out whether he talked to anyone, and if so, learn what he said."

"Let's get Ignacio and Julio in and brief them," Briones suggested. "If there's any chatter, they'll be the ones to pick it up."

Ignacio Roto and Julio Brava were the two most senior plainclothes investigators on Cruz's team. They spent much of their time in the streets, carousing and mingling with the criminal element of society in order to keep current on trends and rumors. They were a vital part of the intelligence-gathering apparatus Cruz had painstakingly woven in over the last five years, which, though controversial, was highly effective. The tactics consisted of spreading money around and nurturing informants, as well as buying drugs, soliciting kidnappers and murder for hire gangs, and generally wading waist deep in the cesspool that was Mexico City's seedy underworld. Cruz's squad had twenty plainclothes officers working the streets at any given time, and their presence was a lynchpin of his overall strategy – the tip about the meeting with Santiago had come up through the streets, first surfacing as a rumor of a cartel boss seeking to establish a new channel for methamphetamine trafficking into Michoacan, the state that bordered Jalisco, to the south.

Both Julio and Ignacio answered their cell phones and agreed to meet at headquarters in two hours. They both showed up wearing hats and sunglasses, with the diminutive Julio sheltered beneath the folds of a hooded sweatshirt. It wasn't unknown for the cartels to hire private detectives to take photos of everyone going into the building, so both men avoided it as much as possible. But a summons from the boss couldn't be ignored, so here they were – sitting in Cruz's office, along with Briones.

Cruz laid out the meat of Santiago's claim, and instructed them to try to get intel on a contract killing commission targeting the president. He told them to search for a conduit to *El Rey*; there had to be someone who acted as his agent, handling the hit requests and vetting the clients. That someone would be in Mexico City or Monterrey, the two hubs for criminal activity.

Julio asked to see the interrogation report. He read it carefully before placing it on Cruz's desk. "If this is genuine, I can tell you where the assassination attempt will take place," he said blithely.

"Really? And how would you know that?" Briones asked. He had always thought the little man pompous and arrogant, although he was undoubtedly a brilliant detective.

"Simple. The only place I can think of where the American president and ours will be together is at the G-20 conference. It's obvious. At least, to me," Julio explained. He shot Briones a smug look of superiority.

"How…where did you get that information?" Briones countered, smelling a rat.

"I have friends all over, and one hears things," Julio replied mysteriously. The truth was less dramatic.

"Shit," Cruz exclaimed. "If that's true, you're probably right. That's…what, five or so weeks away? In Cabo San Lucas?"

"Actually," Julio said, "the location's in San José del Cabo. They've been hard at work building a conference center for the last seven months – there's a late May deadline."

"How do you know all that off the top of your head?" Cruz asked.

Julio decided to come clean. "My cousin got shipped over there to help. He's a civil engineer working on the security systems and presentation equipment for the conference. They've got a crew of six thousand trying to get the project completed – it's been a train wreck to date, with all the usual incompetence and corruption. I hear about it from my sister almost every week when she calls. It's about the worst kept secret in Mexico by now, and that's saying a lot…"

"That's ominous," Cruz observed. "We have Santiago claiming he's going to take out two of the most heavily protected heads of state in the world, and the summit taking place a short plane ride from Mexico City in a little over a month, with the U.S. president in attendance? That's a little too coincidental for comfort…"

Julio looked at each of the men in turn. "I think we need to treat this as a genuine threat. Santiago's cartel has more than enough money to hire *El Rey*, and has the motive – the current president's war on the cartels has probably inconvenienced his group's resources over the last four years, especially after the grenade attack in Morelia in 2008. Even though that got pinned on Los Zetas cartel, Santiago's crew has likely been given a bloody nose, at least – so he'd have reason to want to make a big splash." Julio considered his next words carefully. "Taking out two presidents would send the message he was one of the big dogs, and a lot of people would support him, at least emotionally. The president's war on drugs hasn't exactly bestowed peace upon the country, and he's pretty unpopular with many."

"I agree. Put a task force together on this," Cruz said. "I want to know everything you get, no matter how seemingly inconsequential. There has to be a way to find this *El Rey*. The key to this will be in neutralizing him. The equation's simple. No *El Rey*, no Santiago anymore, equals no threat…"

Ignacio – aka 'Nacho' – shook his head and frowned. "Forgive my ignorance, but what is the G-20? Why are both presidents going to be there?"

"It's a financial summit held every year, where the world's finance ministers meet to discuss economic issues," Julio told him.

"So, why is the president going to be there?"

"Because it's a national honor that it's being hosted in Mexico," Julio answered, patiently. "It's a really big deal. And the American president is planning to show up at the opening ceremony as a sign of solidarity between Mexico and the U.S. That's the only event that will bring the U.S. president to Mexico this year that I know of, so it's a safe bet that if *El Rey* is going to take a shot, that's where he'll do it."

"Then we have a serious problem," Nacho said, back in his area of expertise. "*El Rey* is a ghost. He's like smoke – you catch a whiff of him, then he's gone. It's scary, because he would definitely be the right man for the job – his assassination of *El Gallo* is still discussed in the—"

"He isn't a ghost, Nacho," Cruz corrected. "He's flesh and blood, which means he can be stopped. He's not a magician, he doesn't have superpowers, and he can't fly. I'm not saying it will be simple, but I've taken down enough big swinging dicks to know that no matter how much positive press they've gotten, they all bleed just like we do…"

Julio held up his hands. "Fair enough, but it's not going to be easy. This is a smart, savvy professional, and he's probably got loads of money from his hits. That means he can hide forever if he wants. But I agree that he has to have a network, which means somebody has to know about it. We should talk to the *El Rey* taskforce and see what they've got, although rumor has it they're worse than incompetent – my buddy was with them for a year, and said it's like a game over there to see who can do the least amount of work."

"I've heard the same thing, but you never know. Maybe they cranked up the heat after *El Gallo*. That was a major blow for the party, and an embarrassment for all concerned," Cruz admitted.

"Did you see the footage of the shooting? I swear it looked like *El Gallo* was doing his usual head butt. It was uncanny—"

"We're all familiar with it," Cruz cut in. "But the point of this meeting is to ensure the same thing doesn't happen to the president. And imagine the consequences if the American president was killed on Mexican soil – it could start an invasion…and I'm not exaggerating. At the very least, it would destroy Mexico in the eyes of the world, as well as our relationship with the United States. The more I think about this, the more I believe we need to treat this as a genuine threat and take appropriate steps. I want you to give it top priority, am I clear?"

The men all nodded. The stakes were obvious.

They had to find *El Rey* at all costs.

CHAPTER 5

Los Cabos, Mexico

The man reclined in the dilapidated dentist chair as the tattoo artist poured ink into small plastic cups. The walls were painted a lurid burgundy, with swirls of black intermingled to create a gothic effect. Gloomy lighting was provided by tin pails hanging upside down from the ceiling, with light fixtures mounted within them. On the street outside, a boisterous group of drunk revelers made their way to one of the clubs on the main drag; loud peals of female laughter were punctuated by slurred male *Gringo* voices shouting, "Tequila!" He caught a glimpse of the group through the shop window – two brunette women in their thirties wearing shorts that were misguidedly optimistic as to how time had favored their physiques, and a younger redhead in a jean mini-skirt accented by a white 'wife-beater' undershirt tied provocatively to highlight her pierced navel. The men were universally cut from the same bolt – overweight, red-faced, wearing baseball caps and colored T-shirts with fishing logos on them. All had been out in the sun for far longer than advisable – their skin color varied from salmon to lobster-toned.

The man guessed they'd been fishing all day, given the distinctive pale outline where their sunglasses had rested on their faces. Fishing, of course, being a euphemism for guzzling beer and tequila while going for a boat ride. This was the typical weekend crowd, in town to let their hair down and misbehave like they couldn't back home.

"Quite a night, huh, *Jefe?*" the tattoo artist commented in a tone that belied a complete lack of interest in any response. He was just making idle chatter while he prepared the drawing and busied himself removing the sterilized tattoo gun tip from the sealed paper envelope. His Spanish accent placed him as Argentinean. Not unusual in Mexico, because when people emigrated from Argentina, they generally went to countries where Spanish was the native language.

Sinewy muscles rippled under the artist's gaunt forearms, which were covered from the wrists to his shoulders in vividly articulated tattoos, as was his neck. His nose was pierced and held a stainless steel horseshoe suspended from the columella, complemented by the rows of studs that adorned both ears from top to bottom, visible because his two feet of dyed black hair was tied back in a ponytail. The squalid ambience of the little place was fortified by the speed-metal of Slayer blasting from the overhead stereo speakers, which was in keeping with the shop's name: Metal Ink.

"How long will this take?" the man asked impatiently.

"Figure an hour and a half to two hours. Two to be safe. Why, you got somewhere pressing you need to be?" the tattoo artist replied.

"Nah. Just want to know what to expect."

"It'll hurt a little, but shouldn't be too bad. This area of the chest isn't nearly as sensitive as a lot of areas I've done," the artist said, with a suggestive leer that revealed decaying teeth and badly receded gums – telltale signs of a chemical romance with methamphetamines.

"I'm not worried about it."

"You want a shot of meanstreak before I get going?" the artist asked, gesturing with his head at a bottle of *Chinaco* tequila sitting on the small bar that was part of the establishment's limited charms. Several shot glasses were aligned next to it, like small glass soldiers standing at the ready.

"No. I'm good," the man replied.

"Suit yourself."

The artist sterilized the spot on the man's bare chest where he'd indicated he wanted the tat and pulled a disposable razor from a drawer in the small stainless steel work table. He thumbed the plastic blade cover into the garbage and quickly shaved the area, then applied some neutral deodorant so the artwork would leave a clear impression. Satisfied with his work, he held up the stencil and placed it carefully on the newly shaved area, just above the left nipple on the pectoral muscle. When he removed it, he tossed it into the wastebasket and applied a film of ointment over the blue outline, humming to himself in time with the incomprehensible noise blaring from the stereo. After inspecting his handiwork with satisfaction, he opened a package of surgical gloves and expertly pulled them over his dexterous fingers. Grinning again, he looked at the man and rubbed his latex-sheathed hands together with anticipation.

"So now we begin," he said, grasping the tattoo gun and activating it.

The high-pitched hum of the gun droned against the machine-gun bursts of staccato guitar riffs as the artist swiveled his stool and wheeled to the man's side.

From the trash bin, the watchful eye of the crow depicted on the stencil seemed to follow the artist's movements as he lowered the gun to skin and started to draw.

❧❧

Mexico City, Mexico

Cruz had called a meeting with CISEN to inform them of his suspicions, but it wasn't exactly going as planned. He'd driven to their headquarters and was escorted to a conference room, where he'd waited impatiently for half an hour before four men emerged from the large building's cavernous depths. Nobody had apologized for being late, although they'd been polite enough, at least in the beginning.

The bonhomie had quickly degraded into an adversarial exchange that hadn't gone anywhere good.

"Hmmm, yes, well, I see how you could draw that inference, but the problem is that you have not one iota of evidence to support your, hmm, intellectual leap," the oldest of the men and the director of the agency, Armando Serrate, pointed out.

"I understand. But I'm telling you that standing in the room with the man…it wasn't something he just tossed off. He was telling me, no, he was *bragging*, that he was going to kill the president and that there was nothing I could do to stop it. He didn't seem to care whether I knew. That's part of what makes me uncomfortable. He was convinced it would happen no matter what steps were taken because of the assassin involved. *El Rey*," Cruz repeated.

"Yes. We heard you the first time. But all of this is purely guesswork on your part, gut feel, if you like, absent any proof. Would you agree with that?" Serrate's right hand man, Guillermo Trudo, asked.

"I'm currently gathering evidence, gentlemen. But the man's dying statement, coupled with the mention of *El Rey*, should give you all pause for concern," Cruz fired back.

"*Capitan* Cruz, while I appreciate you coming to us with your, hmm, theories, I think we're probably better equipped to gauge what should concern us than you are," Serrate declared.

"You can't discount this. We're talking about a plot to assassinate the president, confirmed by a cartel chief," Cruz insisted.

"Who are well known for their veracity, I'm sure. Look, you told us that this man, Santiago, died of a brain injury, correct? How do you know that his flight of fancy wasn't an early sign of his brain malfunctioning? Or that he wasn't simply lying in order to torment you, or so he'd appear to have some valuable information to bargain with?" Trudo reasoned.

"You weren't there. You didn't look into his eyes," Cruz said, feeling lame even as he uttered the words. "I know how far-fetched this sounds, but the summit is only five weeks away so we don't have a lot of time. I could use your help. You have resources I don't. You can partner with the Americans, and use technology we don't have, to pinpoint this man—"

"Yes, I'm quite sure the National Security Agency will be anxious to step in and assist the Mexican government with their domestic murder-for-hire problem," Serrate offered, glancing at his associates in an openly skeptical manner. His tone softened. "You have a hard job, Cruz. We all do. If you get some concrete evidence that there's a plot, you're welcome back to present it to us, and we'll be happy to hear it. But right now, you have nothing. You have a hunch, yes? And we don't trade in hunches, hmm, when discussing our business with the Americans. They already think we're a bunch of savages due to the drug violence – we don't need to add superstitious fools to their list of our deficiencies, you see?"

"So this is all about how you're afraid it might look to your counterparts in the U.S.? Haven't you heard a word I've said? This isn't my first week on the job, and—"

"Nor is it mine, *Capitan*. Do you have any idea how many false alarms or threats against the president's life we field in any given month? No. You probably don't. Let's just say it's a fair number, and that most are more solid than what you've brought." Serrate pushed back his chair and prepared to terminate the meeting. "Thank you for coming, and stay in touch – keep us up to date on any progress, hmm, yes? We'll take the *El Rey* matter under advisement and enact appropriate safeguards. Now, perhaps you can go back to solving the nation's drug crisis, and we can return to our humble tasks…"

"You're making a horrible mistake," Cruz, furious, managed through clenched teeth.

"Noted, *Capitan*, noted. Now, if there isn't anything else, Trudo here can show you the way out," Serrate said.

"I know the way. I found my way in, didn't I? Oh, and I hope you don't mind if I contact the American Secret Service and alert them to my suspicions, all right? Perhaps they would be more receptive than you," Cruz threw out as his final leverage.

"Well, *Capitan*, if you think that they'll be any more courteous or receptive to your baseless suppositions and wild theories than we were, by all means, embarrass yourself further. But my advice is to wait until you have something besides emotion to contact them with, or you're quite likely to be laughed out of the room, or treated like a slow child. I deal with them on a regular basis, and you can trust me when I tell you they won't be nearly as gracious," Serrate warned.

Cruz stalked out of the building, fuming at the treatment. He'd never been so humiliated in twenty-something years as a *Federal*. These arrogant pricks had acted as if his interrogation evaluation was toilet paper, unworthy of their time.

He started the Charger engine and sat staring at the wall of the building, thinking. He needed to come up with some evidence, and quickly, or nobody would take anything he said about *El Rey* seriously. The problem was that, if his hunch – okay, he'd concede they were correct on that – was right, by the time they got something solid it could be weeks from now, which would put them all at a tremendous disadvantage. Cruz knew that if a trained assassin was hell-bent on taking out a head of state, and was willing to die in the process, then it was practically impossible to stop him – he'd heard that again and again as a police officer, and later, as a detective. So the more preparation, the more of an edge they had.

But nobody was going to put any credence in his theories – certainly not if it meant humiliation if they were wrong. It was far more prudent for a bureaucrat to take a conservative stance, even if it meant endangering the president. Cruz wondered if they would have been so nonchalant if it had been their son or daughter who was in danger of being killed, but still…he was arguing a loser, until he had proof.

Maybe he would still go to the NSA or the Secret Service, but only once he'd done some more homework. In a way, Serrate had done him a favor. He had forced Cruz to build a real case if he was going to be taken seriously. Cruz had hoped to sidestep that process and fast-track some action, forgetting everything he knew about human nature and the way that the system worked. He couldn't afford to make the same mistake twice.

Swinging out of the parking area, he almost collided with a woman pushing a baby stroller, chatting on her cell phone. His brakes locked, causing his tires to screech to a stop, inches from the pair.

Shaken, he waved in apology. The woman gave him a look that could cut glass.

He needed to cool down. Being angry because his colleagues hadn't embraced his ideas was a luxury he couldn't afford. His strength lay in being analytical and thorough, not in being a cowboy. Serrate was right.

Cruz needed proof.

And he needed it now.

He stabbed a speed dial button on his cell phone as he pulled into traffic. Briones answered on the second ring.

"It didn't go well," Cruz reported.

"I'm sorry to hear that, sir. How should we proceed from here? Did they give you any guidance or suggestions?"

"Yes. We need to get something tangible. So it's of paramount importance that the men working the streets understand they are to have unlimited resources. If they need to offer money to curry favor or to get someone to talk, bring me the request. I don't care what it takes, but we need to stir the pot and shake something loose. Pass that on to Roto and Brava. Tell them I want them to do whatever it takes. Use those exact words, Lieutenant," Cruz emphasized.

"*Whatever it takes.* Got it. Are you coming back in to the office?"

Cruz peered at the digital clock on the dash. It was already five-thirty. By the time he got to headquarters in traffic, it would be six or later.

Then again, what did he really have waiting for him at home?

"Yes. I'll be there shortly. You don't need to wait for me. Get some sleep, chase women or whatever you young men do, and I'll see you first thing in the morning."

CHAPTER 6

The midnight horizon glowed with leaping licks of fire as the meager improvised shacks around the hidden field burned. Dense, acrid smoke belched into the night sky, carrying with it all the earthly possessions of the simple farming family huddled together, their wrists bound with plastic ties, the children sobbing as they watched their home vaporize. A pair of armed men stood next to a lifted four-wheel-drive pickup truck, watching the blaze as they shared a bottle of mescal while admiring their destructive handiwork.

The mother tried in vain to comfort her panicked children – two little girls and a small boy – as the father mumbled a prayer to the Virgin of Guadalupe, who had been conspicuously absent in assisting him lately. This year he'd planted a cash crop instead of tomatoes – marijuana bringing with it a substantial premium over the edible harvest he'd always grown in the past. He'd needed the money for his youngest girl's operation, to repair a congenital deformity; Michelle had been born with a cleft palate that would limit her chances in life due to the effect on her appearance. He had realized that cultivating cannabis carried a risk, because the other drug growers and their distribution network didn't want competition, but he hoped to be able to get away with it this one time, and then go back to tomato farming.

The farmer's luck had been bad ever since the arrival of his newborn two years ago. First there was her birth defect, then a bad harvest, and just a few months ago, news that another baby was on the way. More mouths to feed diminished the miracle of birth somewhat. It wasn't that he didn't love his children, but the financial pressure was immense, and the last thing he needed was another one. And in the back of his mind lurked a darkness – what if this one also had some problem; an even more expensive one to care for? He'd tried to banish the thoughts, but they had recurred and grown to dominate his days.

Two of the men approached – rough-looking, wearing cowboy hats and carrying pistols. These were the foot soldiers of the local distribution network; in 1986, there was only one cartel, operated by Miguel Ángel Félix Gallardo, also known as The Godfather, who lived in nearby Culiacan and controlled all drug traffic of any note in Mexico. Everyone answered to him, including these men. In a few years, Gallardo would divide up the country and create a more fragmented cartel scheme, doling out territories like a multi-level marketing magnate, but at this point, he alone was the ultimate authority, with close friends and family members handling the local day-to-day operations.

The mother pleaded frantically with the two men to forgive them, to at least release the children – they were helpless babies, the boy the oldest at five years old. One of the men backhanded her, splitting her cheek open. The father begged for them to show mercy in a burst of rapid Spanish, his tense formal and respectful of their obvious dominance. He acknowledged that he knew it was wrong to grow marijuana without their consent, but there was the baby's operation to consider, and to please, in the name of all that was holy, not punish the innocent for his bad judgment.

The men were unsympathetic, and drunk, flushed with the power of life and death over their miserable captives. The distraught children were dressed in rags, and the parents weren't much better – their poverty and desperation was palpable.

The heavier of the two men moved towards the kneeling prisoners and kicked the two year old in the head with his heavy cowboy boots. The snap of her neck was audible, the additional blows with his heel unnecessary. The mother shrieked in blind rage, screaming her baby's name into the deafness of the night. The two men laughed harshly, and the kicker wiped the blood from his boot onto the dead child's tattered peasant dress before moving to the father and silencing his hoarse yells with a brutal pistol blow to the head. Dazed, he fell over, blood flowing freely from a gash in his scalp.

Grabbing the mother by the hair, they forced her to her feet, and the kicker tore at her dress. She struggled in protest, hysterical with grief and fear, and was rewarded for her efforts with a savage punch to the throat. The men hauled the now-silenced woman off to a flat patch of dirt near the flaming main dwelling, and took turns raping her while the father and children watched helplessly.

Eventually tiring of the sport, they dragged her back to her muted family and discarded her beside her toddler's mutilated corpse. The woman had gone into shock, barely registering the abuse or the mangled body of her baby, her awareness shut down as a self-preservation mechanism for what remained of her psyche. She raised her head from the dirt, and in her delirium saw Satan dancing in the house's flames; the dark one had come to claim them for his own.

The kicker moved to the little boy – the only one of the family who wasn't crying. The child radiated a piercing look of pure hatred at the man, but there were no tears. Already, he'd been hardened by the demanding life on a rural farm, where he worked beside his father from dawn until dusk.

"Hey, look here, we have a tough guy, Hmm? What a tough character, this little *cabron* is, huh? He looks like he wants to kill me," the man taunted, slurring as he waved the pistol in the boy's face.

"I think he would, if he had a chance, Paco," his companion confirmed.

"All right, little man, you want to kill me? You want to kill someone? Let's see you do it, you goat prick." The kicker flipped open a long wooden-handled folding knife, freeing the little boy's hands with a single slice of the razor-honed blade.

The little boy rose to his bare feet, glaring defiantly. The kicker spat dismissively and cuffed the boy, knocking him back a few paces, but the little boy remained on his feet, although obviously stunned by the blow.

The man strode to him and flipped off his pistol's safety, jamming it into the little boy's tiny fingers while maintaining an iron grip on it. He forced the child's hand towards the back of his father's head, holding the knife at the boy's throat. He reeked of onions, alcohol and sweat, and the little boy gagged at the powerful stench of his bear-like captor.

"Go ahead, *cabron*. Be a man. Blow his fucking head off. Either that, or I'll cut your throat and fuck him in the ass for good measure. After I'm done fucking you, too," the kicker hissed in his ear.

The roar of an engine arriving in the field startled the group, and the kicker reflexively squeezed the boy's hand, depressing the hair trigger of the automatic. A spray of blood spackled the little boy as the father fell forward, his struggle on the planet finally at an end.

A stately older man approached the scene from his Ford Bronco, taking in the carnage with a practiced eye. Like the others, he wore a cowboy hat, but his bearing was one of authority that immediately commanded the men's full attention.

"What the hell are you doing? What's going on here?" he demanded, as the kicker scrambled to his feet, fear spreading over his face, as well as his partner's.

"Uh, nothing. Just cleaning up the job, *Jefe*. Having a little fun," the kicker mumbled sheepishly.

The man slapped him, his look radiating contempt as he shook his head. He regarded the boy, who watched the scene impassively, his face smeared with his father's blood, a fleck of brain stuck to his cheek near where two rivulets of tears had trickled a channel in the gore.

"Your fun is over. Finish this." The leader studied the child carefully for a few more seconds. "The boy will come with me. Hurry up with this mess. I haven't got all night." He kneeled in front of the small face, and flicked the errant cerebral speck off his stern countenance. "This is a lesson for you. Your father took a chance and didn't think through the consequences, so now everyone has to pay. I don't want to hurt them anymore than they want to hurt me, but the law of the land is that if you cross me, you die. So we all pay the price. I've spared you because you're brave, and I can use brave men around me. So remember tonight, and remember that I saved you from this." He gestured at the burning hovel and the bodies.

The boy glared at the man, unable to process much after the horror of the execution. The roof of the main house collapsed in a shower of amber sparks; both man and boy turned to look at it. A crow took flight from the field, its startled, raucous cry piercing the silence as it beat its wings over the slaughter. The man grabbed the boy's chin and returned the child's focus to his mustached face.

"I will be your new father, and the only god you will worship. I am the law, and I am the judge and the jury. Don't forget it. Remember that I saved you, and could have killed you with a snap of my fingers." The man stood, nodding at the kicker, who was obviously relieved to have gotten off with nothing more than a little humiliation and a slap. He took the boy's trembling hand and turned, the child padding by his side as they walked to his vehicle, his mother and sister left behind.

Neither turned when two gunshots fractured the night.

❧❧

Present day, Los Cabos, Mexico

At six-thirty a.m., the old school bus creaked to a halt at the side of the dirt road in the *barrio*, just off the street that led to the small municipal airport. Its front door opened to the waiting group of workers, who shuffled groggily towards their ride. They were dressed in ragged jeans and T-shirts, and most of the men wore hooded sweatshirts in spite of the daily ninety-degree heat. There wasn't much talking as they climbed aboard, and most conversations died once the small portable radio at the front of the bus was turned on, blaring ranchero music from its tinny speaker.

Thirty minutes later, the bus arrived at its destination, a gargantuan construction project on the slope of a hill just off the main highway, near a toll road leading to the international airport. A golf course stretched off into the distance, the perimeter of which was dotted with homes. A school sat below the project, dwarfed by its scope. Across the highway, a shopping plaza loomed over the surrounding buildings, housing a grocery store and a host of shops, with aboveground as well as underground parking areas.

When the bus pulled up the service road to the drop-off point, the site was already a swarm of activity, with workers milling about everywhere. Twenty other buses similar to the new arrival waited in line to exit, having discharged their loads of workers. Still more were queued to gain entry. A long line of personnel transport wound its way from the construction zone to a dirt field a quarter mile away that had been set up as a longer-term parking facility for the rickety conveyances.

The supervisors appeared at seven-fifteen and passed out hard hats – an unusual requirement for workers in Baja, but mandatory on this particular project. The different trades grouped together according to specialty – to the right were the masons, to the left the carpenters, in the middle the painters, in the back the electricians. A sense of controlled pandemonium pervaded the air and the pressure to perform was high. They were a little over four weeks out from show time, and scrambling to catch up to the schedule. Crews were being run round-the-clock, the prior eighteen hour days of nine hour shifts having proved insufficient to meet deadlines. A host of new arrivals waited on the perimeter for their assignments, bewildered somewhat at the underlying chaos that rumbled in the heavy atmosphere.

The project had been plagued with labor problems, and disputes were now being settled with summary firings of the sub-contractors. The company chartered with making the project happen was in a state of raw panic; there was no higher a profile build in all of Mexico. Many companies had underbid to get the work and had failed at every turn to perform. The lack of certainty in the employees created an unhappy labor pool. This in turn resulted in yet more mistakes or overruns, resulting in more firings, which generated a negative chain reaction.

The work orders were handed out to the *peritos*, the supervisors for a particular trade or section of the project, who in turn issued a list of the day's concepts to their workers. At the end of the day, the *peritos* checked the work and verified that the tasks had been completed, then reported the status of their jobs to the main supervisor, who had a team of engineers working to stage the various projects to be completed on the following day.

Turnover had been high in the skilled trades, especially the plumbers and the engineers, who were essential to the building's completion. Most of the companies that had begun the project were no longer there, their attempts to wrangle more money out of the project once they'd won the bid having failed.

The new electrical supervisor for zone seven nodded as the harried engineer in charge of the myriad electrical details for the build curtly handed him his day's assignments along with a rolled-up plan for his area, before moving to the next man in line. There were thirteen electric sub-contractors who acted as supervisors to the actual electricians; six of them had only been hired within the last three weeks.

The zone seven supervisor signaled his men, and together they moved up the concrete ramp to the upper tier of the main entry, where they would be working on the lighting conduit for the massive reception area, which would double as the stage for any opening festivities. The men moved to their assigned work spots, and the supervisor called two of his more senior workers and handed them a set of detailed drawings containing a list of minor modifications. Specifically, eight of the conduit runs were going to be rewired to accommodate a central switching system for the new runs the detail plans now showed. The men nodded to one another – this would be easy to install at this stage, and wouldn't be much more work, so it would be possible to complete it within the timeframe allocated by the schedule.

El Rey slapped two of the electricians on the back, and they moved to begin the modifications. He watched as they added the desired wiring and strung the modified sections with the existing ones. Ensuring that none of the engineers were around, he studied the new plan he'd had drawn by his consultant in La Paz. It would enable him to mount high explosive nodes to simultaneously detonate with a single flip of a switch, blanketing the reception area in a lethal shower of shrapnel that would slaughter everyone in the vicinity. It would be a killing field when they went off – no one would be able to survive it.

Normally, he favored more surgical methods for fulfilling a contract, but with all the security that would be in place, none of them were feasible. There were no surrounding buildings where a sniper could hide, so the most surefire method was the scorched earth approach. He had no objection to killing many versus only a few. To him, the number was immaterial. He just loathed inefficiency and slop – bombs and poisons, as with radiation, were imprecise. This approach flew in the face of his preferred techniques, but after considering all the possibilities, the mass explosion was the most surefire way of fulfilling the contract.

He would position the custom-made nodes several weeks before the G-20 was to commence along with the detonator caps. All he would need to do was wait for the targets to get within the kill zone, and then push a button. He'd have to be proximate in order to confirm that the targets were actually where they were supposed to be when he detonated, but that was relatively simple to execute. He already had his army uniform, and in all the confusion, one more running soldier would never be missed.

El Rey prided himself on detailed planning, which was one of the reasons he'd had a one-hundred-percent success rate on all his sanctions. It was one of the justifications for his high fee – this time, enough to retire on for good, when combined with his savings.

Under normal circumstances, he got half his fee in advance, no negotiation, and the other half upon successful completion; but this was no ordinary hit, so he'd gotten eighty percent up front. The nodes would be made for him by a specialist in Honduras – he'd already been in contact, and they would require a ten-day turnaround, so next week he'd place the order and then his cartel contacts would take care of smuggling them to

Baja. They were to look like lighting fixtures, only with a deadly coating of easily splintered metal that had the explosive power of ten hand grenades per fixture. For the surface area, three would have done the trick, however he'd decided on eight based on worst case assumptions. At fifteen thousand dollars per node, they weren't cheap, but then again he wasn't price sensitive.

Once the hit was completed, he'd have to go to ground for a long time, perhaps forever, so he wanted to ensure that he had double the amount he'd need to live comfortably anywhere in the world. Mexico was his first choice but would be far too hot for him, so he'd made arrangements to be transported to Brazil, where he could live in luxury in a waterfront villa until the search went cold. He figured three to five years, minimum.

That was fine. After this final job, his swan song, he'd have nineteen million dollars. With that kind of swag he could stay disappeared for a long, long time. He'd already flown to Rio the prior year and spent a week there. It had everything he could wish for – first-class restaurants and infrastructure, beautiful women, great wine from Argentina, and a host of more stimulating, esoteric pastimes available for a discriminating young man of secure means.

He wasn't worried about getting paid his final twenty percent for the job, even though the cartel boss who had hired him was dead. Whoever took over for him was unlikely to test the patience of *El Rey* or invite his wrath.

That was one perk of being notorious, he mused. Collections issues disappeared when you had the reputation for being able to kill anyone, however well they were protected. His clients were actually eager to pay him.

Perhaps, in time, the furor would die down, but he wasn't betting on it, which was one of the reasons he still needed to deal with a few loose ends, and cover his tracks. A door closed, a window opened. It was all part of life.

He watched the men working and felt a sense of quiet satisfaction. He was a lucky man. After all, how many people in the world could honestly say that they truly loved their job?

Julio Brava swaggered along the sidewalk in downtown Mexico City, fully immersed in his role as a fast-money criminal. He'd spent a lifetime around miscreants so he knew all too well how they behaved. That was one of the hardest parts of his job, in truth – separating the pretend from the real. He had a generous amount of walking-around money and little in-depth scrutiny of how he parceled it out, and would stay underground for months at a time, so it was dangerously easy to get caught up in the game and lose track of himself.

The job had cost him his marriage early on – it was hard to explain to a wife why you needed to disappear for fourteen weeks. She'd hung in for the first year, but quickly tired of being married to a phantom. There were no hard feelings from his end, although she claimed he'd ruined her life. That perceptual dissonance was probably just one of the many examples of how men and women differed.

He'd been in the game now for over a decade and had been instrumental in busting a lot of bad guys, but there was literally an infinite number of new ones to slot into the place of any he put away. That was the depressing aspect of his job. There were many positives, though, if you could deal with the constant threat of being killed.

Julio was thirty-nine, and had three different girlfriends who didn't ask questions of the free-wheeling entrepreneur. He drove a lemon-yellow Humvee with every imaginable option, and he kept whatever hours he felt like. Every club in the city recognized him as an A-lister, and he had access to whatever vices he cared for.

Now that he ran his own squad he was autonomous, and nobody complained as long as he delivered results. His operating budget was vast, and the opportunities to make additional money on the streets as a function of the contacts he'd cultivated were substantial. More than once he'd made a loan and seen double the money come back to him within a month. That added up when you were funding your loan shark business with government money; it really was a perfect cover for a cop. It wasn't his fault if he never seemed to be able to turn a profit, at least when reporting to his supervisors. Fortunately, his superiors didn't question things too closely. A man had to earn a living, after all, and lending money to those in need was pretty benign compared to most. It was like being a bank of last resort, really – a liquidity mechanism for a booming economy.

He was on his way to meet a man who was rumored to know how to get in touch with *El Rey*, which didn't mean much at this stage, as most of the hustlers on the street would claim to know how to get you a meeting with

Santa or Jesus for a fee. But this contact was different – he was higher up than most of the contacts on Julio's roster.

Felipe was loosely affiliated with the Gulf cartel, and handled some of their distribution logistics, in addition to managing some of their love-for-sale venues, so he probably dragged down thirty grand U.S. a month, no sweat. That kind of money suggested that you were unlikely to be a time-waster or a con artist. If you were in the game at that level and you said you knew a guy who knew a guy, you probably did. Julio's challenge would be to get to the next stage. That sounded easier than it would likely be.

Julio knew how the street worked – if you were responsible for bringing someone into a circle and they wound up burning someone, you paid the price as the person who vouched for them. It was a brutally effective approach. If Felipe knew anyone affiliated with *El Rey*, he'd be very reluctant to admit it unless the reward far exceeded any risk.

He'd known Felipe for three years and had partied with him more than once, bringing in the dawn as they'd left one club or another together. It had been a mutually beneficial relationship – Felipe passed on prospects who really needed money in a hurry for investment, generally in a product he was selling, but who he was unwilling to provide with credit. Everyone benefited; Felipe got his needs met, Julio got his profit, and the borrower got to play with other people's money. None of his referrals had defaulted, so it was a relationship built on love. The truth was that Julio could lose money on occasion to support his cover and there would be no ramifications, but it offended his sense of business acumen – it was more the principle of the thing.

Felipe greeted Julio with a hug when he walked into his bar. He immediately called over two girls for Julio's consideration. They were enticing beauties, but Julio waved them off – he was there for business. He did accept a glass of *Don Julio 1942*, and waited until they were comfortably settled in a corner booth at the back of the club before he began the discussion he'd come for.

"I hear that you can get just about anything a man could want, my friend," Julio began.

"Very true. Thank goodness that most men's imaginations are limited to things I can readily provide – for a price, of course," Felipe remarked.

"It's the way of the world, is it not?"

"Indeed, my friend, indeed. So…how can I help you today, Raphael? What could I possibly have that you might want? Just mention it, and it's yours," Felipe offered magnanimously. He knew Julio as Raphael – his undercover name.

"I have need of a delicate specialist, for a friend. A very wealthy, powerful friend who can afford the absolute best, and demands it."

"Sounds like my kind of people. And what does he want, exactly?" Felipe asked.

"He has a business partner who has been less than candid with him about the profits of one of their operations, and he's grown tired of having to wake up every morning, distrustful and angry. So he wants to retire his partner…with prejudice," Julio explained.

"Ah. I see. Well, there are many discreet professionals who can accommodate that sort of request," Felipe observed.

"An additional wrinkle is that the partner is his wife's father, so it's precarious; he can't afford the chore to be botched. So he's willing to hire the very best in the business, no matter what the cost," Julio elaborated.

"Hmm. That could be very, very expensive. How much is at stake here?"

"They're involved in a variety of large-scale real estate development projects, domestically, and in Dubai. So it's a great deal of money, my friend, a very great deal. I don't get the feeling he's price sensitive," Julio said.

Felipe considered Julio with interest.

"And why did he come to you?" he asked.

"He knows me as a fixer – someone who can handle problems. He felt that I might be able to better navigate these difficult waters than he could. And he is very generous with his gratitude. I have a feeling the love on this one could be, well, almost embarrassingly large."

"How serious is he? When you get to a certain level, the client risks angering the contractor if he isn't prepared to meet the terms and conditions. And when you're talking about the best, and I mean the very best, you don't want to trifle with the contractor. It would be bad for one's health," Felipe explained.

"I'm fully aware of what's required, and I've gotten sufficient assurances to be comfortable acting as the client's representative."

Felipe leaned back, staring at the ceiling as he thought about the proposal. Julio waited patiently, his anxiety now they were at the tipping point masked by a cultivated indifference crafted through years of experience. Appearing to make a decision, Felipe leaned forward, clasping his hands together as if praying.

"I do have a contact who attends to these sorts of matters. Let me make a call and see what his schedule looks like. But Raphael? Once you go down this road there's no turning back. Even my friendship won't do much good if something sours on your end once the contract is made. I would think long and hard about this particular contractor. He's the best – notorious, actually – but he is very particular about the projects he takes, and he is insanely expensive; as in multiple-seven-figure-American insanely expensive. Is that a problem?" Felipe asked.

"It depends upon who the contractor is. There's no way that kind of money will change hands unless there's a reason for the fee to be that high. We both know that. So unless this is, say, *El Rey* we're talking, I think I can tell you that he won't want to play. That's the level of talent he's used to dealing with – he had the Black Eyed Peas play for his daughter's wedding, as an example," Julio shared.

Felipe sat back, impressed.

"That's exactly the level of talent I'm referring to. There's really only one number one in any game, isn't there? When number two won't do?" Felipe said.

Julio's pulse quickened. "And you can make an introduction?"

"Not with the contractor himself, obviously. But I think I could make contact with someone who could speak for him," Felipe said, lighting a Marlboro with his solid gold Dunhill lighter.

Felipe liked his little luxuries, Julio mused. He wore a platinum Lange & Sohne watch, Gucci loafers, an Armani blazer. Business must be good. Then again, both of their businesses were relatively recession proof. And what was the point in having real money if you couldn't treat yourself to the things you loved?

"I'd be in your debt if you could make that call," Julio stated, locking eyes with Felipe. "And I would be very generous for your trouble."

"But take my warning seriously, Raphael. I would hate to see you get yourself into something you couldn't get out of. Once the call is made, you're on the road. Do you fully understand?"

"I wouldn't be imposing if this wasn't extremely serious. I think we both know that there are dozens of also-rans who would jump at the chance to help my client for a fraction of the numbers you're tossing around. But if you can afford the best, that's what you want. And there's a lot at stake here, Felipe. So I know exactly what I'm getting into, and like I said, I'm completely confident, both in the client's seriousness as well as his gratitude. A gratitude that I will gladly share," Julio assured him.

"Spreading the wealth is always best, *n'est-ce pas*?" Felipe quipped.

"I would have it no other way."

They toasted, and Felipe called the stunning blond female bartender over and requested a refill of their drinks. She smiled at them both, eyes hinting at possibility.

Julio and Felipe exchanged knowing glances.

"Just bring the bottle, Amanda. And pull up a chair. Do you know my good friend Raphael?"

CHAPTER 7

Four men in a silver Dodge Durango with stolen plates approached the offices of Gustavo & Sons, importers and manufacturers of fine stone products. Anxiety flooded the vehicle's atmosphere with its distinctive buzz as the men checked and rechecked their weapons – Kalashnikov AK-47s purchased in Guatemala, a residual of the Nicaraguan and El Salvadorian actions. Gun ownership in Mexico was illegal, with very few permits issued for hunting weapons, and yet the country abounded with automatic assault rifles. The cartels never seemed to have any issues getting their hands on guns, so the law was perplexing to many.

Juan Carlos Batista sat in the passenger seat with the air conditioning blasting in his face, barely denting the perspiration that was a by-product of his preparation for battle. This was far from his first armed assault, but he always felt a flutter of nerves in the moments before the shooting started. It was his variant of performance anxiety. But once bullets were flying, he was eerily cool and dispassionate. The four lines of cocaine he'd snorted in the parking lot seven minutes before had heightened his awareness, but done nothing to still the butterflies in his stomach.

Batista had come up the ranks of *La Familia Michoacana* before that cartel had dissolved into several others, including the Knights Templar cartel, in which he was a high ranking lieutenant, commanding dozens of enforcers in addition to hundreds of traffickers. The dissolution of *La Familia* had been a bloody one, and civilian casualties had been high. Many of the cartel's foot soldiers had a propensity for shooting before they confirmed a target, and some of the more reckless had taken to tossing grenades into crowds where they suspected their targets were standing. It had been a troubling time until Santiago had asserted his authority as the new leader – a result of a grisly catalog of executions of his foes: other pretenders to the throne from *La Familia Michoacana*. During the most combative month, beheaded corpses left by the side of the road had been a daily occurrence – one of Santiago's favored signature flourishes.

His demise had left a gap in the leadership, and that vacuum would be filled. Batista was a natural for the top position. He was as vicious as they came, had proved himself in armed conflict time and time again, was a sociopath who killed without regret, and had good organizational skills. In cartel parlance, he was a born leader who was feared and respected by his subordinates. He had just turned twenty-nine.

Many cartel members never saw their thirties, so on his next birthday he was going to be an old man in that shadow world – a survivor that time had tested with every imaginable obstacle, all of which he'd overcome. He'd been shot twice and had come back to kill his assailants, so he had a reputation for being unusually tough. Most of the time when you shot a man, he stayed shot, but Batista seemed to have the angels on his side.

Batista had grown up watching American movies, and not surprisingly, his favorites had been Scarface and Goodfellas. In an obscene example of life imitating art, he'd aspired to being not only a rich and feared *narcotraficante*, but also to emulate the fictional characters in his favorite films. There was a part of him that believed real life was supposed to be as portrayed in those fictions, and so he'd created an environment where it was – to the detriment of society, as well as most of his rivals.

The *narcotraficante* lifestyle was so celebrated in some segments of popular culture that there were numerous songs glorifying their exploits, and a whole generation had grown up believing that an existence involving routine murder was the new normal. Batista was one of them, and he'd long since lost count of how many lives he'd taken. It was just one of the things he did, until it was done to him. He didn't dwell on things he couldn't change, preferring to live in the moment. It wasn't a highly evolved philosophy, he knew, but it worked for him.

The SUV pulled up to the side entrance of the warehouse that doubled as the Gustavo & Sons showrooms, and the men exchanged glances before pulling ski masks over their faces, on the off chance that anyone remained alive once they were through. They got out of the Durango and moved stealthily to the side door, assault rifles held at the ready. Two of the men had been army soldiers before deserting, so they had gotten formal military training, which they'd used to ascend the ranks as enforcers and executioners.

Disputes were routinely resolved by the parties butchering each other, as well as their enemies' families, so every cartel had its armed forces and its operational group. While the two could co-mingle, often the personnel chartered with smuggling avoided the armed clashes, to the extent they could. The armed contingency lived, as did all armed organizations, to fight, and they did so with abandon, turning many of Mexico's larger cities into shooting galleries. Internet sites in hot zones routinely posted safe routes for travelers to use to avoid armed encounters, and social media followed the skirmishes in real time, as did the police and cartel members.

It was a kind of economically-driven guerilla civil war memorialized on Twitter and Facebook. The summary brutality of the cartels was just a part of living in some Mexican cities, especially the large metropolitan areas near the border and key stops along the smuggling routes – Acapulco, Morelia, Culiacan, Monterrey, and a host of others. Even relatively safe areas like Guadalajara and Puerto Vallarta and Mazatlan saw violence, as the clashes expanded into secondary towns.

Batista swung the door open and quickly moved inside, his enforcers following him. The receptionist uttered a stifled scream and put her hands up, as did the two office workers. Batista considered her momentarily, then gestured for her to exit through the front door. She didn't need to be asked twice, and the two clerks gratefully followed her out, running to their cars the moment they were clear of the building. One of Batista's lieutenants nudged his arm and pointed up to the corner of the room, where a small security camera captured everything for posterity. That was a serious problem, because if anyone was watching real time they would now be forewarned.

They quickly discovered that was the case. A steel door at the back swung wide and a hail of gunfire belched from the opening. Batista's men took cover behind the heavy wooden desks and returned fire, peppering the now-darkened warehouse beyond with slugs. They heard a man cry out in pain – then came a lull in the shooting – possibly due to clips being changed. One of the ex-military men ran crouched towards the opening, and narrowly avoided being stitched with a new burst of fire. He took it in stride as he calmly extracted a hand grenade from his windbreaker and

73

armed it, extracting the pin with his teeth. He waited silently for a few beats, then threw the metal orb through the door. The ensuing explosion deafened them all and cloaked the warehouse in a cloud of smoke.

Sensing their opportunity, Batista ran through the door, firing indiscriminately in all directions. Pausing when his weapon ran dry, he fished another banana clip from his pants pocket and jettisoned the empty one while scanning the area. Three men lay bleeding on the warehouse floor. But not his target.

He saw movement from the periphery and swung around just as a shotgun poked out of the upstairs offices behind him and fired, catching him full in the chest. Batista was knocked backwards as his soldiers sprayed a hail of lead into the upstairs suite. Rapid bursts of machine-gun fire answered them, and one of the ex-military men took a slug through the neck, dropping his weapon with a gurgle before crumpling to the floor near Batista. The two remaining men exchanged glances, and one pitched another grenade through the now-shattered upstairs office windows, to be rewarded with a muffled detonation.

Shooting stopped, and the two cautiously ascended the stairs, listening for movement before kicking the door in. A burst of shooting spat from inside; the front man flew off the landing, falling to the hard cement a story below with a wet *thwack*, bullet holes stitched across his chest. A pool of blood spread from behind his head, creating a halo effect to frame his now sightless eyes. The second man crouched by the side of the door and stuck his rifle into the room, firing blind. His weapon snicked empty, and he was fumbling with a spare clip when the shotgun appeared from around the doorway and boomed, taking half his head off at point blank range.

An eerie silence permeated the space, still echoing with the residual energy of the gun battle. A bald man in his thirties with blood streaming down his face peered from the office, and seeing nothing but bodies, carefully moved around the corpse on the landing, probing it momentarily with his toe before descending the stairs, his SPAS-12 combat twelve gauge shotgun sweeping the warehouse for other assailants.

Satisfied he was alone, he strode over to the fallen ex-military Batista soldier and fired a round into his head, liquefying it. As the smoke from the shot cleared, he spotted Batista lying on the floor twenty feet away, his chest shredded from the double aught buckshot blast. Grinning, he sauntered over and sneered at his fallen rival, pausing to spit on his body before blowing his head off.

The round caught the bald man by surprise. He regarded Batista unbelievingly as he touched the smoking hole in his sternum, directly over his heart. Blood seeped through his fingers, and he held his hand over the wound in a futile attempt to halt the spurts of life from leaking out of his body. He fell to his knees still clutching his chest, until the light went out of his eyes and he slipped to the floor, gurgling a death rattle before finally lying still, a sightless stare of shocked disbelief frozen for eternity on his pallid face.

Batista sat up and rolled his head from side to side, massaging his neck with his left hand while he kept his gun trained on the dead man. He stayed like that for a few seconds, then slowly stood, testing his reflexes and balance. Satisfied he was intact, he slipped the Springfield XD(M) .40 caliber assault pistol back into his shoulder holster, pausing to probe the depressions from the shotgun pellets in the Kevlar vest he wore under his sweatshirt. He blew out a sigh and scooped up his Kalashnikov and then made for the exit at a jog, anxious to be rid of the place now that his rival was dead. The shrill warning cry of sirens keened in the distance, but he knew from experience that by the time the police made it to the building he'd be long gone.

He moved carefully through the vacant offices, AK sweeping the space, ready for anything, but sensed and saw no one. For good measure he fired up at the camera, blowing it to pieces with a burst, and watched with interest as the bulk of it hung by its cable for a few seconds before tumbling end over end and shattering on the floor. He smiled for the second time that day, and felt for the car keys in his pocket. Losing three good men was unfortunate, but he'd succeeding in taking out one of the primary contenders for the throne of the Templars. On balance, it had all been worth it.

The big HEMI V8 cranked over with a deep roar, and Batista pulled out of the parking area as neighboring business occupants nervously exited their buildings, panicked by the sound of the gunfight. He'd need to switch cars, and had provided for that by parking a Honda Accord three blocks away.

Batista had prevailed again. He'd need to call a meeting of his chiefs to fill them in on his latest exploit and secure some reliable replacements – never a problem, because the wages of a cartel enforcer exceeded those of the military by a factor of twenty. Every year, roughly ten percent of the Mexican army made that same calculation and deserted, many to go home, but others to sign up with the very adversaries they'd been fighting.

A matter of simple economics.

Just as everything ultimately was.

Cruz met Julio at a Starbucks near one of the big commercial malls downtown. They'd chosen the location because they were unlikely to be stumbled upon by one of Julio's contacts. Cruz was wearing civilian clothes that he kept in his office; he looked unremarkable when out of uniform.

Ignacio joined them, and the update began.

"I have good news. I think I found a line on *El Rey*," Julio announced.

Ignacio and Cruz exchanged glances and stared at him in disbelief.

"So soon? That's incredible!" Cruz exclaimed.

Julio filled them in on his meeting, omitting the raucous dalliance with the bartender. Julio looked worked after an all-nighter with her, but it had been worth it. They'd hit a few clubs after her shift and wound up back at his condo, where she'd demonstrated with gusto why Argentina was famous the world over for its exports. Julio looking like warmed-over shit wasn't an unusual occurrence; he often had a two day growth on his face and deep circles under his eyes – in keeping with his persona as a debauched criminal playboy.

"When are you going to hear something?" Ignacio asked.

"Any time. Maybe today, maybe tomorrow. I don't want to push and seem too anxious. Baby steps on this one."

"Did your boy, Felipe, give you any hints as to who the contact is?" Cruz asked.

"No. But he did underscore about a dozen times how fucked I would be if I couldn't consummate. Apparently, *El Rey* doesn't approve of tire kickers," Julio quipped.

"I'll bet. So how would you propose we proceed once we're in?" Cruz asked.

"I think you and I go in together to see him after we gel your hair differently and darken your skin a little, and you play the rich industrialist with the multi-million-dollar grudge. We try to glean as much as possible, and if we can't get a meeting with *El Rey*, we lean on the contact and stick him under the jail. A few nights in the Mexico City Jail can be startlingly effective for bringing clarity to confused folks who are on the fence as to whether to help law enforcement..." Julio said.

"All right, we'll follow your lead. But the clock is ticking, and we're stuck running in place right now. What about you, Nacho? Anything to report?" Cruz asked, turning to Ignacio.

"It's weird. Every time I bring up *El Rey*'s name, even the desperate cases go cold – and these are guys who would sell their mother for a hit of crack. I've never seen anything quite like it. The bastard has everyone terrified of him."

"Let's hope that Julio's channel works, then. I'd stand down on any other overtures now that we're in play – we don't want to spook him, and it would seem a little odd if the streets were suddenly buzzing with clients anxious to throw a few million his way," Cruz observed.

"Which introduces another potential issue," Julio said. "I think we need to make arrangements to be able to transfer a million dollars, minimum, via wire transfer from a clean account. If the contact delivers, the only way we'll be able to contrive a meeting is if we've dropped some earnest money in his lap."

"I'll get on it. Shouldn't be too big a problem. Anything else?" Cruz asked.

"Anybody got a cigarette?" Julio asked.

"I'm trying to quit. Go home and get some sleep. You look like you went nine rounds with a gorilla and lost," Cruz advised.

"You don't know the half of it."

❧❦

Batista swaggered into the nightclub he owned at seven p.m., cocky after having cheated death again. His men were making their way in, and two of his main street operatives were already there, drinking Modelo and smoking as they flirted with the cocktail waitresses, who were arriving in preparation for the night's partying. Cruz had the club swept for surveillance weekly, and disliked cell phones for communications of any note, preferring in-person meetings to lay down the law. Mexican law enforcement was still light years behind the Americans, but they'd started intercepting cell calls, which had become a game-changer for communications.

Batista high-fived the two men, and then bumped fists in a classic
Mexican street greeting. Both of the seated gangsters had garish tattoos
running down their arms, and their style of dress emulated that of American
rappers, with oversized pants and shirts, shaved heads, and flat-brimmed
baseball caps perched precariously askance. These were veterans of the
trade, having run their own operations on the streets for years. Both had
killed multiple adversaries as a normal course of their business.

Three more of his crew wandered in over the next twenty minutes, and
the men retired to Batista's sumptuous office at the back of the club. Most
of the cartels were big in the nightclub and bar scene, as well as in the hotel
trade – such venues offered the perfect mechanisms to explain huge
amounts of cash income. Tourist towns were full of massive discos with
nobody in them, but they still managed to take in millions of dollars every
month. Tougher banking regulations intended to curb the illicit drug trade
had little effect on the industry – there were always plenty of ways around
the system for the big guys, just as in every country. The rules mainly served
as an inconvenience, at best, for the small time hustlers. Just as the cartel
wheelers and dealers had no problems buying tractors for their farms or
Escalades and Benzes for their girlfriends, likewise, they had no issues
laundering billions in cash every year. The economies of many neighboring
countries depended on it, including the U.S., where in spite of protests to
the contrary, billions still washed through the system every year – the Miami
Federal Reserve saw more hundred dollar bills than any other bank in the
world, indicating that either geriatric retirees from the East Coast had
virtually infinite numbers of C-notes stuffed under their trailer-park
mattresses, or the Mexican and South American connections were still
flourishing.

Batista filled the assembled men in on the day's events and ended with a
renewed call for vigilance against attacks from his rivals, now reduced to
two – Miguel 'El Chavo' Herrera and Paolo 'Poncho' Gallermo. Both were
equally as dangerous as Batista, and it was not a question of whether they'd
be coming for him, but rather a question of when and how. The chances
that they'd want to reach some sort of an arrangement or division of power
were non-existent, just as the likelihood of Batista compromising with them
was zero. That wasn't how the business worked. You either fought, or died.
Like dogs or roosters in a ring, all engagements ended in death. That was
the life. And the egos involved prevented any intelligent conversation.

Young macho males for whom killing was a daily occurrence, who made millions every month and who ruled with absolute power, were not willing candidates for building bridges or mending fences. Throw in all the free stimulants you could handle, and it was a recipe for bloodshed.

Never more so than in Mexico.

CHAPTER 8

General Alejandro Ortega watched the soldiers as they got into position around the club from his vantage point a safe distance from the action. The major who was directing the tactical team was good, a veteran of many similar assaults against the cartels. While one could never know exactly what to expect, it was usually a safe bet that their adversaries wouldn't surrender easily, and it was understood that lethal force was going to be used.

Spring evenings in Morelia were generally crisp, and this night was no exception. The soldiers wore gray camouflage, fully decked out in combat gear, replete with Kevlar vests, assault rifles, grenades, pistols and combat knives. The squad the general had assembled for this assault comprised fifty men, most equally seasoned as the major. He didn't want any mistakes. Morelia had seen enough open warfare in its streets to last a lifetime, and he couldn't afford a lot of military casualties for the papers to rail about. This had to be surgical and over in minutes, or it would get messy, as they always did when events degenerated into a stand-off situation.

The major's voice murmured over their closed-channel, encrypted radio. His aide handed the general the microphone so that he could speak.

"Yes, Major. I see you're in position. I have both sides of the street blocked off, but you'll need to move quickly in case one of their mob sees the roadblocks and warns them."

"Requesting permission to begin the operation, sir."

"You have a green light, Major. Repeat, you have a green light."

"Roger that. Commencing assault at twenty-hundred hours on the nose." The major's transmission went silent.

A minute later, he watched as the troops moved into the club. He heard the distinctive rapid popping of M4s and M16s, with interspersed small arms fire and the chatter of Kalashnikovs. A grenade sounded, its detonation booming down the street, and then after a few more rounds were fired, quiet returned to the area.

Four minutes went by. Then five. Finally, the major's voice crackled over the com line again.

"We are in possession of the club. All hostiles are down. We've taken fire, and three of our men are dead, two wounded. Nine hostiles terminated. Over."

"I'll be in momentarily. Congratulations on a job well done," Ortega intoned.

The general got out of the command vehicle and strode towards the club, flanked on either side by armed soldiers, weapons brandished lest any unseen assailant decide to pop a few rounds at them; the trio's heavy combat boots thudded ominously in time on the pavement. Army emergency ambulances screeched to the curb, where they waited as the medics darted in carrying stretchers and triage packs.

The interior of the club was a scene of carnage, with blood pooled where bodies had lain. The cartel members had been left in place for photographs and definitive identification, but the fallen soldiers had been moved to an aid area with their wounded colleagues. It was their blood on the floor and walls. Several of the cocktail waitresses were wounded and two were dead — regrettable yet acceptable collateral damage. This was a war, and sometimes civilians got hurt in wars, especially if they frequented cartel strongholds. That was just the way things rolled.

Battle-frazzled soldiers leaned against the wall and lounged on the red vinyl booth benches, their guns pointed at the floor or resting on the tables. Combat was an odd thing, the general mused. Time compressed and minutes seemed to take an hour to pass. Once the adrenaline rush of being under fire diminished, your body felt like it had run a marathon. He knew the feeling, although it had been over a decade since he'd been in a firefight. A ranking general was far too high-profile and strategically important to take risks of that sort.

Two soldiers stood at attention on either side of the battered office doorway, the walls around which were pocked with bullet holes. He entered the room and the unmistakable smell of blood struck him, along with that of voided bowels. They didn't feature that in the movies or on TV, but often when a target was gut shot, the bullets tore through the intestines, leaking bowel fluid everywhere. And equally often, a by-product of dying was a complete loss of neuromuscular control, including bowels and bladder. The business of death was a filthy one, he knew.

It was, after all, his chosen career.

Ortega moved to where the major was standing over a little bull of a man, collapsed behind the metal desk, at least six bullet wounds visible. The room was a disaster, the grenade having hurled shrapnel throughout it; the man behind the desk must have taken cover there to escape the explosion. Judging by most of the other bodies in the room, they hadn't had that foresight.

"It's the target. Batista," the major observed. "He was holed up in here with five others, and a group of enforcers. They put up a fight, I'll give them that, but you saw how long it took to take them down. Stupid bastards should have surrendered instead of trying to shoot it out with an army unit…"

"When was the last time one of these shit-rats wised up and put a gun down, instead of shooting at us?" General Ortega mused.

"Good point. We'd all be out of jobs if human nature changed that much, eh?" the major countered.

"Not likely. Well done, Major. Carry on," Ortega said, before taking a photo of the dead Batista with his telephone.

The general inspected the other bodies with scant interest and then motioned to his two armed attendants to move out. He had no intentions of sticking around any longer than he had to. The operation was concluded, the target neutralized, the mission accomplished. The rest was just mop up.

They returned to the command vehicle and the driver started the engine of the military edition Humvee H1 – a throaty diesel that would run the vehicle through raging rivers or up the sides of mountains. Ortega donned his reading glasses and fiddled with the buttons on his phone, struggling to make out the menu options. After a few false starts, he located the e-mail function and pushed send, watching in satisfaction as the photograph of the dead Batista winged its way to his rival, *El Chavo*, the lieutenant favored by his sponsor in the Sinaloa cartel to run the Knights Templar operation now that Santiago had gone to his reward.

Tomorrow, if *Poncho* Gallermo was still alive, Ortega would be spearheading a drive to eradicate that parasite from the planet as well.

One had to choose one's battles carefully. It didn't pay to buck the system. The world was an imperfect place, and if two dangerous homicidal psychopaths could be taken out with a minimum of fuss, that was good for everyone. Of course they'd just be replaced by other cutthroats, but that was the way of the world. He couldn't stop it, so might as well make a little retirement money while doing his noble duty.

The Humvee moved ponderously down the road to the checkpoint, where the sentries waved it through and saluted their commander, a legend in the ongoing battle for the safety of the Mexican people.

Julio's phone rang at ten-thirty p.m. He answered it, and was greeted by the blaring sound of house music and Felipe's voice.

"Raphael! Hey, man, glad I caught you."

"Felipe. How are you? What are you up to?" Julio asked, his heart rate increasing twenty beats per minute and booming in his ears.

"You got a pen? Write this down. The guy we were talking about? He agreed to see you. His name's Jaime Tortora. He's got a pawn shop near the main cathedral downtown." Felipe gave him the address. "He says he'll see you at ten tomorrow morning, at his place."

"Felipe. That's great. I can't thank you enough. I won't forget this."

"Be careful what you wish for, my friend. Like I said, from this point there's no going back. You're on your own," Felipe reminded him.

"I know. No worry, be happy, right?" Julio said, alluding to a reggae song they had gotten drunk to on their first meeting years ago.

"Isn't that right! Hey, you want to come down to the club and have a drink? May be the last time I see you..." Felipe teased.

"I don't know. The last time I had a drink with you, your bartender almost sucked the life out of me," Julio said.

"She's here tonight. She's been asking about you. Apparently, once you taste the God of Love, you're ruined for all other men. You're an animal, my friend. I've never seen her like this," Felipe reported.

"Yeah. I'll just bet. No, I think I'll stay in tonight. I'm still trying to recover from our last little soirée." Julio's mind wandered to their spirited tryst. "Tell her I'll call her."

"I will. But will you really? If you don't, you better not come around here until she quits, because she'll be looking to even the score," Felipe advised.

"I swear on a stack of bibles as tall as you are, I'll call. But I can't do it tonight. I'm beat," Julio said, omitting that he would be on the phone with Cruz in a few minutes and likely have to meet him early in the morning to finalize a plan of attack and scope out Tortora's shop.

"Sure, sure. Hey, I'm not sleeping with you no matter how sweet you talk, so save your breath for Monique," Felipe concluded. Monique was the bartender's name. As if Julio could ever forget.

The conversation degraded from there into jousting over each other's claimed prowess, and before long Julio signed off, impatient to share the good news with Cruz.

The next morning at eight-thirty, Briones, Julio and Cruz were at the same Starbucks as the prior meeting, Briones with a laptop in tow. They ordered coffee while Briones got online, taking a few minutes to log onto the server at headquarters. They had run a full profile on Tortora, and he came back squeaky clean. No prior arrests, no suspicious bank filings, a model citizen with a modest but sustainable pawn shop, all licenses current, no violations or problems ever reported. Tortora hadn't even had a parking ticket in the last five years, which was as far back as the system went. The man seemed the least likely agent for a contract killer imaginable, much less for *El Rey*. Julio had a momentary fear that maybe this was Felipe's twisted kind of a joke, then dismissed it. He hadn't seemed like he was making a funny when he'd agreed that he could put Julio in touch with the most infamous hit man in Latin America.

Briones tapped out a series of keystrokes and then brought up a window with satellite coverage of downtown Mexico City.

"All right. The red X is the shop. You can see there's an alley running alongside of it, and it backs onto another building, so there's only the back emergency entrance on the alley and the front doors to worry about. At street level are single story shops, with apartments above, but they're accessed from a separate lobby next door to the shop. According to what information we could get, Tortora leases a one bedroom apartment there, and also owns a home in one of the suburbs. Drives a VW Golf, three years old, paid for," Briones recited, pointing at the screen for emphasis.

"What else do we know about this guy?" Julio asked.

"He's fifty-eight, been in the same location for twenty years," Briones said.

"Where is he originally from? Here?" Cruz asked, his skin subtly darker from discreetly applied base, and his hair slicked straight back under a sheen of pomade. The transformation was subtle, but made him unrecognizable – a tribute to the skill of the theatrical makeup woman they'd hired to alter his appearance. A pair of round stainless steel spectacles completed the disguise, and Cruz had been truly surprised when he'd inspected his made-over profile in the mirror.

"Hmm, no. Sinaloa. Culiacan," Briones said, switching screens to access the information.

"Drug capital of Mexico. Coincidence?" Julio wondered.

"Yeah, but population well over a million," Cruz pointed out. "And fifty-eight years ago, the only thing that was going on in Culiacan was tomatoes and a little marijuana. So, inconclusive at best if we're looking to make him the handmaiden to the cartels."

"Fair enough. I was just making an observation. It's all just information," Julio countered.

"Says he's divorced, ten years. One daughter. Not exactly the profile I would expect for this line of work." Briones finished tapping away, and sat back. "What do you think an agent for a hit man would make, per job?"

"Probably at least ten percent or more, if he's getting the jobs. But in this case it would be the other way around. So maybe less. Why?" Cruz asked.

"And he'd probably deal with the payments for him, too, right?" Briones had ignored the question, obviously driving at something.

"I'd imagine. Where are you going with this?" Cruz demanded.

"What's he doing with all the money? Even if he passed most of it on to *El Rey*, if he's dragging down, what, two to three million a pop, pardon the pun, Tortora should have millions lying around by now, or at least a couple of million, easy. But look at the neighborhood and the business. It's a zero. And his house? Maybe worth a hundred thousand, maybe two on a stretch. Modest. Says here he has a grand total of eighteen thousand dollars in the bank across all his accounts, which is a lot by Mexican standards but nothing in the scale of what we're looking at. So where's he keeping the money?" Briones asked.

Cruz finished his coffee with a swallow. "I suppose if he's sophisticated enough to be money laundering for *El Rey*, he probably has an offshore bank account, don't you think? And that wouldn't show up anywhere. So just treat this like a cartel financier, and you'll be in the loop. All the money is underground, or in cash. So an absence of money proves nothing, unfortunately."

They went round and round on Tortora, but in the end, the obvious course was just to meet him and see what he said. They wouldn't be wearing wires, because a pro would have detection equipment and they'd be instantly blown. So the plan, such as it was, involved meeting him, seeing how it played out, and then come down on him like a falling piano.

They finished their coffees and folded up shop, descending the escalators to the parking garage where Julio's Humvee was parked. They'd agreed they would take two cars and drop Briones off to watch for anything suspicious while they found parking spots – probably one of the most difficult aspects of their foray into that neighborhood.

They drove across town and located Tortora's street using the GPS in the Humvee, and Cruz dropped Briones off a block away so he could meander over and keep an eye on the shop for the ten minutes it would probably take to park. Briones moved into position on the same side of the street as Tortora's, and bought a *churro* from a sidewalk vendor, pretending to be engrossed in a text message conversation while eyeing the target. He felt a brief sensation of apprehension, given the stakes involved in this meeting, made worse by the double dose of caffeine over the morning's briefing. He made a mental note never do that again before a field op.

Briones started, nearly jumping, when he felt a hand on his windbreaker. He spun around and found himself facing one of the city's transient population – a filthy, disheveled woman, obviously high on something, grabbing at him while incoherently muttering a begging mantra. He shook her off and handed her a few pesos, eager to be rid of her. She didn't even register the money as she continued down the sidewalk, hands outstretched to accost someone else.

Thankfully, there wasn't much pedestrian traffic on the street, which made it easier for Briones to eye the pawn shop. If at all possible, he wanted to avoid having to stand conspicuously near Tortora's to monitor things, preferring a discreet distance. He considered moving across the thoroughfare so he could keep watch on both the deserted alley and the storefront, and then he saw Julio and Cruz, walking together down the sidewalk from the opposite direction. It was game time.

Reassured by the weight of his Sig Sauer in his shoulder holster, he elected to stay on Tortora's side of the road and move down the block before circling back and eventually taking up a position across from their objective. Briones strolled towards the shop, figuring he would glance down the alley and then jaywalk across to the opposite side when he was fifty yards past it, and almost collided with another vagrant – this time a man emerging from the squalid alley, wearing grubby brown slacks and a tattered sweater, clutching a satchel that no doubt contained his few worldly possessions. Both men instinctively started when he rounded the corner, and the two haltingly mumbled apologies to each other as they continued on their separate ways.

Momentarily thrown by the near miss, Briones turned and followed the man with his eyes. *Great. Now he was jumping at panhandlers and bums.* He needed to rein in his caffeine-augmented imagination and focus on the task at hand, before Cruz and Julio reached the front door. Briones was going to be no use to them if he let his nerves distract him. He mentally shook himself and pulled his act together, concentrating on seeming nonchalant as he strolled at a measured pace. Crossing the alley, he took a hard look at the two dumpsters next to the emergency exit side doors, noting they were overflowing with trash uncollected for weeks. The alley was short, which he expected from the satellite image, and dead-ended into a brick wall covered with graffiti, the filthy ground littered with stinking refuse around the battered receptacles.

Briones brushed past Cruz and Julio without revealing anything, and continued down the block fifty more yards before seeming to change his mind. Waiting for a break in traffic he jogged across the street, where he took up position with a good view of both the shop and the alley mouth.

Julio pushed the door open and a buzzer sounded from the back of the building, behind the barred window that kept intruders at bay. After a few moments, hearing nothing, Julio called out.

"*Señor* Tortora? *Hola. Señor* Tortora. *Buenos dias.* Is there anybody there?"

Nothing.

Cruz studied the shabby merchandise in two tired display cases while they waited, having registered the mirrored half globe on the ceiling that was a surveillance camera.

"Maybe he's in the bathroom?" Julio suggested.

Cruz pushed a button mounted by the window, and they heard a bell sound in the back, but no ensuing sounds of movement.

They exchanged troubled glances, and Cruz peered through the bars while Julio tried the handle of the heavy steel access door.

"It's locked," he said.

"That figures. What do you want to do?" Cruz asked. This was Julio's show.

"I think we wait a few minutes. Maybe he stepped out to grab a snack or some coffee," Julio said doubtfully.

Ten minutes later they were still standing in the shop, with no evidence that anyone was ever going to show up.

"All right. This is bullshit. I'm going to go around and try the other door, and if that's locked, we fold this up and get someone who can open this. Either he's made us and bolted, or something's wrong," Cruz said, moving to the door while withdrawing his cell phone from his pocket. He called Briones.

"There's a problem. Nobody's here. I'm going to go around and see if I can get in the back way. If not, I need a locksmith and a tactical team down here fast, so we can tear the place apart. Have you seen anyone exit the building – including the apartments?" Cruz asked.

"No, although I did…never mind," Briones said, feeling stupid for even bringing it up.

"What?"

"I almost ran into a homeless guy. He was coming out of the alley," Briones explained.

"When? How old was he?"

"I don't know. Younger than me…," Briones guessed.

"Then it wasn't Tortora. He's older. And he isn't a vagrant, as far as we know."

"Right."

"Okay. Keep your eyes peeled. I'm walking out the front door right now, and I'm going to try the alley entrance. Stay on the line, but watch the surroundings," Cruz instructed, moving down the grim little dead-end street to Tortora's rear door. He tried the knob, and it, too, was locked.

"Shit. Okay, call tactical in, stat, and get someone who can pick this lock."

"All right, boss. I'm on it."

Cruz fumed at how close they'd gotten, only to be stymied at the one yard line. He returned to the shop and briefed Julio. The pair settled in to wait for the tactical team. That could take a while.

"Looks like we got made somehow," Cruz said.

"I don't see how, though. Really. It makes no sense," Julio answered.

Cruz paced back and forth. This wasn't how the day was supposed to go. His phone began ringing, but before he could answer it both Julio and he were startled by a figure opening the front door of the shop. A young woman entered, as surprised to see them as they clearly were to see her.

"Oh. I'm sorry...I...you surprised me. May I help you?" she asked them.

Cruz took her in. Medium height, maybe early thirties at most, huge brown eyes and wavy black hair. A face that was unconventionally beautiful. Conservatively dressed. Counterfeit Dolce and Gabbana purse and sunglasses, he noted – one of the many occupational habits of being a cop.

Julio spoke first.

"What do you mean, can you help us? We're waiting to see *Señor* Tortora," he said with what probably passed in his mind as a charming smile.

"Oh, well, he should be here. Let me go back and see," she said, returning the smile with considerably less enthusiasm. She eyed Cruz and shot him a smile, too, then moved past them to the door. She fiddled with her keys, and turned to face them.

"Uh, do you mind? Could you move over by the front door? I'm feeling a little crowded here, and I don't want to open this with you standing beside me. Security and all. No offense," she apologized, holding her keys at the ready.

Julio glanced at Cruz.

"Of course. I'm terribly sorry. It was thoughtless of us. Please. We'll just be right here." Julio motioned at the area by the front entrance and moved there, pulling Cruz's sleeve. He stepped over as well.

"Will that work for you?" Cruz asked.

"Thank you. I'll see where he is." She slipped through the door as she spoke.

They waited patiently, Julio tapping his foot, Cruz cleaning his nails. She returned to the little showroom area a few moments later, puzzled.

"That's strange. He's not here. He's always here. Hmm. I wish he would carry his cell phone – then I could call him. He leaves it in his apartment upstairs, or in the car. He's lousy with things like that," she explained. "I didn't get your names…"

"I'm sorry. Very rude of us. This is Señor Albon, and I am Raphael Contreras. And you are?" Julio extended his hand.

"I'm his daughter. Dinah Tortora. Pleased to meet you both. Is there something I can help you with since my father has, erm, disappeared for a few minutes?" she asked, shaking their hands in turn.

"We were really hoping to speak to him in person. A delicate matter he was helping us with," Julio said.

Dinah looked confused.

"Delicate matter? Um, okay…you know, if you don't mind, I'll run upstairs and check on him. Now I'm a little worried. Maybe he slipped and hurt himself or something," Dinah said, and made for the front door. Both men stepped aside, Julio making a courtly mini-bow. They watched as she left the shop and made a right, going to the apartments.

"What's with the *Don Juan* act?" Cruz chided.

"Are you kidding? She's gorgeous. What, are you blind?"

"Her father is *El Rey*'s agent. We're working. Does that ring any bells?" Cruz reminded.

"Party pooper. I didn't get the hit man vibe from her. Did you? I don't think she knows anything. That's where my money's at." Julio winked.

"Maybe. But there's no way to be sure—"

They were cut off by a scream of horror from the apartments.

CHAPTER 9

Cruz and Julio raced to the small apartment's foyer, to be greeted through the glass door by the sight of Dinah staggering down the stairs from the corridor above, obviously in shock, with blood on her hands and dress. The street door was locked, so they had to wait for her to reach them and open it, tears streaming down her pale face as she grabbed at the handle reflexively.

Once the door was open, Cruz grabbed her by the shoulders.

"What's wrong, Dinah? What happened?" he asked, processing the blood on her and fearing the worst.

"It's…my father…"

Julio looked up the stairway with trepidation, and then back at Cruz.

He nodded, and Julio mounted the stairs while Cruz hugged Dinah, who was sobbing against his chest and howling her agonized grief. He had done this hundreds of times in his career, but it never got any easier; each time took a little out of him. Her slender torso shuddered as she struggled to breathe, fighting for air between strangled exclamations of pain. Any doubts he had about whether she was involved in her father's business slipped away – this wasn't a woman accustomed to the business of death.

Julio returned from the apartment looking wan. He was in the streets every day, dealing with the parasites of humanity, not in a combat squad, so he wasn't used to seeing corpses on a weekly basis. He looked like he was going to be sick.

"It's bad."

"Call Briones, and have him get a full crime scene team here. Take care of Dinah. I want to go take a look at what we've got," Cruz instructed, gently pushing Dinah into Julio's arms.

At the top of the stairs, he was greeted by a short corridor with four entries, one of which was now ajar, and one of which squeaked on its hinges as he slowly walked to the open door. An old woman's head poked out, scowling with disapproval.

"What's all the yelling about?" she demanded loudly.

"There's been an accident. Go back inside and lock your door," Cruz answered.

"What, are you fighting with a girlfriend? Did you hit her? Is that the story?" the woman stormed, sure that Cruz was up to no good.

"*Señora*, please. This is now a crime scene, so go inside, bolt your door, and an inspector will be by later to take a statement."

She spat an expletive under her breath, and then the door slammed shut, the sound of multiple deadbolts engaging filtering into the hall. The other occupants were probably all at work, so for a while there would be some peace in which to process the scene. That was the only good news so far.

He pushed the door open cautiously with his toe, careful to avoid touching the knob even though he knew Dinah had already done so. It creaked open. Cruz entered the tiny living room, wishing he had his gun with him, and stopped when he saw the body lying on the floor in a puddle of blood. He'd seen hundreds of corpses in his time, but nothing like this – the man was nearly bisected, from his shoulder to his hip. Cause of death wouldn't be too tough on this one. What the hell could cause this kind of butchery? A splatter pattern at least six feet wide surrounded the body, evidencing that he'd been cut down where he lay.

He scanned the room and answered his own question. A plaque holding a short Japanese dagger in its scabbard was mounted to the wall. The pegs above the dagger were empty, dust clearly indicating where a longer katana had resided. Cruz took several more steps into the room and saw the weapon lying on the floor, covered with blood, the scabbard discarded nearby. The blood was fresh, no more than an hour old, he knew from jaded experience. Soon the flies would come, but as of now, it was just the two of them.

Jaime Tortora, whatever his sins, had seen his last morning, and their hopes of closing in on *El Rey* had died with him. Unless they could find some clues in his shop or his homes, this was, as they said, a dead end. The timing couldn't have been worse, forcing Cruz to confront the ugly thought that had been circling in his head: nobody but he, Briones and Julio had known about this meeting, so either they had a leak within their ranks, or *El Rey* had decided to egress from the business and close down his conduit.

Cruz would like to think it was the latter, because it confirmed what he already now believed: that the assassin was planning a hit on the G-20, and getting paid enough to exit the game for good. Perhaps Tortora had contacted him with news of the new potential client he was going to meet, and that had triggered the ugly murder. Maybe Felipe had bragged to the wrong person, and this had nothing to do with *El Rey*. Possibly, it was a burglary gone wrong, or retribution for something else. Or perhaps it was all coincidence.

But Cruz had long ago given up believing in coincidence.

No, either Briones or Julio had passed on information, or Felipe had talked to the wrong people, or the timing was just wildly unfortunate and it was unrelated, which Cruz didn't believe for a second. He gingerly stepped towards the bathroom and saw a disposable raincoat, covered in bloody spray, discarded on the floor. So much for the burglary theory. Looking at that, he could do a quick equation in his head and piece together what had happened. Someone who knew the apartment, knew about the swords, had entered unbeknownst to Tortora and waited for him, perhaps hiding, suited up to prevent the spatter pattern that would be inevitable when using the sword.

Cruz slowly turned. There was a large armoire behind him that jutted two feet into the room, behind which was the window to the street, framed by long curtains. He closed his eyes and imagined the scene. That's where the killer had stood, waiting. But how would he have known when Tortora would return to the apartment? Cruz thought for a few seconds.

Of course. Because he got a call after opening the shop, instructing him to come to the apartment. From someone whose orders he would follow to the letter.

The killer had waited, hidden in the corner by the curtains, shielded from view by the armoire, confident that Tortora would enter shortly. Tortora had come in, and then walked to the small kitchen bar, and the killer had stepped from his hiding place, taken several long strides, and struck before his victim turned to register his presence.

So how had he gotten him to that location, where he could do the deed within seconds of moving into the room?

Cruz studied the splatter of blood and saw that there was a vaguely rectangular area that hadn't been hit on the edge of the breakfast bar counter. Something had rested there, and was now gone. He peered over the body into the kitchen, but saw nothing amiss. Returning to the bathroom, he noted a bloody bath towel tossed into the small shower stall.

So the killer had wiped off whatever it was, and taken it with him. Cruz considered possibilities, then reached into his jacket and dialed Briones.

"You mentioned a vagrant you bumped into. Think carefully. Describe him to me," Cruz instructed.

"Hmm, he was about your height, maybe a little taller, no beard or mustache, short hair cut like mine, medium brown skin. Wearing filthy brown slacks and navy blue pull-over sweater with holes in it. I don't remember what kind of shoes, but I think they might have been boots."

"Was he carrying anything?" Cruz asked in a quiet voice.

"You know…he was. It was a satchel, one of those old-fashioned types with two straps holding it closed. Dirty brown leather, or suede. You know what I'm talking about?" Briones asked.

"I know the kind." Cruz cursed inwardly. "Lieutenant, do you think you could describe his features well enough for a sketch artist to do a rendition?" he asked.

"Sure. I think so. But why…?"

"I think it might be important. You may have just been one of the only living people to have ever seen *El Rey*." Cruz sighed.

"You're kidding me…you aren't, are you? Shit – sorry, sir. Okay, I'll try to remember everything I can, but the sooner the better. You know how details get lost the longer you wait and the more distractions that take place…"

"Call headquarters and get Arlen down here, and have her bring her pad. I want a face today," Cruz ordered.

"Will do."

Cruz hung up. He could envision the satchel in his mind's eye. Sitting on the counter.

So a call comes in after Tortora has opened his little shop at nine a.m., telling him that a bag full of something important – money, maybe – had been left in the apartment for him to deal with, and to do so immediately. Tortora ducks out of the shop, knowing that there won't be any customers at that time of day, and goes to his apartment. He doesn't have to ask how the satchel got there. The killer is a man for whom locks present no problems, or who has a key. Doesn't matter. Tortora opens the door, closing it behind him so he's not disturbed. He sees the bag where he was told it would be, walks to inspect it, and before he knows what's happened, is cut in two by the trusted caller, whom he had no reason to suspect or fear. The killer grabs the satchel, goes to the bathroom to clean it off, wipes it down with one of the towels, then sheds the raincoat. Perhaps he also wiped off his face, which might have gotten some blood on it. Cruz made a mental note to warn the crime scene unit to check the towel and the curtain for hairs or other DNA trace materials. It was worth a shot.

So then what does the killer do?

Cruz swung around, considering. He probably does a cursory search, and then grabs the keys to toss the shop office as well. Presuming he was looking for something. If that was the case, it would explain why he was in the alley. He had just completed his search of the office and was leaving the crime scene.

The timing suggested that he knew Tortora had a meeting at ten. Again, could be coincidence, but he doubted it. The scenario that made the most sense was that Tortora had contacted the assassin to alert him that he had another gig available, and *El Rey* decided he wasn't going to be needing Tortora or any more jobs, so elected to eliminate the only way to trace him. It all meshed together. Especially if he was going to take out a couple of presidents – he had to know that at that point it would just be a matter of time until someone rolled and they got to Tortora.

The puzzle pieces gelled and he saw the whole picture.

Only problem being that it wasn't proof. It was circumstantial evidence that a skeptic could explain away a dozen different ways. So they were still screwed on securing anything they could use to sway the arrogant pricks at CISEN, much less the NSA.

Cruz had seen enough.

He returned to the foyer, drawn by the sound of Dinah crying, and decided it was time to show his cards.

"Dinah, I'm Federal Police. I came to have a discussion with your father about a matter I thought he could assist us with. I've ordered a forensics team, and they're on their way to process the apartment." Cruz's heart fluttered when she looked up at him, eyes huge and streaming tears, the minute amount of mascara she'd worn streaking her face. "I'm deeply sorry for your loss. Believe me that we will do everything possible to find your father's murderer. But I need your help. Can you open the back of the shop for me so we can process that area as well? I didn't see any keys upstairs, so it's possible that the killer did this to gain access to his office," Cruz said.

"Police?" Dinah was in shock, her skin now the color of alabaster. She wasn't really with it, her tone tremulous, speaking as though from a great distance. "Yes. I'll open it…" She grabbed at the door handle, nearly collapsing in the process. Julio attentively held her elbow, helping to steady her.

"Did your father have any enemies?" Cruz probed, as they proceeded to the shop next door. "Do you know anyone who might have a grudge or a reason to kill him?"

"Enemies? No…no, everyone got along with him," she replied absently as she fumbled with her keys. Julio held the front door of the pawn shop open for them, and they eased through it. Dinah approached the back office door with the key held out, but couldn't steady her hand sufficiently to insert it into the lock. She extended an arm and supported herself against the wall, holding the key ring out to Cruz, silently seeking his help.

He took the keys from Dinah and put his arm around her, opening the door with his other hand. She was going to crash hard soon, he knew from harsh personal experience, and would probably need months of counseling and medication to make it through this ordeal in one piece. Cruz still vividly remembered the period following his family's murder; a Kafkaesque, surreal odyssey of catastrophic collapses punctuated with valleys of despair and rage, and occasional moments of compassion and hope – regrettably, all too few.

"Dinah, was your father afraid of anyone? Did he have any suspicious dealings or any secrets he might have been keeping?" Cruz was now fishing, but it couldn't hurt.

"Secrets? No. He owned a pawn shop, for God's sake. What kind of secrets could he have had? He didn't even drink, didn't have any girlfriends…," she trailed off, remembering her father, lost to Cruz for a time.

The questioning wasn't going anywhere. He surveyed the back room, which was neat and organized, with new inventory Tortora had taken in on one side, and files on the other. A simple mahogany desk sat at the far end of the room, near the rear exit door, and a large gun safe stood open near it.

Cruz moved to the gaping strongbox, which had been equipped with a number of shelves, upon which sat more valuable trinkets; watches, a few gold chains, other treasures of nominal value that had been traded for ready cash.

"Is this the only safe?" Cruz asked Dinah.

"No. There's a floor safe under that rolling file cabinet." She gestured in the direction of one of the cabinets lining the wall behind the desk.

Cruz moved it and found the safe, which seemed large for the size of the establishment. He grabbed a blank sheet of paper from the desk, bent down and tried the handle, but it was locked.

"*Señora* Tortora. I need you to open this, please."

"It's *Señorita*, and you can call me Dinah. I'm sorry...I don't remember your name. And I can't open it. I don't have the combination," Dinah explained.

"It's Romero. Or Cruz. Everyone calls me Cruz." He avoided introducing Julio, and motioned with his head for him to make himself scarce. They wouldn't have to explain his identity if he wasn't there. "Don't worry about the safe, then. I'll just need your permission to drill it open. It's not a big deal, and we're going to be here for a while, anyway..."

"Do whatever you have to do, *Señor* Cruz. Whatever. I mean, what kind of animal can do that sort of thing?" She shuddered. "Just find who did this to him. Please. I'll help in whatever way I can. He was such a good man, a gentle, good, sweet man..." Dinah was fading fast. He wasn't surprised.

Taking the hint from Cruz, Julio slipped quietly through the door, leaving them alone. Dinah didn't notice. She was still fighting to get her sobbing under control, the sight of her beloved father sliced in two winning that battle so far. Cruz pulled one of the chairs from in front of Tortora's desk and offered it to her. She accepted it gratefully, and he swung the other one around, resting his folded arms on the back, leaning his chin forward on them, facing her.

"So what do you do for a living, Dinah?" Cruz wanted to try to get her onto something besides replaying the horror of the sight of her father, over and over again like a tape loop in her head. He knew that was the tendency, and he also remembered how destructive it was to one's psyche. If he could break that pattern early, it wouldn't be a magic bullet, but it might help her later. The sooner she started focusing on something else, the better.

"I teach school. Second grade."

"Why aren't you working today?" Cruz asked.

"It's Saturday."

That's right. He'd been so caught up in the hunt for *El Rey* he'd forgotten that normal people remembered the days of the week. Cruz was often taken by surprise when his calendar showed it to be Sunday, though he spent most of those in his office as well, catching up.

"Ah. Sorry. In my line of work you sometimes lose track…how do you like being a school teacher?" Cruz tried again.

"It's rewarding. The pay isn't great, but I don't do it for the money. I always wanted to be a teacher ever since I was a little girl, so I guess I'm living my dream," she said.

"I always wanted to be a policeman, so same here," Cruz confirmed.

She drifted away again, the brief sojourn into normalcy having lost its appeal.

"This will sound trite, but I'm going to say it anyway, Dinah. I know exactly what you're going through, and there's nothing worse in the whole world."

She seemed surprised, and also angry. That was good. She had every right to be angry. Anger could be good. It had certainly sustained Cruz through some dark times.

"Do you? How could you? Watching people who have had their loved one killed is different than being the one who lost. All due respect, it's not close to the same," she spat.

"I know that, Dinah. I've been through the same kind of thing. I know what it feels like. Nothing anybody says will help. You have to find something inside of yourself, a reason to keep getting up every morning, and focus on that. Maybe it's to teach some youngsters, to pass on knowledge that will form them as human beings. Whatever it is, you'll need to find that thing, and cherish it. After you finish grieving, which will take some time," he offered.

"Easier said than done," she replied, embittered.

"I know. It's the hardest thing you'll ever do. But you'll need to, or you'll lose yourself and make your life about grief and horror, and that's no way to live. I've been there. Trust me on that," Cruz stressed.

They were interrupted by the arrival of the crime scene investigation team. Soon, a pair of technicians were upstairs in the taped-off apartment, sorting through the site's contents, dusting for prints and scouring the area for DNA, while another pair efficiently did the same in the office – much easier given there wasn't a gallon of blood to negotiate. Cruz walked Dinah to the front of the store and brought the chairs there, where they could stay out of everyone's way while they worked.

After an hour, one of the technicians processing the office came out and addressed Cruz.

"Sir, you can have the safe drilled now. We dusted and lifted seven sets of prints, and we'll run them once we get back to headquarters. But the hard disk for the surveillance camera has been wiped, and there's no CD in the machine. Either it was removed, or there never was one," he explained.

"No, he always recorded everything to CD and backed it up," Dinah assured them. "I know. I set up the system for him. He wasn't great with technology, but he'd learned to operate it, and it was the first thing he did every morning…"

Cruz nodded at the tech. "Note it in the report. And send in someone to open the safe," he ordered, rising and taking Dinah's arm. "You may want to plug your ears, but I want you to be here when it opens and we inventory it, so nothing walks off. It's rare, but it has happened."

"All right." She had finally run out of tears, but was distant – the shock was still there in force.

"Do you know what's in it?" Cruz asked casually, watching her to gauge her reaction.

"Not really. He told me once he kept some dollars and pesos in there, and some critical paperwork, but mostly it was for cash."

"Any idea how much?"

"No. I wish I knew more, but I don't. It can't be that much. My father was comfortable, but he was far from a rich man," she said.

A heavyset tech entered with an industrial drill in one hand and a case in the other. He wore safety goggles, and moved past them directly to the safe. After a cursory glance he shook his head. They had many master keys for safes, but not for one this large and of this vintage. Cruz nodded to him; he plugged the drill into the wall, and the clamor started.

Twenty-five minutes later, the driller stepped back, finished. He cranked the stainless steel handle and lifted the door open, then packed his drill and case and moved away from the work area.

Cruz approached the open safe, noting that Briones was now standing guard in the doorway. He'd been so involved with Dinah and the crime scene that he'd forgotten about the lieutenant, who had arranged for the personnel to secure the area without interrupting him. He stared down into the safe, and then with a sigh, began pulling out stacks of thousand peso notes. By the time he was done, there was easily a million pesos sitting neatly on the desk – at thirteen something to the dollar, around a hundred thousand dollars. A lot of money, but nothing that couldn't be explained with the shop, he was sure.

But there were no dollars. And other than a few business-related files and the title to the car and the house, no documentation that could help them. Peering into the safe, Cruz calculated that there was room for a lot more, which if even half of it had been dollars, and somehow *El Rey* had gained access, it could have amounted to at least a million U.S. Unfortunately, whatever else it had contained would remain a mystery to them.

Dinah seemed surprised by the stack of pesos, but lost interest once they were accounted for and recorded – one million six hundred thousand. He signed a receipt for the pesos and handed it to her, cautioning her not to lose it. With his signature, that was as good as a deposit slip. The *Federales* would take the cash into holding, and release it once the investigation was over.

She woodenly put the receipt into her purse, thanking him, and then gazed blankly around the office, lost. Cruz called Briones over and had a brief discussion with him, then handed him the keys to his car. Cruz lifted one of Tortora's cards from the holder on the desk and scrawled his police headquarters number and name on it before handing it to her.

"This is my contact information, Dinah. Please don't hesitate to call, for any reason. This has been a horrible day, and again, I'm deeply sorry for your loss. Hold onto it, if you think of anything that can help, or you need anything. This is Lieutenant Briones. He'll give you a lift home," Cruz said, slipping the card into her purse.

Dinah seemed out of it, and mechanically thanked him for all the help. As they walked out the front door, she turned to him and fixed him with a desperate stare.

"Please find whoever did this to my father, Cruz. Please."

Cruz returned her gaze without wavering. He nodded.

"I will. I promise."

CHAPTER 10

Fourteen years ago, Culiacan, Mexico

The young man pulled himself up on the steel bar mounted in the doorway of his bedroom, his hundredth chin-up in the set of three he did every morning as part of his workout. Three hundred pushups, three hundred chin-ups, forty-five minutes of running, seven days a week, without fail. Sweat poured from his flushed face as he groaned an exhalation, counting the final one and then dropping onto the balls of his bare feet.

He'd completed his run, and also his pushups, so now it was time for his shower, and then he'd begin his day. He padded across the saltillo tile floor to his bathroom, stripped off his sweat shorts and turned the water on — always cold, regardless of the temperature outside. Like everything in his life, the cold water was a ritual, and rituals were important. Rituals had sustained him and given meaning to his life. Rituals meant he was in control, and as the grueling workouts and his straight-A schoolwork underscored, he was always in control — that was his rule, his promise to himself: always maintain control.

He soaped up, noting the six pack abs and professional athlete-level arm and leg muscles with satisfaction. It had taken years of work to create this body, and nothing had come easily. That was fine. He didn't mind effort, and had developed formidable levels of fortitude and commitment. Without commitment, you gave up, and if you quit, you didn't have control. Whatever you'd quit had won, and you had lost. In his mind, it was polarized. Black and white.

The boy had grown into an impressive young man, with a quiet intensity and a brilliant mind, as his teachers could confirm. The private school he attended had skipped him ahead two grades, and he still found the work to be laughably easy. Whenever he was bored, he would read math and engineering books, with the occasional physics textbook thrown in for diversity. He had an insatiable thirst for knowledge, and devoured books like most teens went through sodas.

His life had taken an auspicious turn since that bloody night in the cannabis field. The man who'd saved him had raised him like a son, and provided for him in ways he'd never imagined existed. In return, he'd demonstrated absolute loyalty, and had invested thousands of hours practicing at the estate with every manner of weapon, in preparation for moving into an active role in the family business.

'*Don*' Miguel Lopez was a tough but fair master over his empire, which had grown powerful during the twelve years the boy had lived with him. It now included most of the marijuana crops in Sinaloa and a substantial cut of the cocaine trafficking business. He was respected and feared by his subordinates, as well as his enemies, and had evolved into a legend in the trade – one of the longer-toothed of the cartel heads at fifty years old. He made more in a day than most of his countrymen ever dreamed of making in an entire lifetime, and yet he remained simple, eschewing the ostentatious fast money lifestyle of the new crop of traffickers as evidence of their insecurity and inferiority.

The young man had learned his lessons well. He inspected his reflection in the mirror and liked what he saw. Girls found him pop-star attractive, although his interest in them was limited to sex, and nothing more. He was a loner, and didn't want or enjoy the company of others, preferring to be alone with his books and his thoughts. He'd avoided the traps of youth – shunning the temptations of drugs, and had only taken alcohol on a few occasions, and then only token amounts in accord with the setting. Altering one's state meant surrendering control. He wasn't interested. Likewise, sharing one's thoughts or anything more than some anonymous physical pleasure also involved relinquishing control. And after his one stab at a relationship with his trainer's daughter had inexplicably ended in rejection, he'd sworn off anything that involved getting close to another living human being – love was for the weak and dim, not for him.

Today was a big day. It was his birthday, sweet seventeen, when he would become a man in the eyes of the cartel and could assume a position within the loose hierarchy *Don* Miguel had created. This was a touchy subject between them, because *Don* Miguel had hoped that the young man would go to university to study architecture or engineering, or get a law degree, the better to create a new generation of educated heirs to his empire. But the young man had other ideas. He had expressed a desire to be part of the armed enforcement division of the *Don*'s cartel, and wouldn't be dissuaded. It was difficult for *Don* Miguel to argue against it with much conviction, considering his massive wealth had been created in the burgeoning trafficking industry, but they'd had numerous heated exchanges where the *Don* had told the young man he was throwing his talents away. He had the potential to be whatever he chose, and to waste it being an armed thug was sinful.

It was one of their few ongoing disagreements.

Don Miguel had no children, his wife having proved barren in spite of every medical innovation, and he'd invested much of his parenting drive in raising the young man to be a leader. His wife had died from cervical cancer six years previous, and he'd refused to get married again. He saw no point in it, preferring to have willing young women rotate through his harem rather than staying with any one. *Don* Miguel didn't want the liability of having to worry about a wife – someone that could be used as a bargaining chip in an adversarial situation. The longer he'd been in the business, the more changes he'd seen. It was a different industry than before; more violent, more dangerous. If you loved someone, they could be used against you. He couldn't afford it.

The young man strolled into the main house, dressed, ready for the day, which he'd been told would be a special one. *Don* Miguel wanted to take him to see something: a surprise, he'd said, instructing him to be ready to leave at nine a.m. The young man had complied, punctual as ever. When the *Don* saw him enter the formal dining room, he rose to embrace him.

The cook had made a special breakfast to commemorate the event, and the two sat, eating, looking through the picture window at the river below them. *Don* Miguel owned most of the land in this area of Culiacan, stretching far into the slopes of the distant hills. He was one of the largest landowners in the region. His private *estancia* boasted two hundred ninety-five acres, and featured a stable for his fifteen horses – his one luxury.

Once they had broken their fast, the young man followed the *Don* to his truck – a new Chevrolet Suburban, which was the epitome of luxury compared to the two decade old Ford that was its predecessor. They drove into the hills, on a private road that bordered the estate, and continued for fifteen minutes until they reached a clearing. *Don* Miguel stopped the car, and wordlessly got out, walking around to the rear door and opening it. Inside sat a box, elegantly wrapped, no larger than a large photo album.

"Go ahead. Open it."

The young man moved to the cargo compartment and lifted the package, taking care not to rip the wrapping paper as he carefully removed the tape that held it in place. Inside was a wooden case, highly polished walnut, breathtakingly ornate. He opened the lid and blinked at the gleam of a Colt 1911 .45 automatic, chromed and intricately engraved with eighteen carat gold that complemented the white pearl grip. The young man regarded the *Don*, his eyes moistening at the sheer beauty of the weapon. He'd never seen anything quite like it.

"The slide's been milled. I had my specialist in the United States attend to it himself. There aren't two weapons like it in the world. It's yours, the symbol of your adulthood," *Don* Miguel explained, a hint of pride seasoning his voice.

The young man picked up one of the two magazines that accompanied it in the display box and adeptly checked the rounds, noting they were partially jacketed; his preference. He slapped it home into the grip of the gun and chambered a round. *Don* Miguel retrieved a pair of coconuts from the ground, tribute from the trees that ringed the field, and tossed them thirty yards away. They seemed very small at that distance.

"Go ahead. Let's see if all that practice bought you anything," the *Don* urged.

The young man adopted a military shooting stance, two handed and slightly crouched. Comfortable with the weapon's weight, he fired once at each coconut. Both slugs found their mark and the coconuts shattered. Their ears ringing from the percussive blasts from the pistol, the pair stood admiring the young man's impressive handiwork. A gentle wind whispered through the surrounding trees, rustling the leaves as though they, too, approved of the marksmanship display. *Don* Miguel clapped, delighted at the performance.

"Good shooting. You make me proud. I've never seen anything like that. Really amazing," he congratulated.

The young man grinned, warmed by the compliments, and then spun and shot *Don* Miguel between the eyes.

"That's for my mother and my sister."

He undid his belt and urinated on *Don* Miguel's face, a look of incomprehension still etched into its rigid features.

"That's for my other sister."

He then dropped his pants and defecated on the great man's corpse, using the *Don*'s handmade linen shirt to clean himself afterwards.

"And that's for my father. Now rot in hell, and may the devil do worse to you than you did to them. I'll see you there, you bastard. I'll be the one pouring the gasoline on you."

That afternoon, Enrique, the *Don*'s most trusted lieutenant, was surprised to see *Don* Miguel's new SUV pull up to his luxurious Tuscan home on the outskirts of Culiacan. He approached the tinted windows to greet the *Don* and was startled when the window opened and he found himself looking down the barrel of a shiny new pistol. The boy spoke four words.

"Get in and drive."

In another clearing, where long ago his father's tomato field had been, the boy got out of the truck and trained the weapon on Enrique. Nature had long ago reclaimed the land, eradicating any trace of the event that had changed the young man's life.

"Do you remember this place, you cock-sucking lowlife?" the young man asked, conversationally, his voice betraying no emotion at all.

"Fuck you. If you're going to shoot me, do it, you little cunt. I bet you don't have the guts," Enrique hissed in response, spitting with the curse.

The young man clubbed him across the face with the pistol, and then slammed him in the head with the butt, knocking Enrique out.

When he came to, he was sitting beside a tree on the edge of the field, the young man holding the weapon on him, unwavering. At the top of the tree, a black form rested motionless, its feathers gleaming in the afternoon sun as it watched the humans below it. Neither man noticed, their attention stolen by other things.

The young man offered a wan smile that never reached his eyes as he fished a small bone-handled pocket knife from his back pocket and tossed it to Enrique.

"What's this for?" Enrique asked, rubbing his head and wiping the blood off his face with his arm.

"Last year, I read a book on the American Indians. They had a way of killing their enemies I thought about every time I remembered you raping my mother that night. What they would do is tie one end of their enemy's intestines to a tree, and then force them to walk around it until they'd pulled out all their guts. That's a lot of trips around this small a tree. I want you to slice a hole five inches above your navel, cut the intestine, tie it to the tree, and then start walking."

"You must be out of your fucking mind if you think I'm going to do that."

"You can do it, or I can shoot you in the gut and it will take you many hours to die, in extreme pain. And then I'll tie your feet to the back of the truck and drag you back to your house. By the time we get close, you'll look like hamburger." The young man shrugged. "Your choice."

Enrique ultimately wound up with door number two. When they found his body the following night, it wasn't recognizable at first as human.

After spending two months carpet bagging around Mexico, the young man enlisted in the navy for a three year stint. His aptitude with weapons quickly impressed the officers in his unit, and soon he was receiving grueling specialized training in explosives, clandestine operations, and commando techniques as a special ops marine.

When he deserted after a year and a half, he singled out the Tijuana cartel, offering his services as a hit man. The first few contracts were considered suicide but he pulled them off flawlessly, and in no time he became the go-to killer for tricky situations, at an ever increasing price.

El Rey had been born, risen from the ashes like the mythical phoenix.

૭৵৩

Present day, Mexico City, Mexico

Cruz paced his office, contemplating his next move. Briones was still sitting with the sketch artist, trying to get the drawing closer to his recollection. That was always tough, as it was a highly inexact science, and often when they wound up catching a perp he looked little like the drawings. Still, it was their only lead, albeit a tenuous one.

Dreading the call, he picked up his desk phone and dialed an inside line. Tomas Llorentez picked up – the chief of the *El Rey* taskforce, and in Cruz's opinion, a complete jerk-off. They exchanged pleasantries, and then Cruz got down to business.

"I may have a case related to your boy, Tomas," Cruz said.

"Oh yeah? I didn't hear of any assassinations today," Tomas quipped.

"No, nothing like that. Have you got any photos or sketches of him?"

"Very funny. Yeah, based on descriptions, he's between twelve and ninety years old, shape-shifts into animals whenever he needs to, and can levitate. Oh, and he's got hooves and a tail, and scaly red skin," Tomas joked.

Cruz's generally non-existent sense of humor deserted him further when dealing with nitwits like Tomas.

"That's very helpful. No, seriously. What have you got on him?"

"Not much, other than a chronology of his hits and a collection of rumors, many of them contradictory. He's a crafty bastard, I'll give him that. Every time we think we've got a break, it evaporates and we're back to the drawing board," Tomas groused.

"How long has the task force been operational, Tomas? Is it already three years?" Cruz couldn't believe this lazy drunken shit was still with the force, much less a squad that apparently couldn't find its ass with both hands.

"Three and a half, actually. Tracking this guy has been a long road," Tomas complained.

Cruz wondered whether his supervisors actually bought any of this crap. They must have, because he was still getting resources and funding, much to Cruz's chagrin.

"So, to summarize, nobody has any images of him, or even an idea what he might look like?" Cruz tried one last time.

"There are a bunch of sketches, but no two look alike. We have one from a woman at the church from when *El Gallo* was whacked, and a few stool pigeons gave us descriptions they swear is him, but in the end they all look like a mid-twenties to mid-thirties Latin male. Generic. So, about as helpful as saying that he's Mexican."

"Would you mind having someone drop copies by my floor, Tomas? I know you guys are busy down there, but I'd really appreciate it." Cruz felt the bile rising in his throat, protesting at how nice he was being, but figured he could take one for the team.

"No problem, for you. Give me a few hours and it'll be with your secretary," Tomas promised.

"I don't have a secretary." Cruz realized instantly that Tomas undoubtedly did have one. Probably two.

"Oh, well, you know, then, I'll have them in your office. Always glad to help a fellow officer out, Cruz," Tomas declared with a patronizing flourish.

Cruz couldn't get off the line fast enough.

That went well, he thought. The country had a buffoon running the hunt for the most dangerous man alive, and was paying handsomely to get zero results.

He sat and typed a series of commands into his computer, then clicked his way through a clunky, five-year-out-of-date interface. Entering a name, he waited while the hamsters in the basement pulled up the results. Eventually, another screen popped up, and he was looking at a photo of Dinah, from her passport. That was one hot passport photo, he had to admit. Who looked good in their passport picture? Cruz's looked like road kill, or some sort of animal that had been startled while feeding. Life had indeed been kind to young *Señorita* Tortora. Okay, maybe not too kind, given that her dad had just been filleted with a samurai sword. Still, she really did look great.

He read the rest of the data, more to give his mind something else to focus on while he waited for Briones to get done, he told himself...

Dinah Montaner Tortora was thirty years old, and had graduated from university with a teaching credential. Rented a condo near the school, didn't own a car, had never been arrested. Bank balance was two thousand dollars. Paid all bills on time. Had a cell phone, internet and cable TV, a credit card she paid off every month, and no delinquencies. Had a current gym membership two blocks from her place.

Not a particularly exciting bio. Then again, if you looked that good on your passport, maybe you didn't need much more trimmings. It was a thought.

His rumination was interrupted by Briones knocking politely on his door jamb, Arlen, the sketch artist, in tow.

"Come in. What have you got?"

"This is as close as we could get it, sir. I only saw him for maybe a second or two, so it's a little hazy, but I think it's in the ballpark," Briones apologized. He felt like an ass. He'd known there was something off about that guy...

Arlen put the sketch pad down on his desk, and Cruz studied the drawing.

"Great. So we're looking for Enrique Iglesias?" Cruz asked, deadpan.

Arlen and Briones looked at each other, then at the drawing.

"You know...you're right. It does look a little like him," Briones admitted.

"Are you sure you weren't describing a music video you downloaded?"

"No...although that is kind of funny now that you mention it. But this is as near as I can remember what the guy looked like, only scruffier. Still..."

"All right, then. All we need to do is wait at the Latin Grammies, and we're sure to nail him." Cruz turned his attention to Arlen. "Thank you for doing this. We appreciate it."

She gave him a tentative smile and departed, leaving the drawing on his desk.

"It doesn't look that much like Iglesias," Briones started.

"I know. I'm sorry. It's just been a tough day, and I was hoping for something more distinctive. But it is what it is. You're sure this is the closest you can get?" Cruz asked.

"That's the guy. Or pretty close."

Cruz groaned audibly, and then thanked Briones, asking him to close his door behind him when he left.

Cruz now had to consider the other item he'd been procrastinating dealing with. How *El Rey* had known. It was almost impossible to believe they had a leak in the department, but he had to proceed as though they did. Which meant he couldn't trust Julio, Ignacio or Briones. His mind wanted to veer from the idea that any of them could be involved, especially Briones. He debated back and forth internally, and decided that Briones couldn't be the leak. He'd been with Cruz for five years, and there had never been the slightest hint of anything untoward. No, if there had been a tip-off, it was either Julio or Nacho.

The problem was that Cruz had not the faintest idea how to vet either man conclusively, leaving him with the compromising prospect of having to exclude them from any more involvement in the investigation. That would permanently harm his relationship with them and deprive him of intelligence, but it was the only safe course.

Another knock interrupted him. He went to his door and opened it, and was presented with an x-ray-sized envelope from Tomas.

Cruz returned to his desk and extracted the four drawings from the sheath and spread them out, holding Briones' sketch next to each. The only one that was even close was from the church, and that was a stretch. Still, there was a similarity to the chin and the nose. Which told him that *El Rey* probably looked about like twenty percent of the young males in Mexico.

Some days weren't so good.

CHAPTER 11

Cruz welcomed his associates from the U.S. Drug Enforcement Agency into his office and closed the door. He'd worked closely with John Rode and Bill Stephens for years. While not exactly friends, the men had mutual respect for each other. John and Bill had been doing a thankless job for over a decade – trying to plug a cork into a fire hose of product that gushed daily into the United States. They were world-weary, had seen a lifetime of disappointment, and knew they were fighting an unwinnable battle. The U.S. had been the largest consumer of illegal drugs for generations, and regardless of what steps were taken, it continued to be. Trying to stop that by terminating the supply was akin to the efforts to prevent alcohol consumption during Prohibition. That experiment had not gone well, and neither had the drug war.

John and Bill were in town for a panel discussion on law enforcement in the 21st Century at the Camino Real, and Cruz had convinced them to come by and check out his operation. They'd agreed, arriving at eleven on Monday morning to be given the nickel tour. After making appropriately complimentary noises, they'd retired to his office and settled comfortably in. Both Americans spoke fluent Spanish; they talked shop for a while, comparing notes and sharing war stories, and then Cruz got to the point of the meeting.

"What kind of contacts do you have with the Secret Service or the NSA?" Cruz tossed out.

"Why, you thinking about switching sides?" John asked.

When the laughter subsided, Cruz said, "No, I just was wondering how to proceed with some potentially troubling news about an assassination attempt on your president."

The atmosphere in the room dropped several degrees.

"What are you talking about?" Bill leaned towards Cruz, who now had both men's full attention.

"It all started with a contract killer, a hit man, famous in Mexico for pulling off the impossible. He's called *El Rey* in the tabloids…" Cruz went on to describe his investigation to date, including the theory about the G-20 being the likely assassination spot.

Aside from the frustrated buzz of a fly at the window, there was complete silence in the room. John was the first to break it. "I see your problem. Your security service won't go to bat on the basis of an investigation, even if the circumstantial evidence is compelling," he observed.

"That's probably the same in your country. Nobody wants to stick their neck out and then be wrong, so it's easier to do the safe thing than do the right thing…," Cruz said.

"Some things don't change no matter which side of the border you're on," Bill agreed.

"My thinking is that maybe I can go in through the back door and lean on our relationship. Which is why I need to determine whether you know anyone with either agency who could help me out here."

"My sister-in-law actually works at the NSA, so that could be a decent place to start," Bill said.

"You don't have strong enough relationships with those agencies to get some face time?" Cruz inquired.

"It seems your relationship with your intelligence service is about like ours with the NSA. And we have zero contact with Secret Service. So…no help there. Although, I'd be happy to write this up as a formal report and pass it on. I just wouldn't expect much, for the same reasons you encountered with your team," Bill advised.

Cruz rose, went to the window and opened it to let the bluebottle escape into the heat of the day. He sighed and said, "This is so frustrating. I know

I'm right, and yet I can't get the attention of the agencies chartered with keeping our heads of state safe. It's really unbelievable."

"Welcome to government work," John said.

Once the Americans were gone, Briones approached Cruz's office, standing politely at the door until Cruz looked up from his paperwork and noticed him.

"Yes, Lieutenant. What is it?"

"We got a hit back from our office in Culiacan. They have someone in custody who claims he has information on *El Rey*. He's willing to talk, but he wants to know what he can expect in return for cooperation," Briones told him.

Cruz put down his pen. "What kind of information?"

"About his background. He said he could tell us a lot about where he came from, and that it's verifiable."

"What's he charged with?" Cruz asked, thinking this was too good to be true.

"Burglary."

"What? A lowlife thief knows all about *El Rey*? How likely does that sound to you?" Cruz scoffed.

"Not very. But then again, you wanted to hear about any and all leads, so I thought I'd run it by you," Briones said, preparing to leave.

"Not so fast. What kind of burglary, do you know?" Cruz inquired.

"The usual. Breaking into houses, stealing valuables. Nothing violent."

"I suppose it's worth at least talking to him. Can we get him flown here?" Cruz asked.

"I already asked. They said if we'd pay for the tickets they'd send one of their men with the prisoner. They didn't sound too interested in driving him here…"

"No, I wouldn't think so." Cruz thought about it. "Fine. Make it happen. Just don't book them into first class."

"There's a flight out tomorrow morning," Briones said. "Gets here at noon, and then a return flight at three. So they'll only be on the ground for a few hours. Do you want me to line up a meeting room at the airport? Might be more practical than hauling them around town and having to deal with traffic issues. Last thing we need is for them to miss the plane back."

"Sure. We can be back here in an hour or two."

"He'll want to know what we're prepared to do for him – you have to address that. So what can we actually do?" Briones asked.

"Depends. I suppose we could always trade some favors and get the charges dropped, but it would have to be one hell of a story to get that card played. More likely, we can get a reduced sentence if he doesn't have a ton of priors. Also depends on where he is in the system. If the prosecutor hasn't gotten hold of him yet, it's all internal to us and we can do whatever we want."

"Let me get on the line and talk to Culiacan, and find all this out before we sit down with him." Briones stopped, looking a little sheepish. "Sir, I just want you to know I'm sorry I let *El Rey* slip by me. I had this weird feeling there was something wrong, but I didn't trust my gut…"

"Learn from that, Lieutenant. Next time your instinct tells you something's off, follow it; don't shut it down. It could save your life. Now get out of here, and let's get this robber a plane ride," Cruz said, reluctantly returning his attention to the pile of documents.

"I'm on it. Oh, and maybe we should take the sketches – perhaps slip some placebo ones in as a control? He may be able to identify which is the real *El Rey*…," Briones suggested.

"Excellent idea. If he can, that would be the first real break we've had. I would say we're about due for one."

The following day, Cruz and Briones were waiting at the gate as the plane pulled up to the jetway. The first passengers off were their men – one of the perks of being a *Federal* was that you could command priority, and get it, from the airlines. The escort was a heavily muscled thirty-something-year-old veteran of the force in one of the most dangerous and violent epicenters of the drug wars. He looked menacing and tough, which was probably an understatement. You didn't survive years as a *Federal* in a battle zone by pretending to be a hard-case. Apart from Ciudad Juarez by the Texas border, there was no Mexican city more dangerous than Culiacan, home of the original Godfather, and the capital of not only Sinaloa, but of the Sinaloa cartel.

The prisoner was a skinny weasel of a man, and old – at least fifty-five – and looking like every day of it had been spent in poverty and hardship. He had the hunched shoulders and defeated gait of a man who'd been bludgeoned by life, and was running out the clock, trying to avoid any further suffering. His skin had the leathery look of an existence spent outdoors – the complexion of a day laborer, or a beggar. As he was escorted towards Briones and Cruz, his pronounced limp slowed him, as did the cuffs on his wrists.

The officer extended his hand to Cruz and Briones in greeting, his face unsmiling and impassive.

"I'm Lieutenant Marquez. Nice to meet you both. Where are we headed?" he asked, after shaking their hands.

"We've got a conference room booked over in the old Mexicana club suite. Follow me," Cruz instructed, moving swiftly to the main terminal area. The others followed, Briones lagging behind with the prisoner and Marquez.

They arrived at their destination, where an airport security man opened the room and asked if they'd require anything else. Cruz inspected the space, which had a cooler with water and sodas and some sandwiches wrapped in cellophane. He shook his head. The group settled in around the conference table, and the captive put his gnarled, cuffed hands on the table – his cracked nails and hardened calluses further confirmation of a sustenance-level existence.

Marquez cleared his throat. "This is Rodrigo Moreno. He's charged with burgling several homes in Culiacan, and was arrested four days ago. He was caught climbing out of a ground floor window with a stereo and a few items of jewelry. We put the question about *El Rey* to him, as we have to all detainees, and he indicated he had information he was willing to share." Marquez sat back, his role finished until he had to walk the man back to the plane.

"*Trade*. I have information I want to trade," Moreno said, his yellowed eyes darting from Briones to Cruz, lending him the appearance of a fox, or some other wild animal that lived by its wits in a harsh habitat.

"I'm Captain Cruz. I head up the cartel task force for Mexico City. I'm interested in hearing your information, and if it's of value, I'm prepared to consider some sort of equitable exchange," Cruz said. "But I won't discuss any terms until you tell us what you know. I won't cheat you, but I also don't have a lot of time to negotiate. Either you talk and then I reward you, assuming your information isn't complete bullshit, or you go rot in the Culiacan jail – one of the most lethal places in the country, if I'm not mistaken," he added.

"That's nothing compared to the streets," Moreno commented.

"Maybe. But the question is do you want to spend the next few years there, or do you want to deal?"

"Obviously, I want to deal. But how do I know you won't screw me?" Moreno asked.

"You'll have to trust that I flew you here, at considerable expense, and am sitting in front of you instead of directing Mexico's anti-cartel task force's operations, to hear your account and act honorably if it vets out," Cruz stated.

Moreno regarded him distrustfully. "Talk's cheap. If I had a peso for every time someone told me they weren't going to fuck me, and then did, I'd–"

Cruz pushed back from the table and stood. "Officer Marquez? It was a pleasure meeting you. Sorry to inconvenience you dragging this worthless shit halfway across the country. This meeting's now over. Make sure your prisoner gets the full incarceration experience back in Culiacan," Cruz instructed.

Moreno's face crumbled, and he visibly deflated. He'd played his best hand and lost.

"Wait. I'm sorry. I didn't mean to offend you. I accept your proposal. Please…"

Cruz fixed Moreno with a glare. "Let's be very clear. You don't dictate terms, or complain, or express anything but gratitude that someone as important as me is sitting here, prepared to entertain what is probably an easily debunked pack of lies – in which case, your jail time will make being gang raped in Calcutta seem like a trip to Rio for the Carnival. So here's the deal. You talk. I listen. Then I decide what your story's worth. There's no other deal. You have five seconds to accept or reject it. Now you have four," Cruz dictated.

"All right. Fine. I'll take the deal. Sit down. Please. I promise it'll be worth your time," Moreno said.

"Fair enough. Start talking. And it better be good," Cruz warned.

"Can I have some water?" Moreno asked, chastened from his brush with dismissal.

Marquez handed him a plastic bottle, after twisting the cap open. Moreno lifted it with his shackled hands and drank greedily before setting it, half empty, on the table between them.

"It all started in Tijuana about ten years ago."

ॐॐ

Nine years ago, Tijuana, Mexico

A large walled compound perched on a cliff face near the outskirts of the city, looking over the town below, which bustled with activity in the late morning sunlight. It resembled a small prison, with a dozen heavily-armed men clad in civilian clothes patrolling the perimeter. One of the largest homes in the notorious border city of over a million people, it was an imposing presence at the top of the access road.

A Cadillac Escalade pulled to the gates, and after a glance from the guards through the driver's-side window, the reinforced iron grids rolled open. They had been designed to withstand anything other than a tank running through them. The Escalade eased to a stop in front of the main home's entrance, where three passengers exited the vehicle. The SUV was heavily armored, a special order from a company in Dallas, Texas that built conveyances for heads of state and corporate bigwigs. It could survive a grenade blast, and gunfire would literally bounce off it. The window glass was a special polymer that could take armor-piercing rounds without breaking, and the tires could go twenty miles after having been shot to pieces. All that protection didn't come cheap – the vehicles cost a hundred and fifty thousand dollars a pop.

The compound had three.

The men approached the front door and the youngest, tallest one, who stood between his two older companions, held his hands above his head while one of several armed men frisked him professionally and then scanned his body with an electronic surveillance wand designed to reveal any listening devices or recording apparatus. They were granted access to the house, and the man who'd frisked the new arrival directed the visitors to follow him.

Domestic staff busily cleaned floors and windows as the procession made its way to the great room terrace, where the owner of the property, and one of the most infamous cartel chieftains in Mexico, sat in a white terrycloth bathrobe sipping espresso with a young woman a third his age, also in a bathrobe, though filling it out with considerably more style.

Felix Montanegro eyed the arrivals, then leaned over and murmured something into his young companion's tousled hair. She smiled, then obligingly rose and moved inside, her bare feet padding silently across the oversized Italian marble flooring. Montanegro gestured with his hand for the young man to sit, and snapped his fingers to the service staff, who waited at a discreet distance, out of earshot. One of the maids hurried off, rematerializing thirty seconds later with a cup of coffee for the guest. A gardener studiously trimmed ivy at one end of the terrace, taking care to stay well away from the small onyx table where the two men sat. The pair of tough-looking escorts moved inside the house, twenty feet from the terrace, where they could reach Montanegro in seconds if he needed them.

Montanegro regarded the young man and leaned back in his chair, withdrawing a cigarette from a gold case on the table. The maid scurried to his side and lit it for him. He appeared not to register her, continuing to study his guest's face, which betrayed nothing.

"So you're the miracle man who's been achieving what everyone said couldn't be done," Montanegro started cordially.

The young man nodded, the corners of his mouth almost imperceptibly turning up in a veiled smile.

"It's impressive. Really impressive. I've never seen anything like it. I would have guessed it was impossible to fulfill the last three contracts without being killed yourself, but here you are…and without a scratch on you." Montanegro flicked ash from his cigarette into a rectangular metal container adorned with highly stylized skulls, commemorating the Mexican Day of the Dead, *Dia de los Muertos*. He took a drag and continued, exhaling the smoke skyward.

"I wanted to meet you. I wanted to see the phantom who's causing such a stir among the illustrious members of my group, as well as in the population of Tijuana. I understand the restaurants and cantinas are abuzz with talk of your exploits – of the man they call, *'El Rey'*."

"What people gossip about is of no consequence. What matters are results," the young man reasoned, speaking softly for the first time since he'd gotten into the Escalade.

"Ah. So you do have a tongue. Good. Yes, you are correct, it's the results that count. Everything else is noise for fools and dullards." Montanegro sipped his espresso. "But I understand that you've increased your price for the next contract, yes? May I ask why? This is a competitive field, so you may be pricing yourself out of the market, at least from my perspective."

The young man ran a hand over his face, which sported a two day dusting of growth. He adjusted his black long-sleeved shirt. "I've shown what I can do. When you hire me you get guaranteed results. That's worth more than someone who will try, and perhaps fail," the young man said reasonably.

"Ha! Well, you're right about that. You have delivered impressively, my young friend. So much so, I'd like to offer you a position with my group. You can name your price," Montanegro said.

The young man appeared to consider the proposition, and then reached over and carefully turned the coffee cup, seeming captivated by the pattern in the china. He didn't speak, and a few seconds turned into an uncomfortable half minute of silence.

"I'm flattered by the proposal, but I'm afraid I can't accept. I do my best work alone, on a contract basis, and it wouldn't work for either of us to have me acting exclusively for you. I mean no offense, and if I was considering ending my career as an independent contractor, you would be the first person I'd approach. But no, it would never work, and we'd both be unhappy with the results. So I must respectfully decline."

Montanegro glared at the young man as he spoke, and when he was finished, slammed his hand down on the table in a gesture of fury.

"You little shit. Do you have any idea who you're talking to? It wasn't a suggestion. If I tell you you're working for me, you'll work for me, and the correct response will be, 'Thank you, *Don* Felix, I'm honored you'd want me.' I've rarely had anyone turn me down, and all those who did are dead. So this is a one time, one-way-trip offer. You either accept, or my men will put a bullet in your brain and feed you to the street dogs. Are you reading me?" Montanegro hissed.

The young man's expression didn't change. If anything, he seemed almost angelically serene, untroubled by the turn the discussion had taken. He appeared to consider Montanegro's words, and then leaned forward, ensuring that only the cartel boss could hear.

"I don't drink coffee. I don't like it."

Montanegro was confused by the statement.

"What the fuck do I care whether you like coffee or not? Did you not hear me?" Montanegro growled.

"No, I heard you. I just wanted you to know I don't like coffee, mainly because it alters my body chemistry in a way I don't find useful." Montanegro looked like his head was going to explode. "But there's another reason. Last night I slipped into your house, bypassing your laughable security, and treated your coffee grounds with a nerve toxin that will kill you within seven hours of ingesting it, unless I give you the antidote, some of which I've already taken in case you force me to drink coffee, too. It will take any laboratory in Tijuana days to figure out what the poison is, or what the antidote is, by which time you'll be long dead. Even in the U.S., it would take more than seven hours. And my guess is that isn't your first cup this morning, so you have less time. Maybe six?" the young man estimated, his voice so low that Montanegro had to strain to hear.

Montanegro's pupils contracted to pinpoints, and his hands started shaking with fury.

"You're a dead man, you little fuck. Dead."

"*Don* Felix. I took this step because I understood that you might be less than understanding if I refused your offer, which I had heard through the grapevine would be forthcoming. I mean no disrespect. I simply had to ensure I had something to negotiate with." *El Rey* leaned in even closer. "I was approached three days ago by one of your enemies, who offered me a half million dollars to kill you. I told him I'd consider it. I haven't responded yet. My point is that if we reach an accommodation, and I continue to work on your behalf, I'll decline these sorts of requests. Truthfully, I could have cut your throat last night and pocketed the half million after the fact, but I didn't. Instead, I came here, listened with respect to your proposal, politely declined, and then things started down an unfortunate road."

Montanegro said nothing. Merely glared at him. But the young man could see that he was now calculating instead of reacting. That was good.

"I like my work," *El Rey* continued. "I enjoy it. I also enjoy clients who pay on time, and who do as they promise. You're an honorable man and have always paid as agreed, so I enjoy working for you. I don't want to see anything happen to you." The young man sighed. "Here's my counter-proposal. We agree I won't kill you. I give your men the antidote when they've dropped me in a location of my choosing. It will be enough antidote for you, your companion, and whoever else drank your coffee this morning. There will be no ill effects, provided you take it within the next…" the young man checked his watch, "…hour or so. And as a further incentive for you to take a more positive approach, I'll also terminate your enemy, one of the cartel bosses you've been at war with for the last six months, within forty-eight hours, for a contract price of one million dollars; satisfaction guaranteed. The reason the price is a million is because I will be foregoing the half million for your contract, so I'll expect you to subsidize that." The young man sat back, eying Montanegro impassively.

Montanegro seemed to fight an internal battle, a struggle in his mind.

"You're insane."

The young man's face took on a smile that chilled Montanegro's blood – the blood of a man who had killed dozens himself and ordered the execution of hundreds.

"That may well be. But the question is, do you want me on your side, or working against you? If against, you have nothing to do but wait, and you'll see the result of that choice by two o'clock today, maybe two-thirty. The effects are quite painful, and at that point, irreversible. The Iranian who sold it to me said prisoners they tested it on tore off their own skin in an attempt to reduce the…discomfort." He fixed the *Don* with a penetrating stare. "I don't care whether I see tomorrow or not. The real question is whether you do. From that understanding will flow the correct answer."

Montanegro now saw him in a new light. The young man imagined that was the way he would regard a cobra poised to strike, coiled on the table. Gone were the anger and the hubris. He already knew what the answer would be – *Don* Felix was certainly a man who wanted to live.

Montanegro slammed the table with his palm again and threw back his head and laughed; a laugh hollow with nervous relief.

"Fuck you. You really are good, you know that? I've sat across from many, and you take the cake. All right then. It's a deal. One million, he's dead within forty-eight hours. I get the antidote within the hour. Who am I paying to exterminate, as a matter of interest?"

"Antonio Palomino. The head of the Chiapas cartel. I know where he's staying. Not in Tijuana, by the way, but that's not your concern. I want half the money now, and half when I close out the contract." He glanced at his watch again. "I'd be inclined not to waste too much time getting it."

Montanegro rose, and shook the young man's hand.

"It will take a few minutes to count it."

Half an hour later, the Escalade dropped the young man off in a seedy neighborhood near the infamous wall that divided Mexico from the U.S. He instructed the driver to cruise around the block, and that he'd meet him on the corner, in front of the small market, in ten minutes. The heavy SUV roared off down the dirt street, and once it was out of sight the young man ducked into one of the squalid little cinderblock houses, emerging a few minutes later with an empty aspirin bottle half-filled with clear fluid. He hefted the shoulder strap of the laptop bag with the cash and ambled to the market, stopping to buy a bottle of water with the few loose pesos jingling in his pants. The Escalade pulled up two minutes later, and he approached it, motioning for the driver to roll down the window.

The blackened inch-thick glass slid down.

"Wait until you see me walk round that corner. When I know I'm safe, I'll call this phone and tell you where the antidote is. Be careful with it. Don't drop it. That's all there is. Tell *Don* Felix to shake it well, until the white powder in the bottom is completely dissolved, and then to take one tablespoon orally, and to have anyone else who's affected take one as well. As long as they do so in the next forty minutes they'll be fine. There are only enough doses to treat eight people, so don't waste it. Do you understand?" the young man asked.

The driver nodded and took the proffered cell phone from *El Rey's* outstretched hand.

Satisfied the men weren't going to shoot him, he strode across the street, and then down a block, glancing back over his shoulder before turning the corner and disappearing from view. The men sat restlessly. A few minutes later the phone chirped.

"Go into the market. I left the antidote with the woman at the counter. Oh, and you owe her five hundred pesos for holding it. Let *Don* Felix know I'll be in contact within forty-seven hours to confirm my successful closure of our contract, and to arrange payment for the second half. Again, be careful with the bottle of antidote, and no more than one tablespoon per person. Any questions?"

"No. I understand."

The young man terminated the call and pulled his truck down the dirt road, snaking his way to the highway that would take him south, down the coast. He wondered if the cartel boss would figure out that the antidote was water with a little Viagra dissolved in it. Probably not. In the end it wouldn't matter. Montanegro would be pleased his rival was executed, *El Rey* would have established his new price as a cool million, and he would only have to do one hit a year to live like a king. He suspected he'd actually have to raise his price again in a few years just to keep up appearances.

One thing that was for sure was that Montanegro would use him for any other high-importance executions he needed carried out, regardless of price. Money was nothing to the man. But having the absolute best in his pocket, deferring to him, with the tacit agreement he wouldn't turn on him and fulfill a sanction against him? That was priceless.

As had been the look on Montanegro's face when *El Rey* had concocted the story on the spot, about the mythical toxin.

He hummed as he pulled onto the toll road, headed for Ensenada.

CHAPTER 12

Cruz stared at the little man, trying to decide whether he believed him or not. He rose and began pacing the room, as was his habit when he was thinking. Briones looked like someone had stolen his wallet.

"How do you know any of this, and more importantly, how can it help us find *El Rey*?" Briones sputtered.

Moreno smiled, revealing a near absence of teeth. "I was the gardener that day. I was the one trimming the ivy. I worked at Montanegro's compound for four years, until he was executed by the Sinaloa cartel. You probably remember that. It was a bloody assault even by Tijuana standards. *Don* Felix was always generous with me, but over the years I fell on hard times, and, well, you know the rest," Moreno said.

Cruz finally stopped walking and returned to his seat. He fixed the prisoner with a harsh stare and fired a question at him.

"How do you know about the Viagra?" Cruz asked.

"I overheard it. Seems *Don* Felix sent the 'antidote' to San Diego for testing. He about blew a gasket laughing when telling his brother a few days later. I don't think I ever saw him so amused. He had tears rolling down his face. I think that impressed him more than when he read about the Chiapas cartel boss being executed the next day."

"So you've seen *El Rey*? You could tell us what he looks like?" Cruz demanded.

"It's been a very long time, but I think I could – but it will be what he looked like then. Time can change a man's face, and I only saw him for a few minutes. I was working, and only glanced over occasionally. If you paid too much attention, it could be bad for your health," Moreno explained.

"If we showed you some drawings, could you pick him out?" Briones asked.

"I can try. Only one thing. If I do, what will I get in return? I can wait for you to check my story if you want. You can look up the details of the death of the Chiapas cartel's boss – and the date. That's the only thing I can think of you can verify," Moreno offered.

Cruz considered it. There was no way a man of obviously limited intellect and prospects could invent a story like that; not with so much detail. Cruz was willing to bet it was true.

"If you can help us, I'll speak to Culiacan and ask that your charges be dropped. I'd also suggest that you stop burgling houses. You're too old for that shit," Cruz said.

"I believe you. And thank you, *Capitan*. Thank you so much," Moreno said, close to tears with relief.

Briones opened his briefcase and spread the five drawings out on the table along with a few placebo drawings they'd had Arlen draw in preparation for the meeting. Moreno squinted at them for a few minutes, seeming undecided. Finally, he put his scarred index finger on one.

"This one's the closest. He looks older here, and a little heavier, and there's something about the nose and eyes that isn't right, but this is the most similar to what I remember," Moreno said.

They all looked down at the sketch Moreno had selected.

It was Briones' vagrant.

☙❧

Sarah Wilford checked her e-mail, intrigued when she saw the message from her brother-in-law, Bill Stephens. She racked her brain for the last time Bill had sent her anything and came up dry. This was a first.

She read the short introductory message, then opened the attachment, which was a formal meeting report with the Mexicans. Sarah skimmed it, and then a phone call distracted her. By the time she finished it was already five o'clock, and she needed to get going to pick up the kids from daycare. She thought about what to do with the message, and then forwarded it to her boss, Carl Rugman, who would know better than she how best to proceed. Satisfied she'd done all she could, Sarah gathered her coat and purse and headed off to collect her darlings.

Carl was in a meeting with two communications specialists going over the latest satellite surveillance grids for Iraq, which took until six o'clock. Once finished he did a cursory scan of his e-mail and noted the attachment from Sarah. After a quick read, he picked up his phone and dialed his counterpart at Secret Service, who was out of the office, and left a brief message that he was forwarding on a report from the DEA. Next, he called a friend at the CIA, which also went straight to voice mail.

"Humphrey, this is Carl. I know it's kind of late, but I just got a report from DEA I thought you might be interested in. It's about a possible threat to the president, involving Mexican cartels. I'm forwarding it on. Hopefully, you'll know who to hand it off to."

After re-reading it again, he sent the e-mail to three other men within the NSA, and two more at the CIA. Between those contacts and the Secret Service, they should have the bases covered.

He switched off his computer and donned his jacket before flicking off his lights, tired after another grueling day of meetings and briefings. Keeping the nation safe from terrorism and whatnot took it out of a guy, especially at his age.

Three hours later, a phone rang in the private office of one of the most powerful men at Langley, a CIA assistant director for the entire Middle East.

"I sent a report to your encrypted anonymous box. Read it and call me back. We have a problem." The line went dead.

Kent Fredericks dutifully logged into his alternative mailbox – a blind address for sensitive matters he didn't want on record – and carefully read the report before dialing the phone.

"We need to meet. Can we get together this evening?" Kent asked. He looked at his watch. "Maybe tell the missus that you need to have a cocktail with an important constituent?"

"Ten-thirty, at my club. I'll see to it we aren't disturbed. Shouldn't be many people around at that hour."

"I'll see you there."

That gave Kent a little over an hour to get prepared. He needed to carefully consider how to deal with the report. It would be simple to put out a verbal dismissal of it as an unverified hunch by some Mexican nobody – he could spin the word 'Mexican' with a roll of his eyes to depict incompetent peasants. It wouldn't be hard, given that many of those considering the findings would be older Caucasian males, whose embedded cultural prejudice would be simple to manipulate into a facile rejection of the data. He wasn't so much worried about that as he was how to proceed. It posed a potential problem, and part of his value to the rarefied membership of the group was in coming up with solutions.

When he entered the elaborate foyer of the club he was struck by how the place reeked of tradition and power. The walls were polished dark wood, with lustrous oil paintings of scowling men staring down from their positions in ornate gold frames – past chairmen, he presumed. A discreet man in black tie greeted him with a soft, "Good evening," and then led him to one of the private meeting rooms, down a separate hall from the club's main area, ensuring complete privacy. The escort opened a door, and Kent stepped into a twelve by fifteen room. The passageway closed behind him, and he found himself face to face with the older man he'd spoken with on the phone, as well as the Speaker of the House.

The ensuing discussion was exactly what he was afraid it would be. Towards the end, he tired of the speculation and accusations, and interrupted the borderline-hysterical dialog.

"Gentlemen, I think it's safe to say that we need to deal with this as quickly and unilaterally as we can. I propose that I contact some of our assets in Mexico and get it handled through unofficial channels," he recommended.

"That's all well and good, but the cat's out of the bag now, don't you think?" the older man growled.

"Not at all. We have a police captain, who has a theory absent any support, based on hearsay from a criminal. It says right in the report that his own intelligence service shut him down. If they dismissed him, that's a good indicator he's got nothing solid. This is just a rogue cop with a wild theory and no evidence. Nobody's giving it any credence in Mexico, and for good reason. It's a non-event," Kent responded.

"Well, what if he gets some proof?" the Speaker of the House asked.

"There is no proof. That's the best part about this. There's nothing to get," Kent replied.

"What about this assassin he goes on about? What if he manages to find him and stop him?" the caller volleyed.

"You mean *El Rey*? The most infamous assassin in Latin America? Don't you think that if the police could have caught him, they would have by now? There's an entire task force devoted to doing so, and it's turned up nothing. No, this is entirely containable. The cartel boss who took out the contract is dead. So nobody to talk there. That leaves a contract killer who's evaded capture for a decade, and the Mexican police, who are about as competent as the D.C. cops…" Kent grinned at his humor.

"I'd say the cartel boss already did enough talking," the older man said.

"Maybe, but he's dead. So he's no longer a problem."

"What about the hit man, this *El Rey*? Will he carry out the contract now that his employer is no longer alive?" the Speaker of the House asked.

"All our intelligence predicts that he will. The new cartel boss who replaces him won't want to piss *El Rey* off – he's considered indestructible in Mexico by the criminal gangs there. So if he shows up demanding payment for a predecessor's commitments, the new guy will pay. Look, the cartels are swimming in cash, so it's a rounding error for them versus a bullet in the head when they least suspect it. No, I think it's safe to say they won't stiff *El Rey*, which means the only thing that's changed is this cop stumbling through matters that are none of his business," Kent said.

The discussion went on for another fifteen minutes, but in the end what the everyone really wanted was reassurance. Kent offered that, and proposed a solution they could all live with. They agreed, and the meeting ended. On the way out of the building Kent glanced at his watch – it was now almost midnight. He rubbed his eyes and groaned as he got into his car. It would be a few more hours before he'd be going home.

He had some calls to make.

Six months ago, Mexico City, Mexico

Francisco Morales, the Secretary of the Interior for Mexico, boarded the helicopter that was to take him to the meeting of prosecutors, convened to discuss new steps to battle the cartels. It was a foggy morning, and as the aircraft waited for the arrival of the other passengers, Morales busied himself with his Blackberry, sending a message on Twitter commemorating the death of his predecessor three years before in an airplane crash. That had been a serious blow to the nation; the Secretary of the Interior was largely responsible for the day to day operations in the war on drugs, and his predecessor had been vociferous in his condemnation of the cartels, as well as his development of innovative strategies to combat them, such as the creation of Cruz's task force.

Two SUVs pulled alongside the helicopter. The occupants alighted – Felipe Zariana, General of Legal Affairs; José Salamanca, Director of Social Communications; René Cantantore, Lieutenant General, and a group of military personnel and secretaries. The flight would transport nine including the pilot, who was an Air Force veteran of fifteen years. Collectively, the group represented the top brass in the government's war against the cartels, and there was excitement in the air – Morales was about to unveil a brave new strategy to cut the criminal syndicates off at the knees.

That it would be effective was without question. After years of half measures, someone had finally decided to get serious and cut the heads off the snakes. It was ironic that the fatal blow would come from a native of one of the most violent cartel towns. Morales had come a long way since his humble working-class beginnings in Tijuana, and represented the best hope the Mexicans had for decisive victory against the predatory miscreants who were crippling the nation.

The chopper's blades picked up speed as the pilot prepared for takeoff. In the post-dawn light, the fog was a thick gray blanket over the airfield, but wouldn't pose any problems for the flight – the helicopter was equipped with all the latest electronics and could easily fly completely blind, as it often did in the dead of night. The distinctive *thwack thwack* of the rotor was muffled by the dense haze as the pilot executed the final checks to verify all was operating correctly. Satisfied, he increased the RPMs of the massive turbine, and the craft lifted skyward, its lights blinking as it disappeared into the cloud.

Seven minutes later, air traffic control lost track of the flight, which had been given priority status given its payload. After several attempts to contact the pilot, aircraft were scrambled to trace the travel route and check for an accident.

The pilot of one of the reconnaissance helicopters radioed in. "Tower, this is flight three-oh-seven. We have visual on a crash site near the side of a hill at grid fourteen. Repeat. We have wreckage at grid fourteen. Requesting permission to set down and evaluate."

"Roger that. You have permission. All other choppers proceed to grid fourteen."

The pilot nosed his craft down, landing near the mangled remains of Morales' last flight, knowing intuitively from its condition that nobody had walked away. Small fires belched swirls of black smoke from the devastation; the metal skeleton of the conveyance was twisted beyond recognition, and there had been at least one explosion when the chopper had crashed. After a few minutes walking the perimeter, he reported his findings, then gazed skyward as more helicopters carefully dropped through the now-receding fog, the only task remaining to scrape up the pieces.

The man watched through binoculars as the crash site was secured by the military and took a photo with his phone to send to the client. This was a contract he'd been instructed not to take credit for, which was fine. *El Rey* already had enough press to last a lifetime, so the hit's conditions worked for him – it had been laughably easy to plant a small amount of explosive near the rotor coupling, detonated with a high frequency transmitter when it came into range. He eschewed using cell phones for triggers; there was always the chance of reception getting blocked or that cell service was spotty – a nearly constant issue in Mexico. Or worse, if a wrong number or text message came in, it could ruin a carefully plotted plan because of a random misdialed digit.

Five million dollars richer, he rolled up the tinted window of his stolen Nissan Pathfinder and continued down the rural road, away from Mexico City and the slew of emergency vehicles he knew weren't far behind.

࿐

Present day, Mexico City, Mexico

The following afternoon, Cruz called an all-hands meeting for his squad chiefs in the big headquarters conference room. When he walked in, carrying transparent slides for the overhead projector, the suite was nearly filled to capacity. The murmur of conversation quickly died, and when Cruz took the floor he had everyone's attention.

He nodded at Briones, who extinguished the lights, and fiddled with the rear of the projector until it displayed a bright white square on the wall. He pulled the top slide from the protective folder and placed it on the display screen. The sketch of Briones' vagrant sprang larger than life on the far wall.

"This is a depiction of the assassin known as *El Rey*. To the best of our belief, this is a good likeness, or as good as we'll get until he's lying on a slab in the morgue," Cruz began. The gathered officers tittered and breathed a few hushed discussions before silence fell again.

"As you may know, *El Rey* is responsible for a host of executions and assassinations, most recently of the politician known as *El Gallo*. He's expanded his reach beyond the drug cartels, which appeared to be his specialty until recently, and is now believed to be actively targeting political figures as well. The chances of *El Gallo* being a singularity are slim," Cruz assured them.

"As part of our ongoing sting operations against cartel members in Mexico City, we recently held a raid on a warehouse where the leader of the Knights Templar cartel was meeting with some local traffickers. The information that led us to him came through our intelligence network on the street, as part of our plainclothes undercover project. When the smoke cleared, we had captured the top man: our target, Jorge Santiago – one of the most vicious psychopaths operating in Mexico." Cruz removed the foil with *El Rey* on it, and replaced it with a photo of Santiago. "We sustained casualties during the raid, and Santiago wound up being the only survivor of the assault. He subsequently went into a coma and died, but not before he boasted of hiring *El Rey* to assassinate our president, as well as the president of the United States."

The assembled officers burst into animated discussion, and Cruz nodded at Briones. The lights flickered back on, and Cruz held up his hands in a bid for order. The hubbub eventually subsided, allowing Cruz to continue with his presentation.

"I'll be happy to answer questions after I'm through. Here's what you need to know. First, we have no proof that Santiago's claims are true, so we can't expect any support from the other branches of law enforcement or our intelligence agency. Second, I believe that the threat is genuine. We were able to locate the man we believe was *El Rey*'s representative – his agent, if you will, who purportedly interviewed prospective customers and dealt with them on behalf of *El Rey*. That man, Jaime Tortora, was murdered on the morning we were scheduled to meet with him, posing as interested clients." Cruz nodded at Briones to shut off the lights again. Cruz slid a transparency with a driver's license photo of Tortora on the projector.

"This man owned a pawn shop downtown. I stated that Tortora was believed to be the agent because we found nothing when we searched the crime scene. Yet I'm confident he was involved with *El Rey*, given the method and timing of his execution. He was sliced nearly in half with a Japanese katana – the sword used by Samurai warriors in prior centuries. Now, it may be coincidence that the 'King of Swords' was represented by a man who was killed with a sword, but that seems more like the poetic gesture of a deranged mind. It's a given it would hold significance for a killer who had chosen the moniker King of Swords for himself." Cruz replaced the Tortora's headshot with a photo of the corpse. The room fidgeted nervously – even seasoned veterans of the drug wars, who'd seen countless decapitated bodies, were affected by the grisly image.

"Before I open the floor up for questions, I want to make a few comments. I know our charter is to go after the cartels. I understand our mission, better than most, and I further can see how it could appear that these events aren't our concern – the president has his own security forces responsible for his safety, and the American president has his Secret Service. So why should we stick our noses where they don't belong? The answer is, in my mind, simple. Because we're the only agency preventing the cartels from taking over Mexico; and an assassination of our president would represent a catastrophic blow to the rule of law. Our job is to fight the cartels, and if this plot is real, it represents a new stage in our war against them." Cruz stopped to take a swig of water before finishing. "I believe that this assassination attempt will take place at the upcoming G-20 financial summit in Los Cabos. That's the only time the American president will be on Mexican soil this year. The summit is in four weeks, so we have no time to waste." Cruz took a deep breath as he observed the rapt attention of his men.

"This scheme is the ultimate expression of evil from men who peddle death, and behave like barbarians – like animals. I don't personally care whether our bureaucratic security force figures out that an assassin is planning to kill the president. I have already concluded the threat is genuine, and I plan to act accordingly. And I'm asking for your cooperation. I need everyone to shift their focus and make this the priority in the days ahead. I'll have meetings with each of you to lay out plans of action, but I want everyone to understand what we're up against so I have your support. Thank you." Cruz took another sip of water, then sat down in a chair at the head of the long conference table. "Questions?"

A chorus of voices clamored for attention, and Cruz motioned for quiet. He pointed to a man at the far end of the table. "Arturo. Yes?"

"Where did the image of *El Rey* come from, and are we working in conjunction with the task force that's chartered with bringing him down?"

"Good question. This image is based on a brief encounter by our own lieutenant, Fernando Briones, who all of you know. I've been in contact with the task force, but their success level to date, after years of working the case, has been less than spectacular. So while I'll brief them periodically on our efforts, I believe that to involve them in our operation would be counterproductive at this stage. They'd just get in our way."

"And Briones is still alive to tell about it? What a lucky bastard," Arturo quipped.

"Yes, that's probably true." Cruz pointed at another man, a fat, balding fellow halfway down the table to his left. "Miguel?"

"You mention that this is all theoretical. Do you anticipate getting any data that would make it move from theory to fact?" Miguel asked.

"That's the whole point of this operation, which I am naming 'mongoose'. *El Rey* is a snake: clever, deadly and silent. We shall become the mongoose that finds and kills such snakes. We need to use all of our resources to get leads on where *El Rey* is, so we can neutralize him. I'll go into more detail in our individual meetings, but for now, let me just say that I need everyone to mobilize their networks and support the effort to gather information that will lead to his capture." Cruz pointed at a woman standing by the back wall with her hand raised. "Yes, Cynthia?"

"Will we be working with CISEN any time soon on this? It seems that would be the appropriate group, given the threat to a foreign head of state."

"I'm hopeful we will. But it may be too little and too late. Our job is to build a case, which we will present at the appropriate time. So that's what we'll do."

The questions went on for another half hour, largely centering around logistical issues. Cruz patiently took all questions, answering them honestly, with no hiding from the tough ones or appealing to the authority of his position to justify his actions. This was a personal plea to his loyal staff, and they deserved to understand what he'd gotten them into.

Cruz finished by referring them to Briones for scheduling and necessary materials, such as copies of the sketch, and a case summary. When he walked out of the room, the confidence he'd displayed evaporated, and only one thought raced through his mind. They had less than thirty days to catch the assassin – the blink of an eye.

He'd never admit it, but he didn't like their odds.

CHAPTER 13

The next morning, Cruz began his one-on-one meetings and the day lurched along in a predictably painful manner. Answering the same questions over and over, fielding the doubts many had about the validity of the operation, advising how to proceed from their current position, which amounted to being dead in the water.

Cruz wanted to allocate resources to the two most promising areas – Los Cabos, where the summit was going to be hosted, and Culiacan – the drug capital of Mexico. It was possible *El Rey* was holed up in a cabin by a lake somewhere, but if Cruz was *El Rey*, he'd be in Los Cabos at some point, scoping out the lay of the land and devising a plan of attack.

Accordingly, he called the *Federales* outpost there and alerted them to the situation, adding that he would be deploying resources within the next week to establish an operational base in the area. The officer in charge didn't sound too thrilled – Cruz wouldn't have been happy either, were situations reversed. Cops were territorial, so an incursion by outside parties was never appreciated. And given that hundreds of *Federales* were going to be descending upon the area the week before the G-20 for security, yet another group arriving to complicate the locals' lives earlier than they had expected wouldn't go down well. He understood the reception to his team would be less than ideal, but his job wasn't to make friends; it was to battle the cartels.

Los Cabos consisted of the two towns, Cabo San Lucas and San José del Cabo, and was off the radar of the cartels, other than as an attractive money laundering destination. The issue was one of geography. Drugs weren't shipped from the mainland on the ferry, because they'd have to run a gauntlet of almost a thousand miles of military checkpoints on the only road that stretched north to the border. The only other way of getting there was by plane. So the cartels just used the location to wash cash. Cabo was a ghost town, filled with large restaurants and clubs that were devoid of clientele, yet managed to turn huge profits year round. Some of the hotels were the same way – five percent occupancy at best, and yet wildly lucrative.

Cruz recalled, from the six weeks he'd spent in Los Barriles wasting away, that you could walk down the street at three a.m., drunk as a lord, and nobody would bother you. There was just no crime to speak of. The *Federales* in San José del Cabo were the equivalent of the Highway Patrol, cruising the highways and cleaning up after accidents, issuing the occasional speeding ticket when money was tight or Christmas was coming. Their ability to do anything meaningful in terms of real law enforcement or preventative action to deter a professional like *El Rey* was effectively nil, so they'd be of no use to Cruz.

He intended to fly a group of six into Los Cabos, who would put out feelers in the community and work with the existing infrastructure of police as they searched for signs of *El Rey*, without arousing undue attention. Technically, he didn't have jurisdiction anywhere outside of Mexico City, but his mandate from the president carried with it the ability to commandeer resources anywhere in the country, and to extend his reach should it be required. In this case, Cruz had made the judgment call that it was necessary – he'd worry about documenting the details later.

Cruz wished he could go directly to the president and voice his concerns, but he didn't have any relationship there. When he told criminals the president had given him the power to do as he liked, a more accurate description was that the president created his job and imbued it with that power, and then Cruz had been awarded the position. The truth was that he'd never been within a quarter mile of the president in his life.

No, he was effectively on his own on this one, and he knew it. His staff had continued to give him their support, for which he was grateful, and he had a larger group of officers at his disposal than any other agency, so he was hopeful that would be sufficient.

Briones stretched his arms and yawned, three quarters of the way through the day and four more meetings to go. "Have you asked yourself what the political consequences would be of the president being assassinated? I mean, we're assuming this is some sort of a vanity play on Santiago's part, but what about if it's more subtle than that?" he asked Cruz, who was brewing coffee on his side table.

"Well, if the president is killed, leadership shifts to the Secretary of the Interior – the equivalent of the speaker of the house," Cruz explained.

"Wasn't he just killed in a plane crash?"

"Helicopter. Just outside of the city. Last November eleventh, to be exact," Cruz confirmed.

Briones studied his boss, astonished at his recall. "How can you do that? Remember the date of something obscure?" he asked.

"It's not as hard as you'd think. His predecessor, the man who hired me for this position, died in another plane crash the same month, five years ago. A Lear jet that crashed into the heart of Mexico City. You probably heard about it," Cruz reminded.

"That's right – I just didn't remember who was on board. Seems like being Secretary of the Interior has a history of air accidents, doesn't it? Am I just being paranoid, or is that another of those coincidences you don't believe in?" Briones speculated.

"The black boxes were taken off the jet to the U.S., but that's the last I heard of it. Like so many cases, everyone just moved on to other things and the matter was forgotten. If there was foul play, the government is keeping a lid on it – so we'll probably never know the truth. They wouldn't like to advertise it, if the cartels had brought down the number two guy in the government. Bad press and all…" Cruz observed cynically.

"If you're offered a plane ride with the Secretary of the Interior, sounds like a polite, 'No thanks, I'll take the bus,' might be better for your health, no?" Briones suggested.

"Haven't gotten that invite yet, but thanks for the tip," Cruz quipped dryly. "So what else do we have for today?"

"A few more meetings, but the lion's share of the instructions have been handed out already. We'll establish a hub in Los Cabos and begin surveillance on the site. We'll also get a few undercover operatives to burrow around the strip joints and *barrio* drug-dealing areas to probe for chatter."

"But not from Julio or Ignacio's groups. I want them out of the information loop. As far as they're concerned, it's just business as usual," Cruz underscored.

"I know, I know. We have four guys from Paolo Arriata's squad who are going in. So it's compartmentalized," Briones assured him. Arriata was another veteran of the undercover street operations Cruz had initiated.

"Good. All right, let's get the next one in here and go through the drill."

Briones rose and went to find their three o'clock appointment.

❧❦

The temperature was beginning to soar in Culiacan, although it would get far hotter in a few months. Still, it was uncomfortable enough in the poorly ventilated confines of the jail, where prisoners awaiting trial or sentencing wiled away the days languishing on sparse mattresses in the general population area.

Moreno had been given his own cell once he'd returned from Mexico City, and the quality and quantity of treatment had improved significantly. Instead of being forced to sleep in a room with twenty other men, many hardened lifelong criminals incarcerated for murder and kidnapping, he got his own, more comfortable bed and a private toilet, including a sink. This was akin to a suite in the Ritz Carlton to Moreno, who'd been living in a bleak lean-to on the outskirts of town, surviving hand-to-mouth on whatever he could steal and sell.

As he'd gotten older, it had become more difficult to find legitimate employment; the only opportunities that had come his way over the last two years had been grueling construction jobs that required him to spend ten hours a day in the sun hauling concrete cinder blocks and mixing mortar with a shovel on a slab of plywood. With his pronounced limp and attendant complications, a lingering result of an unlucky two seconds on a tall ladder trimming plants on the second story of a home in town, he just couldn't do it anymore.

Mexico didn't have a safety net for its poor or unfortunate, beyond medical care at the notoriously shabby and inept social security hospitals – where one could easily die while waiting to be attended to. There were no social programs, no food stamps, no unemployment checks, no lobbyists sucking prosperity out of the economy for redistribution to the huddled poor. If you didn't work, you starved to death. The only buffer was the family structure, where caring for the old or the infirm was considered obligatory, but Moreno's four children were no help. One daughter lived in the United States, where she was struggling as an undocumented alien in Southern California, doing housework for wealthy housewives too occupied with their busy schedules to attend to chores like cleaning their own homes; a son was a fisherman in Veracruz who was barely keeping his head above water; and the other two were dead, one a victim of a traffic accident, and the other of Dengue fever, which cropped up in outbreaks from time to time, and for which there was no cure.

His daughter occasionally sent a hundred dollars, but it wasn't anywhere near enough to live on, and there were no gardening jobs for a fifty-something-year-old gimp with a poorly healed pelvis. So Moreno did odd jobs here and there when he could, and had taken to alleviating the pain from his injury with the readily available Mexican brown heroin, a habit that had rapidly consumed any savings he'd amassed. So he'd begun a career as a burglar, pilfering opportunistically – though he wasn't very good at it, as proven by his recent capture. He couldn't even run away from the two cops, who'd been alerted by a neighbor and were standing, waiting at the sidewalk when he'd climbed awkwardly out of the window.

He knew he'd been incredibly fortunate that the police captain, Cruz, had found his story valuable, and he resolved to set himself on a more productive path once he was released. There was a Catholic church organization that would feed him if he did work at traffic lights soliciting donations, and while that was a dead-end prospect, it beat rotting in prison for most of the remainder of his life. No, he'd been given another chance, and this time he wouldn't blow it.

A guard came by his cell to inform him it was exercise time, followed by lunch in the general population. He pulled on his prison-issue shirt and followed the man out into the yard, where the scorching sun beat down on the assembled felons, dishing out further punishment for their abundant sins. He took up a position on the periphery of the yard, in one of the areas where the roof overhang provided some meager shade. A breeze would have provided some relief, but the surrounding twenty-five-foot walls topped with razor wire and broken glass effectively blocked any, converting the jail into an oven. The concrete block construction made an unbearable proposition even worse, because the walls and roof absorbed the sun's energy all day, and then continued to radiate heat throughout the sweltering night.

Moreno pulled one of three cigarettes he had left from a packet he'd been given by the guards upon his return and, stooping over, retrieved a match from his shoe and struck it against the ground. A shadow moved across his, and as he stood, he was assaulted by a spike of searing pain. A burly prisoner with a ragged scar across his face plunged a shank into his abdomen with machine-gun speed, again and again, puncturing multiple organs before Moreno fell to the ground in a puddle of spreading blood. The assailant moved hurriedly away from the twitching form, melting into the prisoners, all of whom averted their eyes out of self-preservation.

Moreno's vision swirled as the world tilted and blurred, his lifeblood spilt in a miserable hellhole just as things were turning around for him.

By the time the uninterested guards arrived and called for a medic, Moreno was sliding into oblivion, struck down by an unknown assailant for reasons nobody would ever piece together. His last thought as he slipped from the world was that the whole mortality experience had been vastly overrated.

⁂

The flight from Mexico City to Los Cabos contained a surprising number of serious, well-muscled police officers distributed among the passengers. The men were traveling in civilian clothes, their weapons safely transported in a special locked container in the belly of the plane, which they'd collect once at their destination. They weren't chatty and kept to themselves, avoiding interactions with their seatmates, preferring to study the in-flight magazine or close their eyes during the short flight.

As the plane descended into the arid desert of the southern Baja peninsula, the plane bucked and bumped from the updrafts of hot air rising off the baking scrub below. Off to the left of their approach, the deep azure of the Sea of Cortez stretched into the distance; over a hundred miles of watery gulf washed between Los Cabos and the nearest point on the mainland.

The wheels scored the tarmac with a smoking streak before the aircraft decelerated down the long runway, recently lengthened for the G-20 as well as to accommodate Boeing 777 flights from the mainland: the final stopping point between Mexico City and China. As the plane turned to loop around towards the terminal, the men noted a phalanx of private jets of every description at the far end of the field, a testament to the money concentrated in the region. Everything from King Air twin-engine prop planes to Gulfstream G-5s nestled wing to wing, and even as high season wound down and the town headed into the dog days of summer, dozens of jets of all shapes and sizes jostled for space.

The men disembarked, and in the baggage claim area met their local counterparts, the Baja contingent of the Federal Police, who'd retrieved their case of weapons and were waiting to take them to headquarters a few miles from the airport.

After a cursory orientation in their temporary new home, the team broke for lunch at a nearby open-air seafood restaurant situated under a huge *palapa* with a thatched roof. When they had eaten, they drove to the site of the newly constructed convention center that would host the G-20 summit. It seemed that the workers milled about aimlessly amid the constant stream of vehicles that came and went, as deliveries were made and supplies distributed.

The lay of the land seemed relatively easy to secure, given that there weren't any structures in the immediate vicinity of the complex. The only locations that were a concern were the school at the bottom of the steep slope and the surrounding hills. A sniper could possibly take a shot from the crest of the nearest bluff, but it would be extremely iffy at such a distance.

In the end, securing the site wasn't their problem. The army and a special security detail would shoulder most of the burden for keeping the dignitaries safe during the summit, given the dearth of experienced police personnel. There were no armed conflicts with cartel members in southern Baja, so the local cops had never dealt with anything more dangerous than a shootout with a local dope-dealing gang, an occasional drunk with a knife, or a furious wife hell bent on decapitating her wayward husband with a gardening machete.

Satisfied they understood the geography, the team moved to the surrounding outlying areas, which were largely residential. Two and three-story condominium complexes lined the highway, interspersed by occasional soccer fields and small commercial centers, and the occasional shop or restaurant. The large grocery store and attached mall across the intersection that led to the G-20 was almost a mile away with a hill between it and the convention center, so posed no obvious threat.

After completing their day's orientation, the men checked into a nearby hotel. The undercover cops took siestas, because their shift would start at the fall of night, when adult entertainment began at the strip clubs as they flashed their neon promises onto the streets of San José and downtown Cabo San Lucas. They'd be up until four in the morning most nights, talking up the girls and trying to see if anyone had spent time with a mainlander who seemed suspicious. It was a long shot, but a surprising number of criminals spent their lazy hours drinking with pros, and perhaps *El Rey* shared that habit. All the undercover officers carried reduced-sized sketches in their wallets, along with some lip-loosening bills, on the off-chance one of the young ladies had something to tell them.

They wanted to avoid passing the photo around indiscriminately, because it could tip the assassin that they were actively looking for him in Los Cabos; once on high alert, he'd vanish, leaving them holding air until he struck from out of nowhere. They would wait until a day or two before the summit commenced to take that last-ditch step of desperation and circulate the sketch to all law enforcement and armed forces in the area.

A big obstacle was that the local police were usually corrupt. Average salary was three hundred fifty dollars a month, so most augmented their income by taking bribes for all manner of favors – letting off traffic offenders, hassling business competitors, demanding money to protect shops and restaurants, and selling information to underworld connections; which presented the problem – *El Rey* would doubtlessly be plugged into the underground buzz, and would hear about a manhunt within hours of their going widespread with it.

Every prisoner taken into custody would be interviewed and shown the sketch, just in case somebody had encountered him. Additionally, the undercover cops would spread the word through the local drug dealers, in case *El Rey* had a habit, which many criminals did. Once the undercover officers had bought a few times, they would show the dealers the sketch, concocting a story that the man had stolen property from a connected cartel boss, who was willing to reward anyone who could help locate him. It wasn't unknown for those hiding to do so in Baja – it was considered the boonies by mainland Mexicans; a wasteland out in the sticks that nobody in their right mind would want to go to if they could help it.

It wasn't a comprehensive strategy, but it was a good start, and as the sun began to dip behind the Sierra La Laguna mountains the undercover team prepared to begin the first of many long nights in southern Baja's dens of iniquity, searching for an elusive man with no name other than that of a tarot card.

CHAPTER 14

Cruz felt like he'd been through the wringer after the last two days' back-to-back meetings. Ten hour shifts were customary for him, but with all the work piling up while he met with his team leaders, he was clocking twelve to thirteen, and it still was not enough. He hated this part of the job, but the administration aspect was an essential part of Mexican management, and whether he liked it or not, he was in Mexico…managing.

Now that the teams had departed for Los Cabos, he felt like they were beginning to become pro-active. But it was an emotional roller coaster. He had the sense of time racing by as the summit drew nearer, yet they were really no closer to getting hard proof than they had been a week before. He'd taken the sketch of *El Rey* to CISEN and described the interview he'd had with the robber from Culiacan, but they'd seemed unimpressed. That didn't surprise him given their first meeting. He knew from experience that, when bureaucrats fought turf wars instead of doing their jobs, there was no way of forcing them back on track. He'd tried shaming them, but they hadn't budged – preferring to spin out lame assurances that all necessary steps to ensure the president's safety had been taken. They'd told him not to worry – they were on the case.

Cruz had left a copy of the sketch and hoped they'd wake up, but he wasn't optimistic. For whatever reason, they hadn't been interested in anything he had to say, so that still looked like a dead-end.

His meeting with the DEA hadn't gotten any traction either. Bill had been noncommittal about the Secret Service's reaction, which Cruz took to mean that he'd fared no better than he had with CISEN. It was possible that the Americans were taking the danger more seriously than Mexico was, but he thought it unlikely, given that nobody had touched base with him or requested any additional information.

It was a classic catch-22 situation. He couldn't prove that the pawn shop owner had been killed by *El Rey*, and had nothing new to report on that slaying, which meant that his sketch could have been of anybody – there was nothing to confirm it was the infamous killer besides the testimony of a jailhouse snitch, which was notoriously unreliable anywhere in the world. And Santiago's statements had carried no weight – a cartel boss who'd died of brain damage after threatening to kill the two presidents was hardly pristine testimony. Cruz understood that. He'd been quick to distrust Santiago's threats as well, until he'd had time to process his reactions and consider the man's tone and demeanor. None of which was proof of anything, even if he thought it was convincing.

Cruz's stomach growled. He glanced at the clock on his wall, surprised that it was already eight o'clock at night. The day had flown past yet again. Staring at the never-shrinking pile of paperwork in front of him, he felt demoralized. He wanted to be in the field, chasing down leads, questioning people, not acting like a damned CPA.

He took a swallow of the now cold coffee from his oversized cup and, grimacing at the bitter brew, decided to call it quits for the night. The slush pile of documents would still be there tomorrow, awaiting his perusal and signature. Of that he was sure. He rose, stretched his arms and rotated his head to get the kinks out, and then experienced a stab of guilt. He was facing another long night in an empty house with nothing but ghosts to keep him company, so he reasoned that he might as well take the work home and plow through it as he ate, rather than watching TV. At least he'd have less unpleasantness waiting for him the next morning, and it would certainly put him to sleep.

Toting his newly stuffed briefcase through security to his car, he decided to put in for a secretary. He'd always dismissed the idea, believing it sent the wrong message to his team, but he couldn't go on like this. Cruz needed to be active operationally, especially now there were less than four weeks till the summit. He made a mental note to have Briones send out an inter-departmental memo notifying the staff, so if there were any candidates internally they'd get first shot. He'd prefer someone familiar with the labyrinthine processes imbedded in the federal police system, otherwise he was just further adding to his task load trying to bring someone up to speed.

He tossed his briefcase onto the passenger seat, then returned to his office and grabbed a cardboard file box crammed full of the week's worth of papers he'd been meaning to attend to, but never seemed to have the time for. The container weighed a good forty pounds. Had he really allowed things to back up that much?

Cruz heaved the container to the car and slid it onto the seat, wedging his briefcase next to it so it wouldn't go flying if he had to stop suddenly. Satisfied, he fired up the big V8, giving it thirty seconds to warm up before pulling out of the lot. He waved goodnight to the guard and swung into the night-time Mexico City traffic, his vision blurred from fatigue and eye strain.

The trip to Toluca was clearer than usual, probably due to the later hour, and he made it to his off ramp in under forty minutes – a kind of minor miracle. Spying one of the ubiquitous OXXO convenience store signs, he calculated the state of his refrigerator and decided to get beer and bread for his dinner; the current loaf had started to turn an alarming shade of green around the edges, and he didn't want to tempt fate any more than he already had. Cruz was on his cell phone with Briones as he rolled into the lot, so he barely noticed the truck that pulled alongside him as he eased next to an ancient Impala that he knew belonged to the manager.

"All right," he told the lieutenant, "I want to fly to Los Cabos next week and spend a couple of days looking over the site before things get too hectic. We're running out of–"

His passenger-side window exploded in a hail of bullets as a burst of machine-gun fire tore into the side of the car. Cruz dropped the phone, momentarily stunned, and felt white-hot lances of pain from his chest and his right leg. Operating on instinct, he slammed the car into reverse and grabbed at his pistol, freeing it as he stomped on the gas. The Charger roared backwards. He spun the wheel to the right, blocking the truck in with his car as he jammed down on the brake. More gunfire glanced off the engine block as the shooter leaned out the truck window in an attempt to adjust his aim. Cruz emptied nine rounds through the vehicle's windshield, noting with satisfaction that the shooter had dropped his weapon on the ground as some of the slugs found home.

A silence returned to the parking lot. Cruz trained his gun on the truck as he swung his driver's door open and stepped unsteadily onto the pavement. His leg hardly supported his weight, and his chest felt like he'd been pummeled with a branding iron as he limped to the vehicle, noting that the weapon the shooter had been using bore the unmistakable shape of an Uzi. The dead gunman hung halfway out the window, his blood streaming down the side of the truck onto the shell casings littering the asphalt, so Cruz was confident that the danger from that side of the vehicle was over. He moved to the driver's door and cautiously opened it, pistol pointed into the cab at point blank range. The overhead light flickered to life, and he was greeted by the sight of the driver, his head cocked at an angle, fighting to breathe, his chest seeping blood from a wound over his left pectoral, and his scalp hanging from his skull where a round must have ricocheted, tearing into his head. He didn't register Cruz or the gun, and judging by the pink foam gurgling from his nose and mouth, he wasn't going to make it. Cruz watched as the man, disoriented and unarmed, struggled to keep his hand up, holding his scalp in place, and then with the distinctive moan of the dying, exhaled his last rattling breath.

Lowering his weapon, Cruz turned and studied the side of his car. It was riddled with bullet holes, the windows blown out; judging from the damage it was a miracle he was still alive – which was his final conscious thought before he slumped against the truck and everything faded.

ॐ◌

Light burst into his eyes, momentarily blinding him, and he registered distorted faces staring down at him, as though from afar, like he was at the bottom of a well. *That's odd*, he thought as he felt a sensation of floating, before slipping back into the quiet place where nobody could hurt him.

A jolt brought him back to awareness. His eyes flittered open. He watched as long fluorescent lights flew by overhead, which he knew to be impossible but found interesting nonetheless. His body conveyed that he was moving from the sense of momentum and the vibration, and hands worked at his shirt and his pants as he struggled to tell whoever this was that he was a cop; but he couldn't find a way to form the words – they seemed foreign, just out of reach. He tried to move his head but he couldn't. His last impression before he lost consciousness again was that the air smelled funny.

Oxygen flowed into his nostrils from two nubs of the connected tube, making his nose itch. He tried to reach for whatever the offending device was, but lacked the strength to move his arm. As he came to full awareness, he heard the telltale beeping of monitoring equipment and realized he was in a hospital.

When he opened his eyes, there stood Briones, waiting at the side of his bed, appraising him with concern. Cruz's voice cracked as he tried to speak. He motioned with his eyes at the pitcher of water by his side, near his left hand. A nurse pushed past them and efficiently poured some into a container, then stuck the straw into his mouth. He swallowed feebly before pulling his head away.

"Why's everyone so glum? Whose funeral is it, anyway?" Cruz asked in a feeble whisper.

Briones shook his head. "We thought we'd lost you there."

"What? From a few scratches? Or the coffee at OXXO?" Cruz asked.

"You took a slug in the chest, and one in the leg. The one in your chest glanced off a rib because of the angle, but you lost a lot of blood. It's a miracle you weren't killed. You can thank work for that," Briones said.

"How so? Seems like the job is what this is all about…," Cruz said.

"The documents you had in your car? They blocked most of the slugs. Otherwise, you'd have been cut in two. There were over a dozen bullets in the box and briefcase, and seven more in the engine area."

"I guess that's a decent excuse to not have those reports done on time."

"I think it should suffice, sir," Briones agreed.

"Do we know who the shooters were?"

"Not yet. We've got the prints in the system, but you know how that goes."

"Well, whoever it was, the party didn't swing the way they'd hoped," Cruz mused.

"It sure didn't."

The conversation seemed to wear Cruz out, so Briones and the nurse moved to the door.

"We've got an armed guard outside, just in case," Briones informed him.

"Great. Look, Lieutenant. Don't bullshit me. How long am I going to be here?"

"Doctor says if you recover quickly, maybe three days. The leg will take some time to heal, and the chest wound tore the muscles up pretty well, but nothing that won't mend. It's mainly for observation and to give your system time to rest from the blood loss and shock," Briones told him.

"Yeah. I feel like a tank ran over me. But I'll live."

"Yes, you will. I'll stop in tomorrow to see you, sir. Do you want anything in the meantime?"

"You got your service piece with you? Do me a favor. Leave it with me. I'll sleep better."

Briones removed his pistol and chambered a round. He slipped it under the sheets, near Cruz's right hand. "You've got one in the hole. But you won't need it."

"I hope you're right. Just call me paranoid at this point." Cruz coughed. "What time is it, anyway?"

"Six p.m. They brought you in last night just before ten."

"Shit. So I've been out all day?" Cruz was visibly agitated.

"You didn't miss anything. Nothing's happened. The job can wait a few days. Everything's on automatic right now. It'll still be there once you're up and around, sir," Briones reassured him.

"I guess I don't have much choice. All right…thanks for coming by. I'll see you *mañana*. Oh – did they get my phone?" Cruz asked.

"It's in the drawer of the bedside table. I turned it off so your battery wouldn't die."

"Thanks again. For everything."

"No problem. See you tomorrow. Try to get some rest, sir."

"Will do," Cruz said, settling back and surrendering to his fatigue.

∾⟋⟍

Kent fidgeted with his coffee cup as the men across from him bickered over tactics. After fifteen minutes, with a sense of the discussion going nowhere, he held up his right hand, signaling a pause.

"The cop has been neutralized, right? So he's not going to be a problem anymore. Early reports are that his car had more bullets in it than a gun store. And he's in critical condition. I'm not sure what all the hand wringing here is about," he observed.

"The problem is that we now have a plot to take out the Mexican president, as well as our guy, documented, floating around in the system. That shouldn't ever have happened," the oldest of the three others commented.

"Agreed. Nobody could have foreseen it. The idiot dope dealer had a big mouth. It happens. The important thing is that nobody's taking it seriously," Kent reasoned.

"It's a concern, though, because it's always possible that the president will cancel his appearance," the older man fired back.

"And miss a trip to Cabo and eighteen holes of golf? Does that sound like our guy? Please. How many legit threats does Secret Service get, per year? Hundreds? Thousands? You really think the ramblings of some taco-breath are going to get any visibility? The Mexicans can't even figure out how to tie their shoelaces. I'd guess this will receive less than zero scrutiny, other than perhaps a heightened security level at the conference and a few more suits than usual. This is noise. We have nothing to worry about," Kent pronounced.

"Let's assume worst case," the older man's associate said. "Can anything be traced back to your group, if they somehow stop the assassin?"

"That's the beauty part. Not a chance. The drug dealer's dead, and he was the point man on this. He's the one who took out the contract, he's the one who hired the killer, and he's the one who's now six feet under. It all goes back to him. If it's successful, then the cartels get blamed – and everyone in the world already knows they're murderous thugs. So it will shock, but not surprise. If it tanks, we can think of something else. We still have plenty of time before the November elections," Kent assured them.

"And what about if they catch him and interrogate him?"

"Highly unlikely. But just for conversation, let's go down that road. They capture him somehow, even though they've been actively pursuing him for years with no success. What do they have? A contract killer paid in untraceable cash by a cartel boss. That's it. The end. That's what made the whole scheme so appealing in the first place: its complete deniability," Kent finished.

The men groused and worried more, but it didn't go anywhere. They discussed some of the finer logistical points, and after another half hour agreed that things seemed back on track after a momentary scare.

Kent was getting tired of having to nursemaid his group of nervous nellies. Like all politicians and power players, they talked big and made bold moves when it was all theoretical, but once hands started to get dirty, they freaked out. The politicians were bad enough, but now he had to act as cheerleader for these second-string wonks, too? He resolved not to let it wear him down. This was a unique chance to achieve their objective in a completely clean manner, with no blood anywhere near their doorstep. It would be a regrettable act of brutality in a savage country run by criminals, and would create exactly the environment they were looking for. He couldn't have scripted it better if he'd tried.

Sometimes he wondered what the hell these idiots were thinking when they green-lit operations like this and got professionals like Kent involved. Did they think he could just push a button and call everything off whenever someone had a case of nerves?

He'd be glad when this was over. If all played correctly, he'd be in line to make a big move up the ranks, and either get the number two spot in Langley, or perhaps even the number one. Maybe next term, after his position as number two had seasoned some.

Nice problem to have.

❧

Cruz slumbered fitfully, the pain in his chest and legs causing him almost unbearable grief. He'd told the doctor to cut his morphine drip; he preferred to tough out the pain than feel the blanket of numbness restricting his ability to function. When the doctor had last checked in at midnight, he'd remarked to Cruz that his recovery was startling, given the condition he'd been in when he was admitted.

In spite of the pain, Cruz had to admit he felt much stronger than when Briones had stopped by. Apparently, the combination of rest and IV fluids was working – he didn't want to get his hopes up too soon, but he was thinking he might be ready to get discharged the following evening, if the hospital signed off on it.

Cruz had a long discussion with the kindly physician overseeing his care, and had been adamant about cutting the narcotics, just as he'd instructed the doctor to keep all staff out of his room unless he was dying. No dope, no distractions, just old fashioned bed rest while his body built back its depleted resources. The doctor had shaken his head and warned him that he'd be in a lot of pain, but Cruz didn't care. If he was feeling pain, it meant he was still alive, and that made it a good day. He knew he'd cheated death by a hair, and maybe wouldn't be so lucky next time. It put things into perspective.

Cruz was acutely aware of the passage of time. He'd lost a day now, due to the shooting; a day he didn't feel like he had to burn. *El Rey* was out there somewhere, not lying about wasting his time. The man was legendary for his meticulously planned hits so Cruz had little doubt that if he wasn't already in Los Cabos, he soon would be. The summit would be the crowning triumph of his assassinations – the Oscars, Grammys and Emmys of executions all rolled into one. Cruz could close his eyes and imagine the killer eyeing the building, the airport, the routes into the complex. He'd probably gotten a schedule of events and knew exactly what was planned for the attendees from the time they arrived until their plane wings lifted into the air.

He shifted and glanced at his watch. Four a.m., and his mind was busy turning over the facts of the case instead of allowing his battered body to rest. That figured. He'd long ago grown accustomed to his nearly obsessive approach to problem-solving; once he got hold of something, he'd worry away at it until he'd figured it out. It was his nature, and he supposed he wasn't going to change now.

One of the biggest question marks for him had been why a cartel boss would want to take out the Mexican president. It was an election year, and he was a lame duck now – he could only serve the one six-year term. There was no re-election bid in Mexico once you'd achieved the highest office; you got your six years, and that was that. So why kill him? To what end? Cruz didn't buy that it was all just to prove a point.

He thought about the chain of command. If the president died, leadership of the government went to the Mexican equivalent of the Vice President – the Secretary of the Interior. And if the Secretary of the Interior also died, as the recent two had in air crashes, then it went to one of the members of the Supreme Court. Cruz considered that scenario – maybe the goal was to eliminate those who were committed to eradicating the cartels, in favor of a judge who'd been bought off? He was far too experienced and pragmatic to believe that anyone in the system was incorruptible. The question was always just, at what price?

Then again, maybe it was as simple as territories, and controlling the playing field. It was obvious to Cruz that the current administration pursued some cartels with far more vigor than others. Santiago's region had been particularly hard hit by government troops, while his competitors went virtually unhindered. There was always the chance that the whole scheme was about money and power, and nothing more – that the goal was to remove a thorn in Santiago's side, and replace it with a politician who would focus on his rivals, rather than his allies.

Cruz knew these were impossible questions to answer, but that didn't stop him from mulling them over as he drifted in and out of slumber. Now that the morphine was clear of his system, his mental acuity was returning to accompany the pain. Which reminded him – he'd need to commit to some regular physical therapy, per the doctor's orders, if he was going to escape without a limp. The wound to his leg had narrowly missed shattering the bone, but had done a number on his muscles and ligaments, which would require patience and attention. The thought of it depressed him. Being around other invalids, casualties of a de facto civil war they couldn't win, wasn't something he was looking forward to.

The door eased open, allowing a sliver of light into the room, drawing him out of his tentative sleep and to full awareness. Cruz peered through squinted eyes and watched as a female form entered the room, pausing to scrutinize him before wedging a chair against the door handle. Something told him that wasn't standard operating procedure for caregivers, and his hand slid the few inches to Briones' pistol still concealed beneath the sheet. The nurse didn't notice, occupied with blocking entry with the chair. Cruz held his breath lest he make a sound and alert her.

The nurse approached his bedside and hastily removed something from her blouse. A pen. *Was she going to try to stab him to death with that puny thing?* She fiddled with it, then extracted a syringe from the casing. She was preparing to inject it into the IV bag when Cruz pretended to come to.

"Oh. Hello. Here to adjust the dose?" he murmured in a drugged monotone, eyes hooded and barely open.

"Yes. *El* doctor wanted to ensure you were comfortable all night and instructed me to check in on you," his would-be killer dissembled, without missing a beat. Cruz looked up at her, standing a few feet away, the syringe that would end his life clutched in one hand as she beamed love at him. The nurse was a stunning-looking Mexican woman, that was sure, with a body that would have stopped traffic anywhere in town. What a shame.

"He's very good, isn't he?" Cruz rasped weakly.

"One of the best. You're in good hands," she assured him.

"I'm glad to hear that. Tell me, what's his name again…?"

Her eyes digested the question, and he watched the split-second it took for her to realize she'd been played. She lunged for him with the needle, only to be slammed in the side of the head with the pistol. Obviously dazed, she fought to maintain her balance, so Cruz whacked her with it again. Her eyes rolled up into her head as she slipped into unconsciousness.

Cruz pushed the red button on his bed control, maintaining an unsteady bead on her as he awaited help. After a few minutes, he heard the staff trying to get the door open, with no success due to the chair. Checking to ensure the woman was still out, he resigned himself to having to do things the hard way. He detached his IV before swinging his legs over the side of the bed, taking a few seconds to get his balance before shuffling his way to the door and removing the chair.

Cruz was almost knocked off his feet by the two *Federales* who burst in, weapons at the ready, followed by a nurse, who grabbed him as he slumped against her. He noted the blood splattered on the floor from where it had leaked out of his catheter, and was reassured that it looked reasonably viscous; a satisfying shade of crimson.

"She's got a syringe in her hand. Careful. Don't let her stick you. It's poison," Cruz instructed the two cops.

Then he fainted.

CHAPTER 15

Briones paced the floor around the chair where the spurious nurse who'd tried to kill Cruz was shackled, much as he'd seen the *Capitan* pace when he'd been conducting interrogations. He smiled inwardly at the impression Cruz had made on him over the last five years. He'd do Cruz proud on this one.

Maria Trigos Gonzalez was twenty-eight years old, with a university degree in mathematics. She was a native of Los Mochis, north of Mazatlan on the coast – a notorious cartel trafficking stop on the route to the border.

"Maria. We tested the syringe. We know you were going to kill him. That's not in question. Judging by your performance it's a safe bet this isn't your first job. So cut the shit, tell me who hired you, and it'll go better for everyone," Briones said.

"I told you. I don't know the man's name."

"How did he get into contact with you?" Briones asked.

"I can't tell you that."

"You mean you won't. You *won't* tell me that," Briones corrected. "And that's the start of our problem, you see?"

"If I tell you who my conduit is, I'll be dead by tomorrow. That's how it works," Maria warned.

"Very melodramatic. But try this," Briones reasoned. "If you don't help me, you'll be dead in the same amount of time, because there's not a chance in hell your conduit will allow you to remain in custody until you decide it might be worth rolling on him. So your only safe bet is to cooperate now, before he knows anything's wrong. Your window of opportunity closes after that, and I believe you when you say nobody can keep you safe then…"

He saw a flicker in her eyes and knew he'd scored a major point. Maria was calculating, he could tell, trying to figure a way out. He allowed her time, confident that he had it right. If she rolled, he'd kill her; if she didn't, he'd kill her. But if she rolled before he knew there was anything wrong, she had a chance.

"You know what I'm saying is true – math degree, right? That's not for idiots. Maria, I can't let you walk after you tried to kill a captain in the *Federales*, but I can figure out a way to have you charged with something less, and incarcerated in a facility that's lax in its ability to hold determined prisoners. We both know that's the best deal you're going to get, but it's only available today, right now. When I walk out that door the deal walks with me, and you'll be dead within a matter of hours. Think it through and make the right decision. Either way, your assassin days are over." Briones studied her face. "You're a very beautiful woman, Maria. I have a feeling you could figure out a way to have a good life without financing it by killing people. There are probably men lined up to court you."

"I'm not a big fan of men. They're pigs. No offense."

"None taken. Okay, then, there's a whole life out there you can live being whatever you want with whoever you want. But it goes away once you're dead on the cellblock floor, which is how this plays if you don't cooperate. So let's save ourselves some time, shall we?" Briones suggested.

She glared at him, but he knew he'd broken her will. Not because he'd tortured her or worn her down physically. He would prevail in this because he'd used stark reasoning. Sometimes that was the best way. Maria was probably accustomed to being the smartest person in any room, so her language was logic; even if she earned her living being a murderer, the math degree meant that she was analytical, and once the equation was calculated in her mind, if the answer was that she'd need to cooperate to stay alive, she would. He fished in his shirt pocket and withdrew his package of cigarettes – tapped one out and lit it, then extended the pack to Maria. She shook her head, declining the offer.

Briones savored the smoke, having trimmed his habit to ten cigarettes a day. The hope was that he could eventually back it off, little by little, until he was only having a cigarette after dinner now and again. It wasn't a bad plan, but the damned smoke did taste good. Sometimes life wasn't fair – the things that were the most fun usually killed you.

Maria looked up at him as he took time with his smoke, in no particular hurry; a man for whom time was on his side. When she spoke, she sounded defeated.

"What do I have to do?"

Maria approached the front door of the antique shop with a measured gait, stiletto heels accenting her perfectly sculpted calves. She stopped at the door and peered through the glass, verifying that her conduit was there before entering. A middle-aged man with a goatee opened the door for her and kissed her on either cheek. He gestured with an open hand to a passageway at the rear of the shop, nodding at the girl behind the counter to hold down the fort while he attended to his guest.

Once they were inside his office, his manner became brusque.

"How did it go?" he asked.

"With the target at Hospital Angeles? Fine. I injected the poison as instructed, and got out before he died." She smiled sweetly at him. "What did you expect?"

He regarded her with puzzled curiosity. "That's wonderful. I'll collect the other half of the fee, and pay you in the usual manner. So why are you here, instead of dealing with this over the phone?" he inquired politely.

"Aren't you happy to see me?" she countered.

"Of course, my dear, of course. It's just not, erm, customary, so I'm a little surprised," he said.

"I want to meet the client, Ben."

Benjamin Del Fuerez stopped stroking his goatee. He gave her a harsh stare.

"That's not possible. You know that's not how it works," he snapped.

"Ben, this was not an ordinary contract. I don't know if you knew it or not, but the target was a prominent member of the federal police. That brings with it a completely different level of risk, and therefore reward, don't you think?" she observed.

"I had no idea," Ben protested, his eyes revealing that he did. There was no surprise in them, no shock. Just duplicity.

"Now you know. I want to meet the client and discuss how he can pay me what the hit was worth," Maria explained.

"I'm sorry; that's not going to happen. What I can do is have a discussion with him, and see about some sort of a bonus for a job well done," Ben suggested.

"No. I need to meet him. Sooner than later. No negotiations on that," Maria insisted.

Ben studied her as he might an insect. "Maria – what the fuck is going on in your head? Who do you think you're talking to? If you want any more contracts, you'll back that attitude off now. Or our arrangement is finished. I mean it."

"Maybe I'm tired of killing people for money, Ben. Maybe I don't need any more contracts," Maria countered.

Ben didn't know how to react to that. Nobody quit the business. Nobody.

"You don't have that option, sweetheart. Once you're in, you're in for life," Ben warned.

"I don't think so, Ben." She stood, and Ben was unsure how to respond to this latest surprise. He was honestly flummoxed by the interaction. Maria was as hard and efficient as pros got. Her announcing that she wanted to meet the client, and now intended to quit, was a complete departure from the script.

"I don't understand. What the hell do you think you're doing? Do you know what happens if you walk out that door?" Ben threatened.

"Let me guess. You kill me, or have one of your other people kill me?"

"You're on dangerous ground, Maria. You know I'll do it," he snarled.

"Yeah, well, I'm betting that it's a lot easier handling money for contract killings than doing it yourself, even though I imagine you've killed plenty in your time, eh?" Maria sneered at Ben, angering him further still.

"You little bitch, I've killed whores like you just for practice. How do you think I got into this business? You do *not* want to fuck with me. You walk out and you'll be dead before nightfall. Am I getting through to you?"

She nodded. "Yes. I imagine that should do the trick. You've made yourself more than clear, Benjamin Del Fuerez," she intoned, and then sat down, removing a small Beretta handgun from her purse.

"What the hell do you–"

A commotion interrupted them from the front of the shop; the sound of boots clattering on the stone floor. The door sprang open and three

Federales in assault gear burst in with their rifles pointed squarely at Ben's head. A moment later, Lieutenant Briones strode in, holstering his pistol.

He looked at Maria. "We've got the whole thing on tape. He's cooked. Give me the gun," Briones said, holding out his hand. Maria placed it into his palm, and he pocketed it before turning his attention to Ben. "As you may have surmised, being an obviously smart man, you're screwed. What I mean by that is that you'll spend the rest of your sad, miserable life being sodomized by AIDS-infested junkie convicts in the worst prison Mexico has to offer, based on her testimony and the recording we just made of you admitting to having killed many, what was the phrase, 'for practice'? You also admitted paying her to kill a federal police captain, and that you handle money in exchange for managing a murder-for-hire enterprise."

"I want my lawyer," Ben insisted.

"No, Ben – I can call you Ben, right? We're all friends here, right? No need for formality." Briones moved around the table to where Ben sat, and leaned in close, invading his space. "Nice cologne there, Ben, if a trifle heavy on the application. The boys in jail will love that. And that's your future – a short life being corn-holed by killers before one of them slices your guts out, well, 'for practice'."

"I was kidding…what I said to her—"

"Sure you were. And the captain will feel much better knowing the man who paid her to kill him was actually kidding when he did so. I'm sure the judge will love that explanation, too." Briones got his cuffs out. "You really do have a pretty mouth. Cherubic. I'm guessing even at your age you'll get passed around the yard like a pack of cigarettes; a nice, soft, civilized *caballero* like yourself." He flicked the cuffs open. "But there's another possibility, unless you're looking forward to living out your prison-rape fantasies…"

Ben swallowed and blinked back at Briones, seemingly receptive to hearing more.

That evening, a short man with a shaved head, wearing a suede dinner jacket and jeans, rang the bell of the antique shop, alligator-skin briefcase dangling nonchalantly from perfectly manicured fingers. An elaborate gold bracelet encircled one wrist, and a Patek Philippe moon-phase chronograph decorated the other. Ben emerged from the rear of the shop with a set of keys and hastily opened the double-keyed deadbolt, holding the door open for the man before relocking it behind him. He motioned to his office area and followed the small man back. Once seated, the man put the briefcase onto the desk and opened it with a flourish.

Ben frowned and said, "The contractor indicated that the target was a federal police officer–"

Ben's statement was interrupted by the muffled sound of the new arrival's small pistol, the subsonic round blowing through his eye. The little man calmly replaced the weapon, a Ruger .22 caliber with a custom-machined silencer, and closed the briefcase, rounding the desk to grab the keys from Ben's lifeless hand so he could let himself out.

When Briones and four armed officers burst through the rustic, hand-carved wood-paneled door at the rear of the office, the small man's composure fractured.

"You're under arrest, for murder and conspiracy to commit murder," Briones said as he stepped forward with cuffs at the ready. The little man bolted towards the front of the shop with the briefcase and the keys, stopping when he saw more police out front. He slowly turned to face Briones, whose pistol was pointed at his head, and tossed the briefcase to the floor with a flourish. The corner of one lip twitched upwards, and he hissed the first words he'd spoken since entering the shop.

"You're making a huge mistake."

CHAPTER 16

"What do you mean, they can't find him?" Briones screamed into the phone. "We brought him in last night, and I'm scheduled to interrogate him this morning. How the hell does a prisoner go missing in lockup overnight?"

"I don't know what to say, Lieutenant. I'm checking it out now. Theoretically, it's impossible. Maybe we filed him under the wrong name, or there was some other administrative error," the duty sergeant speculated.

"Do you have any idea who this man is? He's the one who arranged to have *Capitan* Cruz killed," Briones yelled, still aghast that the mystery man had disappeared.

"I understand, sir. Listen…captives don't just stroll out of here whenever they like. We'll find him. Give me an hour to sort this out. I just came on duty at nine," the sergeant assured him.

Briones looked at his watch. It was nine-thirty a.m. "Call me back as soon as you find him."

He swore as he slammed down the handset. A perfect sting, the perp caught red-handed with the murder weapon while the body was still warm, the killing memorialized on tape, and he vanishes into thin air? What the hell was going on?

Briones recalled the only words the man had spoken. *Gringo*-tinged Spanish in an almost feminine voice telling him he'd made a big mistake. And a smirk that had made Briones' breath catch in his throat.

The man had refused to talk since then, all the way into headquarters and through booking. Not a sound. Just a steady look that projected arrogance and irritation, as though Briones had interrupted a favorite TV show, or demanded to see his license after a traffic stop. What he hadn't behaved like was a suspect who'd just been apprehended for murder in an open-and-shut case. It had been worrisome, and now that he was nowhere to be found, the small kernel of anxiety Briones had felt had blossomed into a full-blown panic.

His phone buzzed again. Briones snatched up the handset. It was the front-desk receptionist.

"There's a woman on the line who's asking to speak to you, Lieutenant Briones."

"A woman? Did you get a name? Did she ask for me, specifically?" he asked.

"One moment please," the receptionist responded and put the call through, further annoying him.

"Lieutenant Briones. Is Captain Cruz all right?" the voice asked, vaguely familiar but not so much so that he knew who it was.

"Uh, yes. May I ask who I'm speaking with?" Briones fielded.

"I'm sorry. This is Dinah. Dinah Tortora. From the pawn shop? My father—"

"Yes, yes. I remember, of course. How can I help you?"

"I called to speak to Captain Cruz, but the woman who put through the call said he wasn't there because he'd been shot," Dinah explained with a worried tone.

God damn it. What did the operator think she was doing? News of Cruz's shooting was sure to end up all over the papers, which he'd hoped to avoid. He made a mental note to go down and beat the woman senseless when he hung up the phone.

"Yes, I'm afraid so, Dinah." That cat was obviously already out of the bag, so he saw no harm in confirming it.

"How did it happen? Is he all right? How badly is he hurt?" Dinah asked in a jumbled rush.

"In the line of duty. He should be fine," Briones said, on guard now.

"Is there any way I can see him?" Dinah asked.

"I don't think so. He's still at…he's still in the hospital, Dinah."

"Oh. Well, I thought he'd want to see what I found. I guess it can wait…," her voice trailed off.

"What you found? What do you mean, what you *found*?" Briones asked, now on alert.

"It's some sort of a diary, with contact names. I was going through a box my father gave me just before he died – it was almost like he had a premonition. I remember I thought it was strange. He asked me to hold on to the box for him. I forgot about it with the shock of seeing his…finding him. But I was thinking about what Captain Cruz said, so I went and got the box and pored through it. There are some bank statements and similar stuff, but also an agenda with names and numbers in it. Names I've never heard of. But I thought maybe it might help you with the case," Dinah offered.

"Dinah, I'm going to the hospital later. What time can you be here?"

જ⁍⳾

Briones was livid. The same sergeant from booking was on the line, giving him an impossible answer.

"What do you mean, he was released?" Briones couldn't believe what he was hearing. "The man's a murderer. We have him dead to rights."

"I wasn't here, but I called the night sergeant, and he remembers the man. A *Gringo*. They let him make a phone call, don't ask me why, and a few hours later the computer updated with a list of those to be released in the morning, at seven, and his name was on it. Nobody questions the computer. If it says release a man, you release him," the sergeant explained.

"How did he get access to a phone? What the hell is going on down there?" Briones was speechless at the incompetence involved.

The sergeant lowered his voice. "You know how it works, Lieutenant. I'm sure money changed hands, but nobody will ever admit it. All I know is what the night sergeant told me. The prisoner made a call, and then the computer listed him as one of the prisoners to release. End of story."

"No, not end of story. I want to know who authorized the release. Someone has to sign the order. And what about the man's name? Surely you had a name to book him under? And prints? You still print prisoners you process, correct? Damn it, man, what have you got? I need to find this prick, and every minute you delay is another advantage for him," Briones warned.

"I'm looking it up. Yes, I see he was booked under the name…oh…you're not going to like this."

"What?"

162

"He gave his name as Juan Perez," the sergeant told him – the Spanish equivalent of John Doe.

"Good God in heaven. Tell me this gets better. Please."

"Well, we did take photos and print him, so that's something," the sergeant said, still reading.

"Send me the prints and everything else you have on him. Now. On the intranet."

"Yes, sir. Again, none of this was my doing. The night sergeant probably had no idea who this man was…"

"You mean Juan Perez? No, I suppose he probably didn't. And now, neither do we. I want that in my inbox within five minutes, Sergeant," Briones ordered, hanging up the phone, incredulous at the exchange. Just when he thought he'd seen everything…

His rumination over the incompetence of the justice system was interrupted by his phone buzzing yet again. He grabbed it and stabbed the offending line button.

"What is it now?" he barked.

"There's a *Señorita* Tortora to see you, here at security, sir," the security team head from the detail in the lobby said.

"Ah. All right. Thank you. Is there any way you can escort her up here?" Briones asked.

"Sure. I'll have one of the men bring her to your office immediately, sir."

A few minutes later, a beaming young officer arrived with Dinah in tow. Briones noticed that most of the cops on the floor had stopped whatever they were doing, their attention riveted on her. She wore jeans and a pastel blue blouse, with only a light dusting of makeup highlighting her features, but the effect was dazzling.

He thanked the officer, who lingered a while before Briones gave him a hard stare as he offered Dinah a seat. She accepted, placing her purse on her lap, and waited in silence.

"One moment please, Dinah. I'm just finishing up something. I need to send an e-mail, and then we can get going," he told her as he studied his screen before entering a series of rapid keystrokes and hitting return.

"No problem. Take your time. I expect you'll tell me what happened to Captain Cruz on the way to the hospital?"

"I'll tell you as much as I'm allowed. Okay, I think that should do it. Did you take the bus here?" he inquired politely, shutting off his monitor.

"Yes. I don't really drive much. It's too terrifying in this city. People are maniacs. Although, now that I have my father's car, I should start. I just haven't worked up the courage yet…"

"Trust me, I know. All right then, I'll drive. Right this way," he directed. He'd sent the prints and photo off for pattern matching, tying in Interpol as well as Mexican national databases, so hopefully the man was on record, somewhere. That was all he could do until they got a match. *If* they got a match.

Twenty minutes later, as they fought their way through traffic, the IT clerk in the basement inputted the data and began the search. He'd send the requestor a message if and when they got a hit. The databases in Mexico were primitive – most weren't linked together – so there were no guarantees that the target would show up, even if he was a known killer in, say, the Yucatán, because the regional offices rarely updated their records with the central system. Sometimes it took years to bring the information current. The operator glanced at the man's prints with little interest, typed in the Juan Perez name, and leaned back in his chair to devour the second half of his sandwich.

❧❧

Cruz was surprised when Briones appeared in his doorway trailed by Dinah. He felt self-conscious lying in the bed with an array of tubes connected to him, looking like an invalid, but Dinah quickly put him at ease.

"Lieutenant Briones was kind enough to tell me about your near-miss, Captain. I'm glad you…you pulled through," she said awkwardly.

"That makes two of us. It's nothing, really. I hope he didn't make it sound like a bigger deal than it really was," Cruz downplayed.

"He said you were shot twice?" Dinah said, slightly puzzled, glancing at Briones for confirmation. He nodded.

"I'd hardly even call it shot. Pea shooters. I've had dog bites that hurt worse than this."

She regarded him skeptically – the IV bag, the pulse oximeter, the heart rate monitor, a crash cart waiting in the corner.

"Must have been some dog," she replied diplomatically.

"So, to what can I attribute this visit? Are you doing volunteer work at the hospital? Am I now a charity case?" Cruz inquired, trying to muster a grin but failing.

She explained about the box and the book. Cruz's eyes widened. She approached the bed and placed the book in his hands. He noticed she smelled like flowers, and honey, or maybe it was caramel. It was good, whatever it was.

He paged through to the last few entries. His eyes darted to Briones. "Lieutenant, please take this and run all the numbers, starting with this last one. It looks like a Mexico City phone number. Can you input the data using your iPhone?"

Briones nodded. He moved to Cruz's bedside and took the book, then took a seat by the door and began snapping photos of each page as Dinah and Cruz talked.

"I'm hoping that this will help with my father's case. Maybe one of these names has something to do with it, or will give you a new avenue to pursue. Has there been any progress...?"

"I have a team working on it, but I've been, well, otherwise occupied for the last few days..."

"Oh. I'm sorry. I should have known. Getting shot would take priority over case updates, right?" Dinah said sheepishly.

"I try to maintain time for both, but sometimes..." Cruz took in her face. "How are you doing? You holding up?"

"It's hard. I try not to replay the image in my mind, but it keeps...well, you know better than anyone."

"I do. But how do you know I do?" Cruz stared at Briones, who was absorbed in the book.

"Lieutenant Briones told me about your family. I have to apologize. I was such an ass the other day," Dinah said.

"Nonsense. You'd just been through an awful experience." Cruz raised his voice so Briones couldn't miss it. "So what else has the lieutenant told you about, besides my family tragedy and shooting? Did he fill you in on my diet, or my vacation plans?"

Briones looked up from his task, guilt tarnishing his face.

"Don't blame him. I can be a ruthlessly efficient interrogator. Ask any second grader. It's impossible to keep secrets from me," Dinah said.

They both smiled. He noticed how her face lit up the room as she did so. He liked it.

"I think that's the first time I've seen you smile, *Capitan*. I'm glad the shooters didn't sever the nerves that do that," she said. They must have been thinking the same thing. His wife used to be able to read his mind in the same way. "Whereabouts were you hit, if you don't mind me asking?" She seemed genuinely curious.

"I got nicked in the chest, and plinked in the right leg," he explained.

"I hope it didn't do any permanent damage."

"No, everything is in as good a condition as ever," he replied. An embarrassed silence hung over them, interrupted by Briones.

"Dinah, can I ask you to step outside for a few minutes? I have a few urgent matters I need to discuss," he said.

"Of course. Forgive me. I know you two must have a lot to catch up on. I'll just go down the hall and get something to drink. I'll be back in a few minutes, all right?" she asked.

They both nodded, captivated by her simple charm. She seemed sincerely embarrassed she'd monopolized Cruz's time. His eyes followed her as she departed, and Briones caught it.

"She's quite a woman, no?" Briones remarked.

"I suppose. I hadn't noticed," Cruz said unconvincingly.

"She seems to like you. You're a lucky man, *Capitan*," Briones teased.

"Your calling me lucky after I've been shot and almost poisoned is beyond the scope of my reasoning, Lieutenant."

"I'm just saying." He flipped his notepad open, and began reciting the events since Maria had been hauled from his hospital room. When he finished, Cruz was stunned.

"Great work on turning the conduit, but…how the hell does a man who shot someone in front of you, and who paid to have me killed, waltz out of lock-up and vanish? Just how can that happen? Am I hearing this right? Or is this humor of some sort?" Cruz's agitation was increasing with each question. The heart rate monitor blipped faster, and his blood pressure was spiking.

"I know. I wish I was joking. Oh, wait a second. This might be something on the case," Briones said, as his phone beeped to alert him he'd received a priority message. He skimmed the contents for a moment, and then re-read it. When he met Cruz's eyes, all the blood had drained from his face and he looked chastened.

"What? What is it? Did they locate the man, or ID him? Talk to me, Lieutenant."

Cruz didn't think the news could get any stranger or any worse than the story about the killer getting away.

He was wrong.

CHAPTER 17

"An American diplomat?" Cruz demanded.

"Yes, sir. The prints matched a set on file for a member of the American embassy in Mexico City. Says his name is Joseph Fitch, and that he's a commercial attaché," Briones said.

Cruz took a few moments to digest the revelation. "Any theories as to why a member of the U.S. embassy would be hiring contract killers to off me, or cold-bloodedly murder antique shop owners?"

"None, sir. Or at least, none of them good."

"Maybe he's working with the cartels? Co-opted? Wouldn't be the first time…" Cruz mused.

"Could be. But doesn't really matter. If I'm interpreting this correctly, he's got diplomatic immunity," Briones said, reading from his phone.

"What? No way. Don't tell me that immunity applies to hiring hit men or shooting people," Cruz exclaimed.

"Uh, I don't think that's what it's supposed to cover, but we'll have to get the Attorney General involved for a definitive…"

"He shot a man while you were recording it on tape."

"Yes. And assuming he's still in the country, we could and should go to the Attorney General. Even if he isn't. Maybe we could extradite him…," Briones trailed off, unconvincing even to his own ear.

"We can worry about the details later. Get the Attorney on the line, give him what you've got, and then let's press the Americans to hand him over. If he's sided with the cartels, he's the enemy, and our 'partner' up north needs to get with the program."

Cruz was processing furiously. He needed to get out of the hospital and back into the field. "Get the doctor in here. I need to determine when I can be released without killing myself."

"One more thing. The identification came back on the two shooters who tried to take you out. They're Knights Templar enforcers. So maybe revenge for Santiago?" Briones reported.

"Maybe. That's the most likely explanation. But it doesn't explain why an American diplomat would be paying to finish the job…"

"…unless the diplomat was working on behalf of the cartel," Briones finished. "I get it. Obviously, if the cartels are penetrating and compromising the U.S. diplomatic corps, the problem just got much, much bigger than only Mexico. Now, we're talking more of a global problem. Certainly for the Americans."

Dinah returned at that moment, a can of soda in her hand. She beamed at Cruz again.

Briones shot him an unmistakable look of admiration. "I'll go get the doctor," he said, making himself scarce.

Cruz sat up straighter with a wince. "We're going to analyze the information in your father's book, and hopefully, it will take us in a productive direction, Dinah. Don't worry. I'm not going to drop this. Trust me when I say that finding your father's killer is my top priority," he assured her.

"I do trust you, and I believe that if anyone can, you can. For now, concentrate on getting better. It's not every day that you get shot. Thankfully," she added.

"I don't recommend it. But I should be out of here soon, and then I'll be back driving things."

Briones appeared with the doctor, who did a cursory exam, and assured Cruz that he would be out within twenty-four hours.

"Well, that's great news, *Capitan*," Dinah enthused. "I bet you'll be glad to be rid of the hospital."

"You don't know how right you are about that," Cruz assured her. "Briones, let me have one more minute of your time before you leave, if you please." Cruz looked pointedly at the doctor and Dinah. She got the hint.

"I hope you get better soon. Try not to get any more dog bites," she said with a wave, and followed the doctor out of the room. Cruz waited until she was gone and the door had closed.

"Get me out of here. Transfer me to another area of the hospital, or to a different hospital, but I want out in the next two hours. I don't like all the weird crap that's going on, and until we figure it out, I want to make myself hard to find. Take Dinah home; don't tell her anything more about me, and send the doctor back in when you leave. Arrange a transfer to a different floor, or a new facility, but I'm not remaining here. I feel like a sitting duck, and I don't want to wait for someone with diplomatic immunity to show up and shoot me, and then give Mexico the finger." Cruz had digested the unsavory information about the American diplomat, and didn't like the implications.

"Absolutely. Will do. And I'm sorry about telling Dinah anything. She just has a way of pulling it out of you…"

"I have no doubt she's very persuasive. Now get out of here. Get me moved," Cruz concluded.

"Will do."

While waiting for Briones, Dinah was innocently enrapturing the doctor – who was just finishing up speaking with her.

"He's really lucky to be alive. A slightly different angle on the chest wound, or a few more minutes bleeding out on the pavement, and he'd be dead," he told her.

"I'll say he's lucky. Thank you, Doctor. You're a gentleman," she cooed; the doctor seemed to gain an inch in stature.

Briones followed after him as he moved to the next room, and had a hurried discussion. The armed *Federales* sitting in the hall eyed Dinah with curiosity and more than a little interest. She didn't seem to notice.

Briones returned, and she fixed him with a look that must have petrified seven year olds.

"Dog bites, huh?"

❧❦

The Citation Ten executive jet touched down at Dulles International Airport and pulled towards the private charter section, where a well-lit hangar awaited its arrival. Even though it was inbound on an international flight, no customs agents were anywhere in evidence. That had been taken care of in advance. This hangar was off the grid as far as niggling details like passports or searches went. Had been for decades.

The plane rolled to a stop and a folding hydraulic stairway descended from the fuselage with a precise hiss as the pistons lowered it into place. The small bald man walked carefully down the steps carrying a hastily packed overnight bag, and continued to the waiting limo – a long black Lincoln with government plates. The driver, wearing a black suit and tie, opened the rear door for him. The new arrival looked inside the car, smiled, and climbed in to sit across from Kent.

"Welcome home, Joe," Kent said, holding his hand out to shake.

"Thanks, Kent. And special thanks for arranging the flight. Nice plane," Joseph said, clasping Kent's outstretched hand.

"It's the only way to fly, isn't it?" Kent agreed.

The car pulled out of the hangar, and soon they were hurtling down the freeway on their way to Virginia.

"So what happened? How did you wind up in Mexican custody?" Kent asked.

"I terminated the conduit, as instructed," Joseph said. "Turned out it was a setup. The *Federales* were waiting for me. I had zero options but to allow them to take me in. Good going on the computer hacking, by the way. They let me walk out in the morning, no questions asked. Stupid bastards."

"Did they get any information from you? Any ID?"

"What, are you kidding? You know I never carry anything on a job. And no, I didn't say a word to anyone. As far as they're concerned, I'm the invisible man," Joseph assured him.

"I should have known. You're a magician, as always." Kent smiled at him. "It's really good to see you again, buddy. It's been too long."

"I agree. Next time don't send me into any hellholes, okay? Maybe someplace fun, like Prague or Buenos Aires?"

"You got it. Hey, I'm sorry, bud. After four hours in the air, you must be parched. You want some water? A drink? I've got scotch and vodka, beer, sodas and H2O. Name your poison," Kent offered.

"I could use some water." Joseph adjusted the air conditioning so that it was blowing on him. "So what do we do now? Where do we go from here?" he asked.

"That's a tough one, Joe." Kent handed him a bottle of water, cracking the bottle top for him. "We're going to have to take you off the board in Mexico. Too high profile. I'm thinking we get you an office for a few months, let you run ops from behind the scene, and then get you back on the ground once this thing has played out," Kent said.

"Makes sense. I don't care if I never see Mexico City again. The air sucks, and it's like living on an anthill. Too many people packed on top of the other," Joseph complained, downing half the bottle.

"Been a while since I was there. I'm with you on the crowds, though. I hate them," Kent agreed.

Joseph wiped his forehead and took another swig of water.

"I think I might have picked up a bug in jail. I'm not feeling too–" he said, and then slipped into unconsciousness, the water bottle soundlessly dropping onto the carpet. Twenty seconds later white foam began trickling out of his nose and mouth. Kent retrieved the bottle and screwed the top back on. Amazing what a little superglue could do to create the distinctive crackling sound that mimicked a factory-sealed bottle. Kent pushed a button on the intercom.

"It's over. Let's drop him at the base and get rid of any trace. Grind him up into pieces so small he'll fit through a straw."

❧

Once the hospital had fallen silent, the bustle of daytime replaced by the hush of night, Cruz propelled himself unsteadily down the hall in the wheelchair that had been left for him by an orderly. He'd gotten the okay to disconnect the intravenous drip and plug the catheter, and had done so a few moments before placing a plastic bag containing his wallet, phone and weapon on his lap. He cautiously wheeled himself through the door. The two *Federales* could have been statues – Briones had briefed them to stay on guard at 'his' room and not to allow anyone in, no matter what, and not to discuss his absence under any circumstances.

The doctor had reluctantly agreed to get him a room that he could lock, and had equipped it with a drip so he could stay hydrated. Cruz had been informed of the attendant risks and had bought off on them; they were considerably less than the odds of him being attacked by a cartel bent on killing him, so on balance, he fancied his chances better as a no-name patient in the maternity wing.

His chest hurt like hell from the exertion, but he didn't mind. He still had decent upper body strength even after the slug had torn through the pectoral muscle. The leg was another matter, but he'd deal with that on a day-by-day basis. If necessary, he could crutch it for a few weeks. He hoped that wouldn't be required. Maybe some sort of a brace or a soft cast could be fitted. They'd go over options upon his release.

The doctor said he could be discharged the following day, but would prefer if he stayed forty-eight more hours. Cruz wanted out of the hospital in the worst way, but didn't want to wind up back in a few days because he pushed it. Tomorrow, Briones would bring a laptop so he could link in to the headquarters' servers, which would make him feel more productive, so he'd resigned himself to tough it out and spend two more nights there.

He reached his new digs, wheeled himself in and locked the door with the key that hung obligingly from the interior of the dead bolt. Now he was safe, or as safe as he could be in Mexico City. Once he was discharged, he was going to have Briones rent a by-the-week executive apartment in one of the fancy downtown high rises while he recuperated. It was pretty clear he couldn't return to his house any time soon without risking extermination.

Cruz climbed onto the bed and hit the button that extinguished the lights. The only illumination came from the window; the soft glow from the parking lot lamps provided just enough visibility so he could place the plastic bag on the bedside table and pull out the pistol, cradling it in his hand as he dozed off to sleep, finally able to do so without the worry of being butchered while he slumbered. His last thoughts were about Dinah, hair gleaming in the harsh fluorescent hospital lights, and the dreams, when they came, featured her smile in all its high-voltage glory.

☙❧

The next day, Briones arrived with the laptop and a bag of clothes to replace the ones that had been shot to bits and sliced off him by the emergency medical team. There were few things as humbling as spending three days with one's ass hanging out the back of a gauze robe, so the sight of real clothing filled him with an optimism that defied rational explanation. Briones also had a special surprise – a brand-new pistol with two spare magazines. Cruz handed back the one Briones had loaned him and hefted the new Glock happily. Only ten a.m., and already it was shaping up to be a good day.

The doctor stopped in to check the dressing on his chest and leg, and promised him he'd be back later to change it and give him another shot of antibiotics. Cruz's color had returned, signaling that his red blood count was back to normal – the tests would confirm that, but his skin told him all he needed to know. The nearly constant infusion of plasma, vitamins and minerals had given his body the necessary materials to rebuild, and he felt stronger by the hour.

Cruz got online and saw that he had hundreds of messages to wade through. That took care of how he'd stay busy for the next ten hours. He turned to Briones, who seemed consumed by something on his phone.

"What is it?" Cruz asked.

"It's not good. The numbers in the final section of Tortora's book? All but one were cell phones that were registered, used once, and then tossed. Sound familiar?"

"Standard cartel issue. Is there anything promising at all?" Cruz asked.

"Well, the last number was a Los Cabos number. A pay phone outside of the old bus station in Cabo San Lucas. It's not much, but if that was being used by our friend *El Rey*, it means he's already in Los Cabos, and has been for several weeks, at least."

"So more circumstantial evidence nobody will want to pay attention to, other than to point out holes in the case," Cruz muttered bitterly.

"Yes, but it tells us something important, I think – that we need to up our surveillance-push in Baja and put more feet on the ground there. That's where all the action's going to take place, now that the summit is coming at us, only twenty-five or so days away," Briones stated.

He was right. *El Rey* had to be there. No question. But knowing that didn't do them much good, unless they could pinpoint it a little better. The population across San José and Cabo was almost two hundred fifty thousand – not exactly a tiny group to sift through. And as they'd discussed many times, *El Rey* doubtlessly had ways of changing his appearance, so the sketch might not do them any good. Something as simple as a change of hair color or cut, or facial hair, could radically alter appearance. They'd had

Arlen draw in goatees and moustaches, but the more you covered the face, the more generic the drawings became.

They spent most of the day going through strategy, and at six, Briones begged off on any more work. He needed to secure an apartment for Cruz, and break the news to the additional officers they'd be shipping out for Baja, so he'd be lucky to be done by nine p.m.

Cruz was grateful Briones had stepped in and picked up the slack while he'd been down for the count. He truly didn't know what he would have done without his help, and was glad he hadn't cut him out of the loop when he'd had his doubts about Julio and Ignacio.

❧

Kent hated phone conversations for anything of importance, but he couldn't just hang up on the Speaker of the House, tempting as it was. At least he was calling from a landline. Cells were fraught with eavesdropping problems, and even though there was virtually nobody wishing to have him under surveillance, force of habit told Kent that discussing anything on the phone was a bad idea.

"You told me there was no way we could be connected to the events, and now you tell me that you had to pull an asset and terminate him? What about the locals? You think they're not going to go crazy when they discover he's gone?" The Speaker sounded far more concerned than the situation warranted, in Kent's opinion.

"He was turned by the cartels, a black sheep, and disappeared. That's the explanation. We can't produce someone who doesn't exist anymore."

"My point is, this is already unraveling. First the DEA memo, now a manhunt for embassy personnel. I don't like it. I don't think you have as solid a hold on this as you pretend," the Speaker said.

So there it was. The anxiety needed somewhere to land, and so they'd gotten out the shit-gun and sprayed Kent with it. He'd put a fast end to that.

"Nothing significant has happened. On any complicated plan, you expect a few random variables. These were ours. But they've been manageable. Have you heard anything more about the memo? No. It's already buried and forgotten. Same as Joe. He was a rogue low-level staffer who apparently was lining his pockets doing the bidding of the cartels.

175

Guess what? Regrettable as it is, sometimes good men go bad. That's the surprised explanation we'll eventually give – and we'll waive diplomatic immunity for him should they locate him, as a symbol of our goodwill. The end. Nothing further to discuss. That's why I'm not worried."

Kent had good points. It was a closed loop. The cop was out of circulation, Joe was sludge at the bottom of a drainage ditch in Vermont, the memo was one of thousands of informational bulletins read and then forgotten, and the cartel boss was worm food.

After a few more platitudes Kent hung up, satisfied that for now he'd talked the great man's nerves down. As the big day approached, he knew there would be more of these displays, but as long as they got no worse, it was water off a duck's back.

All part of the job nobody else wanted, or had the guts to do.

CHAPTER 18

A group of heavily armed men in the distinctive blue uniforms of the *Federales* formed a defensive arc around the hospital's rear emergency room entrance. The afternoon haze from pollution and dust hung over the valley like a shroud, obscuring the outlines of tall buildings only a few miles away. A black Ford Explorer pulled up to the blue wheelchair ramp, and an officer emerged, pushing a seated figure wearing sunglasses and a baseball cap, a blanket draped around his shoulders and down his front. The men closed ranks, and the figure was helped into the SUV before it tore off, followed by several police vehicles.

Cruz watched the charade from his window. Anyone waiting for his departure had just gotten a nice show, and would now be tracking a motorcade that would drive around the city for an hour before making its way back to headquarters. He gingerly pulled on the loose pants Briones had brought for him and examined his reflection in the mirror. Considering what he'd been through, not so bad. He tucked his new weapon into his waistband; a Glock 21 that fired .45 caliber ACP bullets. It was light, accurate and held thirteen rounds with an additional one in the chamber – a lot of stopping power, even if you were being charged by a rhino. He'd need to get a nylon shoulder holster for it, but for now the improvisation worked.

Taking a final gaze around the parking lot and seeing nothing suspicious, he wheeled his chair to the front entrance and called Briones, who was waiting at the far end of the lot. He pulled up to the ramp, and an attendant assisted Cruz into the little Ford Focus.

"That went well, I think," Cruz said, shaking Briones' hand.

"It was very convincing. If I didn't know it was all an act, I would have bought it," Briones agreed.

"Let's hope that anyone watching for me was also taken in." Cruz pulled his pistol out and held it up. "I need a shoulder holster for this. Stuffing it down your pants may work in the movies, but it hurts like hell in reality."

"I've got one in the back seat for you. Are you ready to go to your new home?"

"Sure. And I'll need someone to do some quick shopping and get me some clothes and shoes, and also go by my house and grab my uniforms and a few hygiene items."

"I'll get someone on it. You'll probably be gone for some time, sir, so I'll arrange to have someone go by every week and flush the toilets and run the pumps," Briones said.

"Yeah. I suppose I'm going to be floating for a while – at least until we get *El Rey*."

"The summit's in three weeks, so it shouldn't be that bad. The place I rented is nice. Furnished, with dishes and glasses, a fully stocked fridge…almost like staying in a first class hotel," Briones offered.

"How's security?"

"Locking front door and a large foyer with a security guard, which I've beefed up with a pair of officers. Low key, plainclothes, but armed and ready for anything."

"Good. And what news do we have on Los Cabos? Anything? I can't believe I lost almost a whole week. These bastards' timing on trying to kill me couldn't have been more inconvenient," Cruz complained.

"We have another six men on a plane to Los Cabos today, and we're sticking with the protocol we agreed to. So far, no hits, but you never know. We could get lucky at any minute. It's not that big a town, although the *barrios* go on forever, so if he's holed up in one of them he's as good as gone."

"I had a few thoughts last night. I think it's worth taking a hard look at the crews doing the construction on the convention center for the event. If I was him, I'd be involved, even if just as a day laborer, so I got used to all the ins and outs of the place as well as the surrounding terrain. Nobody would look twice at a construction worker, scoping it out. You see what I mean?" Cruz asked. He'd been trying to think like *El Rey*, and he kept coming back to the build. That would be the natural place for him to gravitate.

"I understand. Let's get you situated at your new place, make sure the internet's working and that you can get around, and then I'll get some men on it."

"I can walk. It's just a little painful. But the doctor said that if I took it easy it wouldn't be an issue," Cruz said.

"I know. I got you a set of aluminum crutches at the apartment, and a cane. Very sporting."

"Too bad you couldn't make them fifty caliber. At least they'd be useful," Cruz said.

"That wasn't part of the ordering options, unfortunately."

The little car narrowly missed a collision with a truck that had run a red light, causing Briones to stomp on the brakes and lean on his horn.

"Your driving is more dangerous than the cartels," Cruz observed.

Briones shook his head, jammed the car back into gear and sped down the busy boulevard.

❧❦

The man pulled into the contractor parking lot, the ancient Toyota Camry groaning as it lurched over the rutted dirt surface. He parked at the far end of the field, all the other spaces already full, even at seven a.m. The pace had increased as the summit drew nearer, and it seemed like, every day, more new arrivals were thrown at the problem in a bid to meet the deadline.

He'd packed a lunch – a *torta*, the quintessential Mexican sandwich, prepared on a large bun and loaded with ham, cheese, chorizo, and a host of other delicacies. He cheerfully swung the plastic bag as he ambled towards the site to get his work orders for the day. The explosive faux light fixtures would be ready in one more week, so now he was actually helping to get the convention center built, which amused him to no end. He was more motivated to get the project completed on time than anyone else on the crew, and so his men were routinely finished with their assignments ahead of schedule. It was a pity he couldn't direct the whole project. The incompetence was typical, with a lot of tired men going through the motions of a thankless job, uninterested in the quality of their work.

Give him two weeks with the crews, and he'd have had the damned thing finished. Then again, he had more important matters to attend to.

He approached the trailer where the electrical team gathered every morning, and clomped up the temporary wooden stairs, swinging the door open with his right hand while clutching his sandwich in his left. He adjusted his security badge – numbered, with his photo laminated on it – and said good morning to the group of preoccupied engineers. One of them looked up at him from his workstation and peered at his badge, comparing it to the list.

"I guess you didn't get the word, huh?" the engineer asked without looking up.

"What word?"

"Your company is off the project. It got terminated," the engineer said unsympathetically. He finally looked up, and held out his hand. "I'll take your construction badge, please."

El Rey stood immobilized for a few moments before collecting himself.

"That's impossible. Could you check again?" he demanded.

The engineer held up his list, and made an X next to the name of the company he'd joined to get onto the project.

"That's you, isn't it? Some sort of a dispute, so they're history. Sorry about that. Might want to take it up with them. I can't do anything from this end. Now, if you please, your badge…," the engineer ordered.

He unclipped it slowly and handed it over, his thoughts churning.

"Is anyone else hiring? I…I don't have any other job. Do you know of anything else on the project? I have a lot of experience…," he tried.

"No. At this point, with only a few weeks left, there's nothing I know of. It's a shame. You've done good work – I have no issues with you. It's your employer that's the problem. Probably trying to shake the builder down for more money. A lot of these guys wait till the project's nearly done and then stick it to them, figuring they're irreplaceable or that the builder will cave. Not these guys. They've adopted a zero-tolerance policy to that kind of bullshit."

"So I can't work as an independent contractor? You've seen the quality of my jobs. They're some of the best here," he said, now almost pleading.

"Nope. All the hiring takes place out of Monterrey, and I know for a fact that you need to have a company with at least a three year history, and a bond. I'm afraid you're out of luck. Now, could you move aside? I need to get these work orders distributed," the engineer finished, dismissing him to his fate.

El Rey descended the shaky stairs and considered his options. He hadn't foreseen the company he'd weaseled his way into having a dispute with the builder. That had never come up in his contingency planning. He cursed inwardly, then calmed himself – losing his patience would accomplish nothing. What was done was done. But this was a disaster for his plan. There was no way he'd be able to mount the light fixtures now, much less stay on to do maintenance up to the big day, ensuring the detonator was in place and functional. He was screwed. And he only had three weeks to come up with an alternative plan; the blink of an eye in terms of this scope of a hit.

All the work and preparation had just been flushed down the toilet by a larcenous contracting company. He momentarily entertained a vision of the company owner, flayed alive and suspended over a fire, and then dismissed it. Satisfying as it might be to take his frustration out on someone, he needed to spend his time more productively.

Opening the door of the junky, beaten car he'd bought in the *barrio* for a thousand dollars, he fumed at his ill fortune, and then reconciled himself to plodding forward. It was a setback, but he was used to overcoming adversity. It's what made him *El Rey*.

Which was all well and good, but wouldn't get the job done. He was running out of time, and the clock was ticking even as he sat in the dusty lot. The engine turned over with a puff of alarm-inspiring black smoke, and he wheeled around and headed for the exit, mind working furiously on alternatives.

He needed a plan. And he needed one fast.

∂∽

That afternoon, two uniformed *Federales* entered the large administration tent that had been erected to house the hundred or so support staff for the project. They spoke with the project director. After a few minutes, he directed them to a computer terminal and brought over an overweight woman in her forties, who was chartered with keeping track of personnel. They unfolded the sketches of *El Rey*, with facial hair and without, and began the tedious process of going through sixty-five hundred badge photos on the off-chance they found someone who resembled their target.

The woman was chatty, regaling them with stories of her move to Los Cabos from San Luis Potosi, where she'd had a travel agency in a past life, before the internet had obviated her business. She seemed singularly incapable of appreciating how little both men cared about her banal history or her opinions of the region's charms, and how they compared with her home town, which to hear her tell it was the Garden of Eden crossed with Shangri-La.

They listened politely, but soon were exchanging glances of annoyance as she kept up a rapid-fire monologue of excruciatingly dull observations, many of which involved the antics of her beloved cats, which she believed possessed magnetic charms and would surprise and delight anyone within earshot. The older of the two leaned in and whispered to his companion, speculating on the ramifications of shooting her, maybe just to wound.

The hours dragged on as they stared at photo after photo, assembling a group of men that came relatively close. By the time they'd seen all the photos they had thirty-seven possible suspects, which they downloaded to a flash drive for forwarding to Mexico City. It was now two o'clock, and Mexico City was an hour ahead, so the photos probably wouldn't be looked at until the next day.

The men thanked their new friend for the hospitality and headed for the exit with palpable relief, intent on getting back to the *Federales* outpost so they could send their findings via e-mail. They stopped at a Burger King on the way to the office, having missed lunch in favor of the voluble babblings chronicling the precocious hijinks of the woman's felines, and wolfed down burgers with air-conditioned relief. It was three before they got to the station and had sent all the photos, and when they were done they sat back, exchanging war stories with the local officers while waiting for instructions on what to do next.

જ⊷ન્ડ

Briones returned to headquarters late in the day, having spent much of it getting Cruz settled in and outfitted. There had been some complications with the internet that had taken time to work through, and then some shopping, so by the time he made it in, it was already five. He checked his e-mail and found twenty-two messages. With a resigned sigh, he began poring through them, sending single-sentence responses to most. The last five were the photos from the Los Cabos team. He rubbed his eyes and began paging through the various shots. A few looked close, and could have been the man. He just didn't remember so clearly – too much time had gone by.

And then he stopped.

Briones peered at the screen, and then enlarged the image. He was almost a hundred percent sure, although there were some differences, most notably the goatee and the hair color, which was considerably lighter than he recalled. But the nose and eyes were the same. Not daring to jostle his mouse for fear of somehow deleting the image, he reached out and dialed Cruz's number.

"I think I'm looking at a photo of *El Rey*, from the construction site in Los Cabos," Briones said excitedly.

"You think, or you are?"

"I'm almost positive. Remember, I only saw him for a few seconds, assuming that was him. But I believe this is the guy."

"Send it over to me," Cruz instructed. "Find out if he's at work or when he's next due in. But let's cover all options immediately. I want every officer in Baja to have that photo within the hour, and if he's not at work, I want the man located and apprehended. Send out a team to the address listed on the manifest. There's the slimmest of chances he didn't use a fake name and address, although I think it's a given that he did. If so, I want everyone on the streets tonight, asking every bar, strip club and restaurant whether they've seen him. It's show time – this is our first real break."

CHAPTER 19

Sergeant Obregon, the head of the team that had been sent to Baja, crouched behind an abandoned car forty yards from the one-room dwelling that had been listed on the security pass docket for the suspect, whose name, Adrian Sendero, was undoubtedly fake.

After discovering he'd been fired from the project, they had been watching the house for several hours, but there was no sign of life. Sergeant Obregon had the sensation in his gut that this was going to be a waste of time, but his job was to run down all leads, and this was the only one they had. So here he was, carrying out surveillance on a hovel in one of the worst *barrios* in San José del Cabo – a section that had originally started off as a squatter camp, with electricity pilfered from overhead power lines and open sewage running downhill towards the ravine, and had gradually become a neighborhood, such as it was, with cracker boxes like the one they were staking out, built from cinderblock and bags of cement purloined from work sites.

It remained a grim area, redolent with the fetid odor of garbage and poverty; the pervasive squalor spoke of a population at the end of its rope. These were life's losers – the sick, the drug-addled, the hopelessly alcoholic, the mentally ill. Nobody with any sort of income lived there; even the lowest of the low, the unskilled laborers, could do better. Crime was constant, and never reported, partially because the police were unlikely to show up and partially because the denizens were mostly criminals as well.

It was the type of area where the residents kept to themselves. Nobody wanted to know what you were doing, and it was best not to be curious about their affairs. It was a place the unwashed came to die, enslaved by heroin and methamphetamines and alcohol. AIDS was a near-constant among the intravenous drug users, and corpses being hauled out by the coroner's office was an almost daily occurrence.

Obregon's ear bud crackled as the com line came to life.

"Car headed your way."

He squinted in the dark and watched as a battered twenty-year-old Buick LeSabre trundled to a stop near the shack. A man swung out of the car, clad in a filthy white undershirt and soiled pants, accompanied by an obese woman in an ill-advised tank top and shorts that strained to contain her modesty. They cackled with inebriated laughter, and the man veered to the front door, which consisted of a slab of plywood held in place by two rusted hinges. He fished a key out of his pocket and unlocked the padlock securing the chain that acted as the door lock, and was caught unawares by the bright floodlights from the assault team as they flashed their dazzling focus on him.

"Stop. Put your hands up. Do not move. This is the Federal Police. Repeat, do not move," Sergeant Obregon instructed through a handheld megaphone.

The couple froze in place, and within seconds, were surrounded by armed men, weapons at the ready.

Twenty seconds after it started, the operation was over. The man was clearly not the one in the photo, given that he was emaciated, filthy, reeking of cheap tequila, and with a profile more akin to a living skeleton than a human being. After a few minutes of interrogation, it also became obvious that nobody lived with him in the little hothouse. The sergeant entered, to be confronted with a soiled mattress, a reeking bucket with a lid fashioned from a piece of sheetrock being used as an ad hoc toilet, and a few odds and ends. Illumination was provided by a single light bulb dangling from a wire affixed to the corrugated tin ceiling with a rusty nail. Two holes in the wall with rebar bent to serve as security bars afforded scant ventilation. Obregon gagged at the smell wafting from the dirt floor.

As expected, it was a dead-end.

The team packed their gear and loaded into the black pickup which had been called in after the operation was terminated. With a final look around at the slum, Obregon gave the signal and the men headed back to the station.

It was unlikely they'd get any traction from circulating the photo around the local prostitutes and drug dealers, but at that point it was the only option they had left. At Cruz's behest, they'd erected road blocks at several key intersections, ostensibly as sobriety checkpoints but in reality to spot-check suspicious travelers; but those were long shots, at best. As the night wore on, the officers grew increasingly frustrated. It was obvious their target had either gone to ground, or had somehow eluded them.

Wherever he was, *El Rey* wasn't there.

῾ ῾

Cruz wasn't surprised. While the badge photo had been a lucky break, their losing streak in the case had held, and it had been too little, too late. That was how things had been going from the outset. The assassin always seemed to be one step ahead of them or had benefitted from pure luck, such as getting fired before they collared him. Cruz began to have a little empathy with the men on the *El Rey* taskforce who'd made zero progress in over a thousand days.

He'd met with them and turned over the photo, in the slim hopes their network could generate a lead, but that was unlikely given they had no presence in Baja. In typical fashion, they hadn't even considered sending personnel to Los Cabos once the photo was in hand, preferring to question whether the likeness was even *El Rey*, considering that it didn't resemble most of the sketches. In truth, Cruz couldn't prove it was him any more than they could prove that it wasn't, so it was a classic stand-off. They obviously felt that Cruz was encroaching unfairly into their investigation, while he believed they were incompetent asses. Relations remained cordial, but strained, and Cruz expected nothing helpful.

The rest of the week was similarly frustrating. There was no buzz on the streets, the flesh trade had yielded no leads, and *El Rey* didn't buy drugs from any of the local substance purveyors. The team continued to go through the motions, but each day brought an increasing sense of hopelessness as the opening date of the G-20 summit loomed with no progress on their end.

The only good news was that Cruz's chest wound was healed and hardly ached at all any more. The leg was also mending, albeit grudgingly. He'd been to the physical therapist for instruction on exercises he could do, and religiously performed them every morning and evening.

The other surprising occurrence was that Dinah had taken to calling every few days to follow up on the case and to see how he was doing. Cruz was unsure how he felt about that. It had been two years since his family's heads had been shipped to him, and life inevitably had to move on, but it had also *only* been two years since the tragedy, and he wasn't sure he was ready for anyone new in his life. He felt guilty over his attraction to her, but also recognized that it was mutual – he could tell by their conversations, where Dinah had subtly but unmistakably indicated interest; women didn't call regularly to see how you were doing out of a sense of charity. Even though he'd been off that horse for some time, he still hadn't completely forgotten how to ride.

Cruz woke up every day with a sense of impatience, and a tremor of doom, as the days to the summit counted down. He'd made scant headway and wasn't kidding himself. At the rate they were going, *El Rey* would succeed in his objective, and life for every man, woman and child in Mexico would forever change, as their neighbor to the north exacted retribution for the nation's savagery. That was a future Cruz didn't want to see, and it was that prospect that kept him getting up early to fight to prevent it with every ounce of energy at his disposal.

怘怘

The Acapulco night cloyed hot and humid, the air scented with the distinctive verdant aroma of the tropics. Off in the distance, the lights of the waterfront strip twinkled as partygoers celebrated their Friday *fiesta*, dancing and drinking until the oncoming dawn chased them to bed. The town was in decline from its heyday in the Sixties and Seventies, when the Hollywood set had made Acapulco and Puerto Vallarta must-go-to destinations, but it still saw its share of celebrants from Mexico City due to proximity – at a hundred and eighty miles away, it was the closest accessible beach resort, and still a popular getaway for those seeking a respite from the densely populated *Distrito Federal* – the term used by locals for Mexico City and its surrounding environs.

Cartel violence had sullied the reputation of the seaside paradise for the last decade. It had joined the ranks of notoriously embattled areas like Morelia and Culiacan, as roving gangs of armed thugs terrorized whole neighborhoods, and the cops either stayed away or were on the drug traffickers' payrolls. Still, the tourist zone along the water was relatively safe, and travelers from the southern Mexican states went there in droves, ignoring the sporadic outbursts of violence.

Booming music and trills of laughter drifted up into the hills, the din amplified as it refracted off the placid water. *El Rey* jabbed at the button to raise his driver's side window so he could hear himself think. He'd been in town for two days and had finally connected with his contact: a minor underworld facilitator who claimed to be able to get him anything he wanted, and had proved useful doing so in the past. The beauty of this transaction, if consummated, was that the local network could reliably get the items he required into Baja with no problems. That was worth the supplier's substantial premium, because delivery was as much of an obstacle as securing the required materials.

The industrial section of Acapulco was ominously dark and seething with menace. It was infamous as an area where people disappeared, where headless corpses with bound hands cropped up all the time. Even a predator like *El Rey* experienced a sense of trepidation sitting alone outside the deserted warehouse at midnight, waiting for the appearance of his host. He'd had a discussion with the man over the phone, where a price had been agreed upon, along with detailed specifications for the order, but he'd wanted to be paid in cash, as was increasingly the case due to anti-money laundering provisions in the formerly compliant banking industry. So *El Rey* had gathered a knapsack and seventy thousand dollars, before driving southwest from Mexico City, sticking to the toll roads in order to avoid the ever-prevalent banditos who haunted the free roads.

The last few times he'd needed something special he couldn't get in Culiacan or Mexico City, this contact had arranged for the goods to come into Manzanillo, the main port on the Pacific side, yet another dangerous town in the trafficking chain that ran up the coast. All shipments from South America that came up the west coast offloaded at Manzanillo, so it was a natural hub for criminality and violence.

El Rey assumed that this shipment would traverse the coastline via shrimp boat or small freighter before changing craft somewhere off Manzanillo, and then move north into the Sea of Cortez from there. The logistics of the smuggling didn't interest him, as long as the items arrived in time, which is why he was willing to pay this source double the price asked by less-established providers.

A Toyota Sequoia with a bank of spotlights across its roof swung around the corner and rolled to a stop at the curb in front of the warehouse. Four men got out, surveying their surroundings before approaching the building and unlocking the multiple locks on the heavy steel entrance door. Two of the men took up a position on either side of the entry and stood with their hands in their loose sweatshirt pockets, the bulges of their pistols obvious.

El Rey waited to ensure that was the total welcoming party, and then pulled up the street with his lights out until he was twenty yards away. He opened his door and stepped onto the wet pavement, slick from a cloudburst a few minutes earlier.

The synthetic soles of his boots gripped the surface securely. He walked confidently towards the two men, the bag and his free hand clearly visible so as to avoid any accidental bouts of nervous shooting. After a brief confirmatory discussion, one of the men made a cell call, and a few moments later, the door opened and his source welcomed him into the dank interior.

"Greetings, my old friend. Glad to see you. You found the place with no complications?" Gerzain, the vendor, asked.

"No problems."

Pleasantries concluded, they walked through the depths of the cavernous expanse until they arrived at a set of wooden crates. Another man waited nearby. Gerzain gestured to him. He approached with a crowbar and wedged it between the crate and the sealed top, then expertly pried it loose. Gerzain reached in and brushed aside the straw packing material, and stood back so his favorite client could inspect the goods. *El Rey* moved to the crate and crouched down, rubbing his hands along the cold smooth surface of the contents. He stood and nodded to Gerzain, who smiled with pride.

"Nice," *El Rey* said.

"You only need the one? I'm having a double-discount sale tonight...," Gerzain offered.

El Rey considered the proposition, but then shook his head.

"And the rest?" *El Rey* asked.

"Being manufactured. It's a very unusual request, and will take every bit of the two weeks I quoted you."

"No problem delivering everything to Cabo?"

"Nope. On time and on budget. Guaranteed," Gerzain assured him.

El Rey tossed him the bag of money. Gerzain smiled and began walking to the door. "Can I get you anything else? Hand grenades? Machine-guns? A tank?" he asked over his shoulder.

"Not tonight. You going to count it?"

Gerzain turned to face him, grinning, a happy man indeed.

"No need. I trust you."

∽∾

Cruz could now walk without crutches, using only the stainless steel cane that Briones had acquired for him, and following his doctor's orders, he walked as much as possible. He'd been driving into the office every day now, after going stir-crazy in the apartment for the first week. He was feeling increasingly fit as time went by.

He'd commandeered another Dodge Charger, and had the doors reinforced with half-inch steel plates at a local body shop – he'd learned a valuable lesson from his OXXO shoot-out, namely that having something that would stop all but armor-piercing rounds could be a life-saver. It still hurt him to operate the gas and brake pedals, but he was willing to suffer in order to regain his lost mobility.

The hunt for *El Rey* had gone exactly nowhere, and as the pages of the calendar turned and the summit raced towards them, Cruz's agitation level increased further still. He knew his hunch was right – the photo had proved it in his mind, even if the other agencies downplayed it. When he'd tried CISEN one final time they'd actually laughed at him when he'd shown them the photo and the sketch. His pride still stung from that one, but he wasn't in this for ego. They had the photo now, and hopefully would distribute it to their personnel leading up to the event. All he could do was push. The director had mocked his efforts, pointing out that the photo looked like a generic Mexican male under thirty-five, especially given the goatee. Not to Cruz, though, but perhaps he was too close to this now. He'd done his best, and would continue the hunt even if CISEN thought he'd lost it.

Cruz forced himself out of the office every night at eight, and was awake by six each morning. One advantage of residing in downtown Mexico City was that he could walk out his front door, turn right, and arrive at a really great coffee shop within a hundred yards. It had quickly become a favorite way to start the day, and the stroll was good for him.

This morning, he was making plans to vacate the apartment at the end of the week and ship out to Los Cabos for the final five days before the summit. He could be of more immediate use there than languishing at the headquarters in Mexico City, armchair quarterbacking from seven hundred and fifty miles away. Cruz would fly over with Briones and ten of his top men, and hopefully, catch a break. If nothing else, he could review the security for gaps and become conversant with the lay of the land – something that would be critical to blocking any attempt in advance.

Finished with his phone calls, he took the elevator downstairs and hobbled out of the lobby, squinting at the sun's already bright light. He was making his way down the block, thinking to himself that living downtown wasn't so bad, when an iron grip clutched both his arms while a reeking rag was held over his face from behind. Cruz fought against inhaling as long as he could while he struggled against his assailants, but succumbed to the urge and quickly blacked out.

CHAPTER 20

When Cruz came to it was getting dark. He slowly rotated his head, trying to orient himself. He was lying on a plush bed in a room with high ceilings; heavy wood beams supported large, flat roof tile slabs above him. Groaning, he stretched his arms to his side, then automatically reached for his weapon. Gone, of course. His skull was splitting, and he felt extremely thirsty, no doubt a byproduct of whatever his kidnappers had used to knock him out. Ether? Chloroform? He couldn't be sure. It probably didn't matter.

He sat up and spied an en-suite bathroom, the mottled marble vessel sink visible through the partially opened door. Cruz cautiously rose to his feet and moved to the faucet, slaking his thirst with several glasses of water. He noticed a needle stick on his left arm – so it hadn't just been the rag that had taken him down. He'd been drugged. He shook his head in an attempt to clear the fuzziness. Peering at his watch, he noted that it was six o'clock, presumably p.m. He'd been out at least ten hours.

Cruz spun around at the sound of the bedroom door being unlocked. It swung open and two muscular men entered. Cruz was largely recovered from his injuries but he was in no condition to fight the pair of goons, so he figured he'd wait for a better opportunity to escape. Besides, he had no idea where he was, so it would be hard to break free unless he could get his bearings.

The uglier of the two hulking men regarded him.

"Come with us."

The trio walked into the hallway of what he now gathered was a large hacienda-style house, the floors finished in three foot square saltillo tile and the walls sponge painted with a heavy hand. The furniture in the seemingly endless hall was rustic and dark, hewn from weathered wood, many of the pieces appearing to be hundreds of years old.

The passageway opened onto a courtyard, and the men led him to a veranda overlooking lush green hills, unspoiled by any other houses. *Where the hell was he?* This wasn't Mexico City, that was for sure. Maybe Guadalajara area?

A man in his sixties sat at a massive circular dining table, easily twelve feet diameter, eating soup from a lava bowl. Cruz did a double take and felt his heartbeat pounding in his ears. He stiffened automatically, causing the man on his right to grip his arm before forcing him into the seat opposite the man.

"I see you recognize me from my fan photos...," the man said.

"I'd know you anywhere," Cruz acknowledged. "Carlos Aranas. One of the most powerful men in Mexico, and head of the Sinaloa cartel."

"*One* of the most? You might want to rethink that. Try *the* most." Aranas grinned, dabbing at his moustache with a multicolored cloth napkin. "Want some soup? It's really incredible. The best tortilla soup you'll ever taste. From a recipe that's been in the family for generations."

"My last meal?" Cruz spat.

"Please. If I wanted you dead, you wouldn't be sitting at my table. I've gone to considerable trouble to get you here in one piece for this discussion. So don't insult me with idiotic assumptions. Now, do you want some of the finest tortilla soup in the world, or not?" Aranas asked equitably.

"I'm not going to dine with my family's murderer."

"Again with the idiocies. For the record, I didn't have any hand in the death of your family. If I wanted to send a message to you, I wouldn't do it that way. I'd chop your dick off and make you eat it. Much more direct. So last time, soup or no? You haven't eaten all day so I know you must be starving. Tell you what, since you're stubborn, I'll just assume the answer is yes." Aranas looked over Cruz's shoulder at one of the men standing silently behind him. "Chacho, have Yolanda prepare our guest a bowl of soup."

Cruz was startled by something wet pushing against his right hand. He jerked it away, looking down to see a boxer snuffling at him.

"I see you've met Frieda. Don't worry. She doesn't bite. Probably wants to see if you've got a treat for her. It's why she's so fat. Always on the prowl for food…," Aranas said.

In spite of the surreal circumstances, Cruz slowly lowered his hand and stroked the dog's head. She licked him appreciatively.

"There. You see? She likes you. Just don't let her get up anywhere near your soup. She's a glutton, and she'll drain it if you drop your guard." Aranas smiled, and slurped another large spoonful.

"What do you mean you had no hand in my family's execution? They had your scorpions in their mouths. That's your signature," Cruz accused.

Aranas sighed, and then his face lit up. One of the weightlifters set a massive black lava bowl of thick brown soup in front of Cruz, then set a spoon and colorful cloth napkin next to it. Aranas scooted a plate towards him on the slick mesquite table surface. It slid almost to the edge, by Cruz's napkin.

"It tastes better with a little lime. Try it. You'll see. I recommend two slices to start."

Cruz reluctantly squeezed two of the cut lime wedges into the soup, and stirred it. Aranas sat expectantly, waiting for him to sample it. He raised the steaming spoon to his lip and took a tentative taste.

"It tastes like shit." Cruz took another sip.

Aranas laughed with genuine merriment.

"I see you have a sense of humor. They didn't tell me that. Unexpected in an anti-drug crusader."

"I'm full of surprises. Now, what about my family?" Cruz demanded, slurping at the delicious concoction. Frieda wagged her stump tail and stared hungry holes into his profile, then sat on the tile floor, hoping for a morsel to come her way. Cruz glanced at her. She was fat, all right. But happy. Definitely happy.

"I had nothing to do with that, like I said. That was probably Santiago. He was a shithead, and he perhaps thought he was being clever. But he was an ally, so we'll leave it at that. You know I've cheerfully ordered hundreds of executions. There's no reason for me to deny this one. But it wasn't me."

"And I'm supposed to believe you?" Cruz waved his free hand, wet from Frieda's slurping. "You kidnapped me. Why?"

Aranas scowled at his now-empty bowl and then dropped his spoon into it.

"I needed to get your attention. I have it. So it worked." Aranas tapped a finger on the table while watching Cruz. "I want to tell you a story, and then I'll return you to Mexico City, unharmed. Your job in this is to listen to the story. I talk. You listen. This won't take long, so indulge an old man, yes?" Aranas reasoned. Without waiting for a response, he continued.

"About three months ago, Santiago approached me for a conference. We did a lot of business together, so I granted his request. He came to this house with a proposal for me." Aranas took a sip of water from the half-full glass. "A proposal that I declined."

Cruz waited for more.

"He'd gotten it into his head to do the unthinkable – an action that would polarize the population against the traffickers, and in my opinion, would result in a catastrophic set of events for Mexico. I tried to argue for reason, but he was adamant. He wanted to assassinate our president, in an effort to sway the upcoming elections for a candidate he had clout with." Aranas sat back. "The frontrunner had been killed recently, so he believed that if he took out the president, his man would have a very good chance."

Cruz nodded slowly, saying nothing.

"As you know, the Secretary of the Interior had been killed in November, and then *El Gallo* was executed…all probably related, but I digress. Santiago was convinced he could get his pet politician elected president, and use his position to take on his rivals while turning a blind eye to his traffic. It was naive and dangerous talk. But it was intriguing, I have to admit, and I wouldn't hesitate to back an idea if I thought it would be effective. But then he came to what I considered to be the deal-killer. He said that he also intended to kill the American president at the same time," Aranas recalled. "I asked him, why on earth he would want to brand Mexico with that, and kill a man who was, at worst, a figurehead? I could see taking out our president, but the American? It made absolutely no sense."

Cruz put his spoon quietly into his empty bowl, not wanting to interrupt the narrative.

"He couldn't explain his reasoning coherently. He just wanted to do it. He asked me if I would fund half the contract price. I wanted no part in it. It was lunacy, and I couldn't see any advantage to be gained by pursuing it.

I told him that if he persisted with the idea, our business together could be jeopardized, and later on, he agreed to drop it. Only I think he didn't. And after recent information reached me, I'm sure of it." Aranas snapped his fingers, and Frieda trotted over to him, her previous resting place a puddle of drool. He broke off a bread crust from the platter beside him and tossed her a piece. It disappeared with a swallow.

"I have my sources, even in your hallowed halls, *Capitan* Cruz. I know you're pursuing *El Rey*, and believe he's the hired gun to take down the presidents. This scheme originated with Santiago, or worse, it was fed to Santiago and he was stupid enough to buy it. It will be a disaster if it's successful. And that's why I had you brought to me. I needed you to hear this from my lips. I have no part in any plot to kill the president," Aranas finished. He'd said what he wanted to say.

"What was the contract price?" Cruz asked.

"Ten million dollars."

Cruz whistled.

"You think he might have been fed the idea. Why do you say that? Who would want to get him to do this?" Cruz asked.

Aranas stood and delivered a loving scratch to Frieda's ears. She looked up at him with unconditional devotion. Capitulating, he gave her another piece of bread. A large one.

He turned to face Cruz.

"That's part of the puzzle, is it not? What I can offer you is a name that I suspect strongly of instigating the scheme. You will need to do your own due diligence. Carefully, would be my advice. The name is Xavier Sorreyo. He had a lot of influence with my recently-departed associate."

"Sorreyo…I've never heard of him. Cartel?"

"Much worse. Now, if you don't mind, I need to attend to some chores that I put off to meet with you. Our business here is concluded. I got my message across to you, and what you do with it is your affair. But I wish you luck, *Capitan*. And I really didn't kill your family. I'm not sure that Santiago did, but it seems like the kind of thing the man would do. Now, if you'll excuse me, I have to run." Aranas smiled his charming smile again, teeth gleaming beneath his gray moustache. "If I ever see you again, I'll kill you like an ant. As I expect you would do with me. So now things return to normal, yes? You fight crime, I create it, and the world continues to turn, the spiders eating the flies." Aranas petted Frieda again and walked to the archway that led to the courtyard. "Thanks for coming, and good luck. You're going to need it."

Cruz braced himself to rise, only to find himself with the now-familiar rag over his face. He instinctively struggled, then gave in, recognizing the futility.

When he regained consciousness, he was sitting in the passenger seat of his car, the keys in the ignition, the doors locked, ventilation coming from the battery running the air. He checked the time. Two a.m. He grabbed at his shoulder holster and relaxed when he felt the reassuring bulk of his new Glock nestled there.

Cruz took a few deep breaths, trying to clear the fog from his vision, and registered an unfamiliar sensation in his clenched right hand. He opened it and stared down at the crumpled piece of paper stuck to his palm. On it were scrawled two words. A name.

Xavier Sorreyo.

❧❦

The next morning, Cruz felt like he'd drunk a bottle of rotgut tequila. The hangover effects of the drugs he'd been knocked out with were substantial. His mouth tasted like lead, his head was pounding, and the body aches were accompanied by a pronounced disequilibrium.

Cruz considered driving to the office, but decided against it. Instead, he called Briones to ask for a ride. Briones had been panicked yesterday by Cruz's absence, but didn't know what to do – and in truth, there wasn't much he could have done.

Briones wanted to know everything that had happened. Cruz promised to fill him in on the way to work.

Once in the car, Cruz recounted the story dispassionately while Briones' mouth hung ever wider in disbelief. Finished, he laid out their battle plan for the day.

"Obviously, Aranas felt that the name Sorreyo was important enough to warrant snatching me, so I think the priority needs to be getting everything we can on him."

"I still can't believe they did it. I mean, I know they're powerful, but that…it makes you kind of want to reconsider being a cop." Briones vocalized what Cruz had been thinking.

"He could have killed me at any point. And still could. I think that was the other part of the message – to clarify how things really stand," Cruz agreed.

"Why do you think he didn't?"

"Honestly? I believe Aranas wants *El Rey* stopped as badly as we do. He's afraid it will be bad for business, and he's right. It would. Especially if the Americans decide to *help* us in the war against the cartels by sending in a hundred thousand soldiers, which isn't out of the question if their president is killed. Can you imagine the outcry? It would be the end of the cartels, and also of Mexico as an independent nation. Aranas is no patriot – he's a killer, and a businessman who doesn't see a benefit in killing the U.S. president. So…he's on our side, for once," Cruz mused. "And I think he understands there will always be someone in my job, so it might as well be me – the devil he knows, if you like. That's the plain truth. We've been so unsuccessful against the cartels, he's not worried."

On that depressing note, they arrived at headquarters, and within a few minutes were entering Xavier Sorreyo's name into the system. Moments of processing later, a screen popped up informing them that the file was classified.

"Classified? By who? We're the damned cops. How can it be classified?" Cruz fumed. He smelled the hand of CISEN in this – and whenever an intelligence service was involved, it was never good. He remembered what Aranas had said when he'd asked whether the man was cartel: "No, much worse." Cruz had forgotten that part of the discussion up until now, no doubt an effect of the drugs. What could be *much worse* than mass-murdering drug traffickers? And be classified?

He'd tried the front-door route enough times and been humiliated out of the building, so now he'd do it the old-fashioned way. His cousin, Laura, worked at CISEN, and occasionally did him favors, as he had done for her. Cruz called her cell, and gave her Sorreyo's name, explaining the problem. She committed to getting information within a few hours, and told him she'd call him back when she had it.

Cruz worked with Briones on the logistics of setting up a functional remote command center in Baja, and before they knew it, the morning had flown by and it was one o'clock. Cruz's cell rang. It was Laura, wanting a meeting in thirty minutes at a restaurant they both liked.

He made it in twenty.

Laura entered ten minutes late. Cruz rose and kissed her. She was a handsome woman, three years older than he and almost as tall, with a full head of curly black hair going gracefully to gray. They sat, and after ordering, she slipped a single folded piece of paper to him.

He read it and stared off into space, puzzled. Then the pieces clicked into place. In a single burst, he understood that this was far bigger than a cartel boss wanting to assassinate the president. Three little letters, and it all came together for him, or at least a chunk of it did.

Cruz would never be able to interrogate *Señor* Sorreyo. He'd been the victim of a hit and run accident in Monterrey a week earlier. Then again, Cruz didn't feel as though he needed to ask him much, or think a meeting would have even been a good idea. There was little chance Sorreyo would have told the truth, about anything.

Xavier Sorreyo had been a CIA asset.

CHAPTER 21

San José del Cabo, Mexico

The hills around the conference center basked in the bright warm glow of the morning sun, a few lonely saguaro cactus standing like sentries, silently watching the unfolding events. The parking area and grounds were crawling with soldiers and security details, as the American Secret Service coordinated with its Mexican counterparts. Over a hundred army personnel formed a protective perimeter around the sprawling building, their M16 rifles ready to combat any threat. Two army helicopters sat at the far end of the field, and an area nearer to the convention center had been cleared and was ringed off by police for the president's helicopter to land. Armored military Humvees were poised like predatory jungle cats around the edges of the property as guards patrolled from station to station.

A crowd of protestors thronged behind barricades as the soldiers stood by impassively, sweat trickling down their necks from the already ninety-four degree heat. Signs in a dozen languages berated inequality, U.S. imperialism, poverty, banking syndicates, and the general unfairness of life. The protestors were a mixed bag – everything from hippies and college students to angry retirees. It was an unruly bunch, made more so by instigators who roused them into chanting every few minutes. The Mexican forces seemed uncertain how to deal with them, and were keenly aware of the phalanx of cameras from the global media cabal capturing the event for international consumption.

The commander of the crowd control squad had radioed for more backup, and two army trucks filled with yet more soldiers barreled up to the staging area. Fifty men leapt down from the backs, many now armed with shotguns loaded with bean bags for non-lethal stopping power. Several carried larger tear gas launchers, and two men moved towards the crowd with a case of pepper spray. The tension was thick as fog as a confrontation loomed and, perhaps sensing that the Mexicans weren't going to be as concerned with PR niceties as some of the prior years' hosting countries, the demonstrators grew more timid. Nobody wanted to catch a bullet or be incarcerated in a Mexican prison for months while a worried family back home paid through the nose to lubricate their release. This wasn't the U.S. or Europe – Mexico's patience was thin and its tolerance for civil disturbance limited in the extreme.

Cruz stalked the area by the building with his team of *Federales*, looking for signs of anything suspicious. With the hundreds of men moving around – soldiers, police, marines, American and Mexican security forces, CISEN, *Federales* – a sense of subdued pandemonium reigned as the hour for the opening ceremonies neared and the arrival of the participants drew imminent. All attendees and workers who approached the massive structure's entry were forced to pass through metal detectors, and two airport x-ray machines had been brought in from Mexico City to scan every item that would get within a hundred yards of the opening ceremonies. Bomb-finding dogs had twice sniffed their way through every square inch of the grounds, and the earnest pooches found nothing amiss.

American Secret Service bodyguards were salted throughout the presentation area, conspicuous due to their pale skin and the suits they wore in the simmering heat, and their protocols had been integrated into the event. The U.S. Secret Service was considered the best of the best, so there could be no more comprehensive protection for the attendees. They murmured into their palms and their eyes roved over the crowd and surroundings, clinically evaluating for possible danger. Between the Mexican special forces commando group, the regular army troops, the *Federales*, and the *Gringo* team, the delegates were safer than in their own living rooms.

Every possible security precaution had been taken, and yet Cruz was agitated. *El Rey* specialized in defeating the best efforts of those trying to stop him. This kind of circus was his specialty. Cruz didn't buy for a second that any of it would prevent the assassin from moving forward with his plan, whatever it was – although he couldn't for the life of him see how he could pull anything off, given the battalion of armed men guarding the event. And nobody could make it to or from the building alive if anything went wrong. All roads for a mile were blocked by armed soldiers and a phalanx of federal police, and traffic had been diverted so only the delegation vehicles would be on the road to the site.

Cruz studied the huge black two story structure. Remarkable that they'd completed it in time. He'd been in town for a week, and right up until the final seconds, crews of frantic workers had rushed to complete details and repair systems that were already beginning to fail. He checked his watch – the delegation would be arriving in a few minutes. The buzz in his stomach increased its strident alarm, but there was nothing obvious he could do now. Everyone had the photos of the man Cruz believed to be *El Rey*, and the convention center was more fortified than a maximum security prison. He'd done everything possible.

He lifted the binoculars to his eyes and scanned the surrounding hills, the bases of which were over six hundred yards away. The conference center was surrounded by slopes on three sides, covered almost entirely by short, brownish scrub that had been grazed to the nub by a herd of wild goats – escapees from the small petting zoo belonging to the school at the bottom of the hill. He scrutinized every cranny. There was no place for a man to hide, and even had there been, the distance would have made a shot tricky; there was a considerable breeze, with gusts whipping at the semi-circle of flags fluttering above the facility's entrance.

A murmur rose from the packed group of media and protestors as a line of limousines drew up the newly-paved road that delineated the fourth side of the compound. The moment everyone had been waiting for had arrived. The cars pulled past the throng and began moving to the entrance, where the opening ceremony was going to begin. A large blue-and-white-striped marquee stood to one side, where the performers and presenters nervously awaited their turn in the spotlight.

The crowd's eyes rose to the beating of rotor blades, as two more helicopters approached and then hovered over the field, finally coming to rest on the designated area of tarmac. The aircraft doors opened simultaneously, and a group of men in dark suits stepped briskly from them both, forming a protective barrier as the presidents of Mexico and the U.S. stepped out, waving at the crowd before moving to glad-hand each other in a staged symbol of friendly solidarity. The crowd of protestors booed and shook their handheld signs while the press corps filmed the arrival.

Cruz eyed the group of journalists nervously. All of their equipment had been searched and scanned, but he still suspected a trick. Briones stood by his side, similarly engaged by the sight of all the cameras pointed at the two great men. They exchanged glances, and Briones unconsciously fidgeted with his sidearm. A persistent fly buzzed around his head, and he swatted at it in annoyance before wiping his brow. On the parking lot, the temperature was blazing, the sun's energy baking the grayish-black surface, multiplying its effects as it radiated heat.

Briones' eyes were drawn to a movement on the periphery of the protestors; something alarming he barely registered. A bearded man had drawn back his arm and was preparing to hurl a projectile. The lieutenant sprang into action, covering the twenty yards to the edge of the barricades in seconds, gun drawn, ready to fire. The soldiers froze, weapons now trained on the crowd rather than pointing at the ground, and for a small slice of eternity time stood still. Briones' eyes locked on the man's face, and he seemed to swivel his head in slow motion to watch the uniformed federal policeman racing at him, pistol aimed at his head. A few of the other protestors, sensing a problem, drew back, leaving him fully exposed.

He slowly lowered his arm, and Briones screamed at him to freeze: not to move. The man looked somewhat like the photo, but it was hard to tell with all the facial hair and the knit Rastafarian cap. The soldiers automatically made way for the lieutenant, who pushed the nearest barricade aside as he stalked towards the man, ready to fire. The crowd had gone silent, and a few of the media had turned their attention from the two world leaders walking to the convention center, to the drama playing out between the menacing, pistol wielding policeman and the peacefully-convened protestors.

The soldiers stood nervously, fingers on triggers. There was a very real sense that the situation could escalate into a bloodbath in seconds. All it would take was a single case of nerves and the area the crowd was gathered in would become a slaughterhouse. The throng sensed this and backed away, as a group, nobody wanting to be martyrs in a desert backwater a thousand miles from anything.

Briones reached the man, and, holding the gun to the hippy's head, cautiously reached down and lifted the man's hand to see what he'd been attempting to launch. He saw a flash of red. A tomato.

Briones removed his cuffs and locked them on the man's wrists as the crowd, sensing the conflict was over, jeered at him. He pushed his captive to the barricade, where two of the soldiers took charge of the dangerous vegetable assailant. Briones marched back to where he'd been standing with Cruz, followed by boos and catcalls of 'Gestapo' from the protestors, his face redder than the tomato. The soldiers relaxed, the fire drill over, and returned their barrels to pointing at the ground, a few of them smiling nervously with relief. The presidents' security details hadn't registered the lightning-like scuffle, although Briones' wooden features would become an infamous symbol of totalitarian abuse of power across most Western television networks that night.

An older uniformed soldier moved over to Cruz from the assembled group of military functionaries, and leaned into him, speaking softly. "You better get your attack dogs on a tight leash, *Capitan*. That almost turned into a disaster over a tomato. Get your shit together, or you're going to be asked to leave." General Ortega eyed Briones through eyes like slits. "I do not want any more outbursts, do you read me?"

Cruz's stare darted to the imposing officer's face, and he nodded, once. Message delivered, the general turned and marched back to his position with the other military brass assembled near the stage.

"What the hell, Briones," Cruz started, still watching the crowd, painfully aware of the cameras documenting the incident, as well as their every move now.

"I just saw the movement and reacted. I'm...I'm sorry, sir."

"I think maybe you should take a walk around the perimeter and verify all is in order. Try to stay as far from the cameras as possible, all right? Hopefully they'll lose interest in a few minutes. And do not, unless *El Rey* is standing with a bazooka pointed at the presidents, draw your weapon again. Clear?" Cruz spoke softly, but the steel in his tone was unmistakable.

Briones moved to do as instructed, glad to have the scrutiny shifted back to the gathered functionaries.

The two presidents had taken seats at the front of the raised platform that would serve as the stage, erected that morning and checked and rechecked by the security forces. The gathered delegates surrounded the two men, and cameras clicked and whirred as the moment was captured for posterity. The Mexican president stood to applause from the delegation, and moved to a solitary microphone on the stage, which faced the assembled dignitaries but was also turned sufficiently so that the media were presented with his left side. He had become polished enough to gleam at these types of events over the five and a half years of his term, and he moved and spoke like a veteran statesman.

Cruz listened to the predictably hackneyed aphorisms about global cooperation and a new era of peace and studied the gathered journalists, eyes scanning restlessly over them before continuing to the roof of the center, where several snipers watched the crowd. He rotated slowly, studying the protesters, and then moved again to the hills. He caught a movement on a far bluff and raised his binoculars, ready to warn everyone to get down.

A baby goat nosed the shoots of a struggling plant at the base of a cactus and was quickly joined by its mother, who scooted it away, back to the others on the far side of the hill.

Cruz lowered the glasses and blinked the sweat from his eyes. The blistering heat wasn't doing anything for his already frayed nerves, that was for sure. His only consolation was that at least he hadn't run in a hobbled trot while brandishing his assault rifle to save the delegation from a toddling *chiva.*

The president finished his speech and the American president took the stage. Cruz spoke passable English from his university years and so understood most of it. A relationship forged through common goals, a new era, commitment to prosperity. About the same as *his* president's spiel. He absently wondered what would have happened if they'd switched speeches, whether anyone would have even noticed. For the first time that day, Cruz smiled.

The American's rendition was blissfully short. He sat to polite applause. Now there would be half an hour of festivities, including the presentation of the key to the city, some dancing by the local high school girls, and a *fiesta* with some first graders, and the welcoming event would be over, and everyone could move into the air-conditioned comfort of the new hall.

His trepidation increased with each passing minute. The governor of Baja California Sur made a mercifully brief set of comments and then presented the key to the city to the American president. Once everyone had taken their seats again, music blared out of the speakers that had been brought in with the stage, and the dancing began, the girls twirling in native garb while the gathered politicians feigned polite attention. Cruz had personally been involved with checking the speaker cabinets and associate audio gear for any booby-traps, so there was no danger there.

Things were going as planned, but he still had a tingling at the nape of his neck, a premonition of something about to go badly wrong. He tried to shake it off, but it lingered like a bad taste.

He wiped more sweat from his face and prayed it would be over soon.

El Rey watched the presentation with little interest. So far, no surprises, although the security detail did seem to be on a more heightened alert than usual. He'd studied hours of footage of speeches and rallies with both presidents, and knew their procedures cold. They were nervous, that much was clear, likely due to the ruckus the federal police captain had raised. No matter. He was within a hundred yards of the targets, and soon they'd be a bloody pulp, and he'd be gone during the confusion.

The girls took the stage, and he watched with a grim smile as they performed their intricate footwork for the leaders of the free world.

Soon to be ex-leaders.

He hummed along with the music, shifting his weight from one foot to the other as he held his rifle at the ready, lest anyone try to attack his president.

Inside the tent, the two teachers were having a hell of a time with the kids. Amped on soda and nearly shaking with anticipation, they were running around their area of the tent like hellions – even the little girls. Normally better behaved, the heat and the large crowd had sent them berserk, and it was all Monica and Lety could do to control them.

Three of the little boys were especially ill-behaved. They kept swatting at the *piñata* with the pole reserved for that purpose, and Lety was afraid they'd break it apart in the tent, which would spoil the whole ceremony. After hearing a particularly alarming *thwack* from the enormous suspended papier-mâché bull, she turned to see the little bastards smiting it with all their might, not two minutes after she'd punished them for doing so earlier. She was worried they'd knock the sorry creature's head off and was already mentally calculating where she could get glue to re-affix it if they got away from her again and succeeded in their assault on the candy-stuffed totem.

She grabbed one of the tiny assailants by the hair to get his attention, tweaked another by the ear, and dragged them away amid noisy protests. Once she had them under control, she confiscated the heavy stick so they couldn't do any more harm to the endangered animal. Monica moved several chairs as an improvised blockade to keep the feisty tikes from doing any further damage. She looked up at the blank bovine stare the artist had created and took a deep breath. It would all be over soon, and then they could return to the classroom and some semblance of order.

The bull was large for a *piñata*, over four feet long by three high, which was part of what made it irresistible as a target for the kids. Colorful ribbons hung from around its neck, and a chrome metal ring dangled from its nose. It weighed a good forty pounds due to all the candy inside, and Monica silently offered thanks to its fabricator for making it sturdy enough to withstand the pummeling from the toddlers' searching blows. Little Stefan, especially, had already delivered substantial punishment to the effigy's shoulders and head, and Monica cursed the little prick as she studied the cracks and gouges the pole had inflicted. She fished in her purse and withdrew a black felt pen, and worked furiously to mask the bulk of the abuse. As long as nobody got too close, it would pass muster. Now she just needed to keep little Satan and his friends from completely destroying it in the next ten minutes, and they were home free.

El Rey yawned as the girls finished their performance to a smattering of lackluster applause. He was glad it wasn't him having to dance like a monkey in the sweltering sun for the amusement of a bunch of suits. An elaborate fabric tarp had been suspended over the seating area to fend off the worst of the June blaze, and large fans blew ventilation across the seated dignitaries, but even so, whoever had thought it would be a good idea to do this outside had been misguided to the point of delusion.

He studied the overhead white linen billowing in the breeze and imagined what it would look like soaked in the assembled group's blood. Now that would be something the media would remember. It was all he could do not to detonate the bull now, just to end the misery.

The *piñata* had cost a fortune to create – a one-inch shell of a new explosive three times more powerful than Semtex. He'd sourced it from Russia, a half-inch thick coating of carbon fiber etched with grooves so that when the animal blew apart hundreds of razor-sharp shards of half-inch square projectiles were created, effectively shredding everything within the blast range to smithereens. And lest that wasn't sufficiently destructive, roughly half the candy inside was in reality carbon fiber bearings milled to match the gum balls they'd loaded the creature with, which would also hurtle outward at near the speed of sound. They'd even tested a sample of the new explosive with two bomb-sniffing dogs from the airport in Manzanillo, and they'd passed by the bull without interest – apparently, they didn't know what prototypical Russian explosives smelled like.

He'd conceived of the design himself after reading about the claymore mines used by the U.S. military, and the devastation they inflicted. The engineer who'd manufactured it had assured him that nothing would survive for a forty-yard radius – and the presidents were seated ten yards away, at most. They'd be hamburger once it detonated, and the resulting carnage would be panoramic – a fitting pinnacle on which to end his already infamous career.

El Rey shifted the M16 to his left hand as the first grade class, dressed in white peasant pants and shirts, pranced out onto the stage, the girls peering nervously at the audience while the little boys' eyes stayed glued to the *piñata* like it was made out of chocolate. The Mayor and Governor took the stage again, and together hoisted the bull aloft, having secured it to a wire suspended from the stage framing. They would hoist the *piñata* provocatively to extend the fun as the children took turns swatting it, waiting eagerly for the payload of candy to come raining down on them.

Not today, kids.

The miniature high frequency transmitter-triggered detonator in the *piñata* was the only problem he'd encountered. He knew everything coming into the area would be x-rayed, and while the carbon fiber would pass through clean, appearing to be nothing more than part of the plaster used to fabricate the creature, and the bearings would resemble the rest of the gumballs, the detonator had to be made out of metal – wires to conduct the necessary electric pulse, a tiny battery to emit it, and an antenna. The nose ring had been the designer's suggestion, and it had worked like a charm. The *piñata* was ready for its denouement on stage, and nobody suspected anything.

Overhead, on the trim at the top of the ebony conference center, the sun's harsh rays gleamed off the black feathers of a silent spectator, its avian eyes coldly appraising the gathered children and the bovine target of their excitement. Nobody noticed the crow in all the pandemonium – it was, after all, only a bird.

A blast of music from the speakers startled it from its position and it took flight, emitting a cry that was lost in the hubbub from the stage below.

El Rey, to all the world just another of the hundreds of soldiers chartered with keeping the world safe from the cartels, cautiously slid his hand into his camouflage pants pocket, preparing to push the button. He'd had a hacker in Ukraine list his new name two days ago on the security force's roster and had spent the last two nights in the temporary barracks that had been erected to house the troops on the road to the airport. He was just another faceless, anonymous drudge, his appearance altered with a military buzz cut and cotton padding in his cheeks. He'd long since shaved the goatee off. To any observer he would look like a hapless Mexican serviceman from the hinterlands, albeit a sergeant – he needed a suitable cover for his age, given that most of the enlisted men were eighteen to twenty-two; and he also wanted to ensure he would have sufficient rank to be able to roam, rather than being stationed too far from the stage for the transmitter to reach.

Steeling himself for the blast, he winced almost imperceptibly, and pushed the button, waiting for the blinding flash and then the horrified screaming.

Nothing happened.

Unbelievingly, he pushed it again. Same result.

He quickly estimated the distance between himself and the stage and calculated that he was no more than eighty yards away.

Fuck.

He moved closer to the stage, eyes fixed on the bull, and depressed the button again.

More nothing.

It wasn't going to work.

He momentarily contemplated spraying the presidents with lead from his rifle, then dismissed the idea. The goal was not to get killed today. It was to kill. Trying to shoot them would be suicide.

No, he had to abort.

El Rey pushed the button one last time, and when the stage didn't vaporize in a blinding flash, he decided to terminate the operation and live to fight another day. All he had to do was wait out the performance.

Except of course, that once the *piñata* came apart and it became obvious that half the candy was in reality custom-crafted projectiles, everyone in the vicinity would be put under a microscope. Even as good as his cover was, it wasn't designed to withstand that. No, it was time to pack it in and slip away. Or in this case, run away. He'd been assuming that the scene would be one of chaotic pandemonium, not calm, when he made his getaway.

Which posed a problem. But not too much of one.

He was, after all, *El Rey*.

❧✿❧

Briones listened as the girls finished up their jig and the music terminated. From his position at the rear of the building, he peered into the hills, alert for any threat. His nerves were shot after the incident with the would-be tomato thrower, and he forced himself to take deep breaths to slow the adrenaline rush. He held out his right hand, palm extended down, and considered the tremor, a byproduct of the fight-or-flight reflex he'd triggered when going after the protestor.

Pull yourself together, dammit.

He was chagrined by the end result of his charge into the crowd. Briones had been a split-second away from blowing the man's head apart – he'd started squeezing the trigger before he'd registered the tomato. Just the memory of it caused the tremor to worsen. He told himself to calm down and focus on the job at hand.

Maybe they'd gotten it wrong. Maybe the entire *El Rey* thing had been bullshit, just as CISEN had obviously thought. Perhaps the *Capitan*, racked by grief over his family and blinded by hatred for Santiago, had invented a new crusade to bring meaning to his life. Briones was starting to doubt the entire hypothesis now, just as he was doubting his instincts after nearly killing the hippy.

Briones wound his way around the structure, noting that the soldiers stationed every thirty feet seemed alert and ready. Soon he was standing by the side of the stage, watching the kids trot out to do a cloyingly cute presentation, replete with a badly out-of-tune song, before breaking open the *piñata*. He wiped his face with the arm of his long-sleeved shirt, blotting sweat, and cursed his fate. There were bound to be repercussions from the tomato incident. He wasn't looking forward to discovering what they would be; probably a shift in his career to working traffic in the desert or something similarly awful.

Briones noticed movement on the far side of the stage. A soldier had inched towards the dignitaries, probably to get a better view of the kids, and now was moving away again. Briones' stomach twisted. He watched the man slowly saunter back to his position, and then continue walking easily in the direction of one of the Humvees sitting at the edge of the grounds, near the access road. Two soldiers rested against the vehicle, scanning the hills with boredom now that the presentation was winding down.

There was something wrong. He couldn't place it, but he knew, just as he'd known there was something off about the vagrant in the alley. What was it that Cruz had told him? Trust that instinct.

Casting aside his doubts, he set off in pursuit, cautiously, so as not to arouse suspicion or create a scene if he was wrong yet again. The soldier was three-quarters of the way to the vehicle now, so Briones picked up his pace to a fast walk. As he closed on the man, he called out to him, his hand on his holstered pistol, ready to draw, but not doing so yet, remembering the admonition from Cruz. The man didn't hear him, so he called out louder.

"*Oye*. You. Wait up. *Federales*. Just a second," he yelled now that they were far enough from the stage he wouldn't disrupt anything with his exclamation.

The soldier turned, gun pointed at the ground, his posture relaxed. Briones got within twenty feet of him, then saw the man's eyes. It was the vagrant – but his face was different somehow, fatter and heavier. He jerked his pistol free and prepared to fire.

CHAPTER 22

El Rey heard the call from behind him but ignored it. Every foot closer to the Humvee was a foot closer to safety, so he kept moving, subtly increasing his speed by lengthening his stride. The call came again, and he turned, resigned that the game was up. There was only one reason someone would be following him, and it couldn't be good.

He watched as the man in the distinctive blue uniform strode towards him, and then their eyes locked, and he watched the man pull his gun.

Two shots exploded out of the assassin's combat jacket pocket, catching the cop in the chest and the shoulder, knocking him off his feet, his gun clattering uselessly beside him on the pavement. The silenced compact automatic pistol was almost soundless, and he turned and trotted the remaining twenty yards to the two soldiers by the vehicle – thankfully, both privates, and both relatively green.

"Men. Quick. Over there. That man – the federal policeman. He's down. Help him. I'll get the truck. We need to get him to a hospital." *El Rey* saw the confusion in their eyes. "Now!" he bawled at them. "That's an order. He's been hit. Get a move on!" They sprang into action, and jogged over to where Briones lay.

El Rey climbed into the driver's seat and cranked the engine, jamming it into gear and tearing across the road and straight to the hills. He only needed a half minute head start, and he'd be golden. It would be just like if he'd been successful, only with more pursuit. The wind dried the sweat on his face as he bounced along, the massive four wheel vehicle's heavily knobbed tires gripping the steep slope as it climbed towards the peak above.

৵৵

The soldiers made it to Briones, who was bleeding heavily from his shoulder. His vest had stopped the shot to the chest, and though there would be a painful bruise, it wasn't a deal breaker – but the arm was: the bullet had nicked an artery, and blood spurted freely from the wound. He tried to speak, but found himself disoriented and momentarily unable to do so. Cruz, having noticed the downed man, came jogging over with a lopsided gait, his leg still hurting even weeks after the shooting. He leaned over him, putting his head close to the lieutenant's ear.

Briones struggled to talk.

"*El Rey*. There…"

He used the remains of his energy to point in the direction of the Humvee, now three quarters up the hill and throwing out a cloud of dust. Cruz looked back down at him, and Briones' eyes rolled back into his head as it fell limp against the pavement.

"Get an ambulance. Run. Hurry. Where's your commanding officer?" Cruz demanded.

"Over there." The soldier pointed to the group of soldiers in front of them, thirty yards away.

Cruz debated for a split second, and then abandoned his initial instinct, which was to commandeer one of the other Humvees and give chase. He moved to the officers, and quickly explained what had happened.

"He's out of range, and I don't think we want to shoot up the hills and cause an international incident. Get the helicopters loaded with some crack shots, and take off. I'll go after him with some men in one of the trucks," Cruz directed.

The officers were taken aback for a few seconds, gawping at the blood surrounding the fallen policeman before snapping into action. The general trotted over to a man holding the rank of major, and gave him direction. The major quickly held his radio to his mouth and barked a sequence of orders.

They were losing time. It would take several more minutes to get the choppers into the air, best case. That was too long.

Cruz limped over to the nearest Humvee and slung his rifle onto the seat next to him, calling to the three soldiers who were approaching.

"Get in. Now."

They exchanged furtive glances, then hopped aboard. Cruz gunned the engine, and then roared pell-mell up the hill in full-on pursuit.

Back at the stage, the kids were still whacking at the *piñata* with all their might, the drama taking place on the perimeter off to the rear side of the building invisible to the attendees. The roar of the diesel motors was muffled by the linen shade element and the dissonant fiesta horns blaring from the speakers.

When the two large military helicopters lifted off, the *piñata* festivities had grown tiresome, and the dignitaries were restless and hot. When the infernal creature hadn't fallen apart after ten minutes of determined swatting, that part of the summit entertainment was concluded by the Mayor, and the assembled attendees moved gratefully into the building interior, where refreshments and arctic air conditioning waited to greet them.

El Rey's Humvee slid to a stop by an old shed two hills north of the conference center. He studied the dust thrown up from a pursuit vehicle, and calculated that it had to be several minutes off. He tossed his helmet into the truck and shrugged out of the uniform, beneath which he wore black cargo shorts and a T-shirt.

He hurried to the shed and disappeared inside the abandoned structure. Emerging a few seconds later, he pushed a heavy-duty off road motorcycle to the side of the Humvee and jumped on the kick start. The motor roared to life. He kicked the gear selector and tore down the slope into an even more remote area of uninhabited brush.

Cruz came over the hill and saw the motorcycle leap into the air, landing with a puff of dirt as it raced into the wilds.

"Shit. We'll never get him in this," Cruz lamented. "How does this radio work? We need to let the helicopters know what direction he's headed, and that he's on a bike."

One of the soldiers jabbed at a button and turned a dial – within moments a voice crackled over the air. Cruz grabbed the microphone from him and barked directions to the pursuers before stomping on the gas and rocking down the hill, past the shed, to the arroyo down which the assassin had disappeared.

El Rey was enjoying the pursuit. The men in the Humvee had to be hating life right now, as they fought a losing battle to keep up with the nimble motorcycle. They didn't stand a chance.

He sped along the dry wash for several minutes, trailed by a cloud of reddish-white dust, and then swung up a tributary gulch that led to the uninhabited mountains that bisected the peninsula. Part of him wondered what had gone wrong with the bull. Everything had been so perfectly planned, and then it didn't explode. It was his first failure ever, which annoyed him more than being pursued by half the Mexican army.

Spotting the *choya* cactus with the streak of yellow paint on it, he made another right turn, and thirty yards farther down the rutted ground, pulled to a stop. All the planning was worth it, he reasoned with satisfaction. They'd never catch him, and even though he hadn't succeeded in his attempt to kill the two presidents, this escape would be spoken of in hushed awe by police for generations.

He killed the motorcycle engine and dismounted, then sprinted into a small cave that had been eroded by centuries of flash floods from the nearby mountains. He couldn't help but grin at the thought of his pursuers' plight.

Cruz saw the motorcycle tire tracks careen off to the left, and he spun the wheel, nearly flipping the burly vehicle when it lost its footing and skidded precariously across the dirt before straightening out. As they tore up the arroyo, they heard a sound from above. Cruz slowed, and the men searched the sky for the source of the clamor.

An ultra-light flew off into the distance, a single man at the controls, the off-white fabric of its wings glimmering against the blue sky. It was already over five hundred yards away, so well out of rifle range, leaving Cruz and the soldiers to gape at it in disbelief.

It banked over San José, and made for the coast and the sparsely inhabited East Cape area, the town receding beneath it as it pulled steadily away from them.

Cruz watched it disappearing from view as he radioed to the pursuing choppers. A few minutes later they *chucked* by overhead, a pair of gunships after little more than a kite with a lawnmower-sized engine propelling it.

A large part of him wanted to celebrate at the prospect of nailing the son of a bitch, but a tiny voice inside him countered that they wouldn't get him. *El Rey* might have been a homicidal psychopath, but stupid or careless he obviously wasn't. Cruz watched the helicopters tearing off in pursuit, and then, finding himself suddenly purposeless, twisted the wheel and headed back to the convention center, his part in the chase over. He wiped dust and sweat from his brow with the back of his sleeve and took a final glance over his shoulder, then shook his head and concentrated on retracing his route.

El Rey soared over the highway and then banked again, heading in the direction of the coast. He was looking for a very specific area and knew he was on borrowed time. The search team would now be looking for an ultra-light, so he'd need to ditch soon. Fortunately, everything was still going according to plan. He fished a cell phone from the knit bag suspended from the chassis and pushed redial even as he rapidly trimmed altitude.

"I'll be arriving in two minutes. Have everyone suited up and ready to go," he instructed into the phone, which he then dropped, watching as it fell two hundred feet to the ground, shattering against the desert rocks below. He was deliberately flying as low as possible so as to avoid possible radar hits, but there was always a chance they'd manage to still track him, so he'd taken an extra precaution.

He rolled onto a dirt road by a large cement factory and braked to a stop, shutting off the ultra-light motor before climbing to his feet. Three men, all dressed exactly like *El Rey*, stood by four all terrain vehicles, their engines putting in harmony. *El Rey* nodded to them and slipped on a waiting helmet. Now all four were indistinguishable. He had paid each ten thousand dollars to participate in a race, over alternative trails, to a common destination ten miles beyond the airport, halfway between that landmark and the coast. Every contestant had a route charted for him, and all had gotten half their money in advance, the rest to be settled when they arrived.

El Rey checked his watch with a flourish, and then gazed up at the riders, who were waiting anxiously for the race to start.

"Good luck, gentlemen. On your mark, get set...go!" He gunned the throttle and took off, as did the rest, each in a slightly different direction.

As his ATV tore across the dirt towards the coast, he heard the choppers approaching overhead. They'd managed to track the ultra-light, as he'd feared. Oh well. He glanced over his shoulder and saw that there were only two helicopters. One peeled off after the pair of racers who had gone north via an inland dirt track, and the other stuck with *El Rey* and his partner, who were taking the shore route. They cut back and forth, and then his partner shot up another dirt path to his left, and now it was just *El Rey* careening along the dilapidated road that followed the coast.

He glanced down at his speedometer; he was doing fifty miles per hour – dangerously fast on that stretch of marginal track. The helicopter, uncertain which vehicle to go after, had gained altitude, the better to follow them both. He knew how the pilot would have to react, and had anticipated that as he rounded the point and made it to the small beach outpost of Zacatitos. The other rider would soon branch even further inland, forcing his pursuer to make a decision. That would be in about three minutes at the rate he was traveling. He could see his twin's dust cloud to his left as they diverged.

El Rey was fairly confident that the soldiers wouldn't shoot at four ATV enthusiasts out for a good time. Even if they suspected one of being him, no officer would give the order to start shooting at civilians, creating an international incident at the most highly visible event of the year, especially absent any assassination. So far, the only crime had been shooting the nosy cop, which while serious, wouldn't justify gunning down a group of unarmed riders. He hoped he had called that one right, as otherwise at any moment he'd have fifty caliber slugs ripping through his back – assuming the Mexican soldiers could hit a fast moving small target from an airborne helicopter, which wasn't a given.

He still liked his odds.

As he rounded the point, the helicopter arrived at the expected moment of truth. He'd know soon enough which racer the pilot had decided to follow, so he slowed a little as he passed the houses in Zacatitos. He pricked his muffled ears for the chopper and heard it heading north, after the other man. His luck had held.

So far.

He continued up the coast road for another few minutes – not so much a road as a single car-width, badly-scarred dirt track with frequent washouts and jagged rocks stabbing out of the loose sandy surface. The ATV was the perfect vehicle for such terrain, and he wondered how the residents got their cars over the ruts, especially during the brief, intense rainy season.

A green beachfront house on his right sat atop a bluff, the ocean crashing below the gentle seaside slope. He approached the wall that ran around the perimeter of the property and then turned down the drive and pulled into the courtyard, taking care to close the gate after him. The house was vacant, the owners having left it empty during the unbearable summer months, which he'd gleaned from talking to a real estate agent who'd shown him the villa two weeks earlier. He'd broken in last week and made the meticulous preparations for his escape, confident that his gear wouldn't be disturbed – he had been the first prospect interested in visiting the home in two months.

The serenity was broken by the shuddering *whump* of rotors as the helicopter followed the road, three hundred feet above the ground. *El Rey* glanced at it and figured he had about twenty-five seconds. That would be more than enough time. He swung the metal garage door open, stepped inside and hefted his insurance policy to his shoulder. He hadn't had time to hide the vehicle. He was hoping they might miss the ATV out front, but wasn't betting on it.

Fifteen seconds later, the chopper was hovering fifty yards from the house, slowly dropping in altitude in preparation to land. When it was a hundred feet off the ground, a streak tore towards it from the garage, and then the aircraft exploded in a molten orange fireball, tearing apart into two immolated sections before dropping and crashing into the rocky soil beyond the road. A second explosion rattled the house windows as the fuel tanks detonated, and then all that remained was an inky-black column of oily smoke billowing from the wreckage.

El Rey set down the Iranian surface-to-air shoulder-fire missile and flipped the laser guide closed. It had performed as advertised. He was a satisfied customer. Maybe he should have taken the purveyor up on his double-discount offer.

Perhaps next time.

Knowing that the helicopter crash would draw more scrutiny within minutes, he pulled the ATV into the garage and shut the door. Now it was just another multi-million dollar house on the beach, sitting uninhabited with nothing suspicious to attract attention.

And what a nice beach it was. White sand, medium drop off, some submerged rocks, little undertow.

He peered out at the navy destroyer patrolling a mile offshore, at least five miles further along the coast towards San José. It wouldn't be a threat. The navy would be maintaining the no-passage area that had been set up off the town's beaches, to keep any threatening vessels from getting into range of the convention center, not attempting to search the dozens of boats fishing outside of the restricted area. They didn't have nearly enough manpower for that.

El Rey quickly stripped and donned the waiting neoprene wetsuit. He retrieved his dual-tank scuba harness and mask from the corner of the garage and after strapping it on, carefully walked down the beach, a pair of flippers in hand. Once in the mild surf, chest deep in the water, he donned the flippers and went under, checking the waterproof compass he'd strapped to his wrist. He swam out forty yards in search of a yellow nylon line with a float on it at the thirty-five-foot depth. Submerging until he could grab it, he pulled himself down until he was on the bottom, next to the two Torpedo 3500 scuba propulsion units he'd anchored there three days earlier. He unclipped them both from the chain and activated one, clipping the other onto the rear of the first. Each unit would run for roughly forty-five minutes, giving him an effective three and a half mile range underwater. And because he'd just be pulled along he wouldn't use nearly as much air as if he'd been swimming, so he'd make it to the waiting shrimp boat, out in the Sea of Cortez, no sweat. Three miles offshore, within an hour and a half, it would be stationed, waiting for his arrival, as arranged, the captain eager to collect the fifty thousand dollars his trip would bring.

Worst case, *El Rey* could swim it. But the Torpedoes were worth their weight in gold, and there was no point in over-exerting himself now.

He pointed the unit out into the open sea and got under way.

It was a good day for a boat ride.

CHAPTER 23

Kent hated his life sometimes. Most of the time he was master of the universe, moving the earth and exerting power over life and death, a kingmaker, a god of sorts. But occasionally he was bitch-slapped by fate and had to grovel and mewl to the real powers that be, who were predictably less intelligent or visionary than he.

This was one of those times.

He pushed the door open to the club, and the perennial, discreet, ageless man in black tie motioned for him to follow without uttering a syllable. They proceeded to a different room than the last visit – this one slightly larger and equally ostentatious. Inside, the Speaker of the House and three other older men sat scowling their discontent.

"What the fuck, Kent? Explain to me what happened, and where we go from here...," the Speaker of the House blurted.

Kent studied each of their faces in turn before replying. He sat down and sipped from the water glass at the side of his place serving.

"We lost this round. Everything was going perfectly, and then at the last minute, something went wrong. It happens. I haven't gotten a full briefing yet, but I expect details will creep in over time. It appears that the assassin who can never fail...did exactly that."

"Are we exposed in any way?" a concerned voice asked.

"No. By using a straw man, in this case the drug lord, Santiago, we created a Chinese wall. Total deniability. It was a Mexican, trying to kill the Mexican president, for reasons only known to Mexicans. End of story.

They kill each other all the time. This time, it didn't happen. And everyone goes on to fight another day."

"This is a disaster. I'm not sure we'll get another chance before the elections," the Speaker of the House complained.

"Probably not," Kent agreed. "A domestic assassination won't fly. This was perfect – our beloved president executed by slack-jawed madmen, our vice president stepping bravely into the breach…shit, it had Lyndon Johnson written all over it. The VP would have been a landslide victory, and we would have been guaranteed another four, or even possibly eight, years. Now, we have to go with the cards we've been dealt, namely an unpopular candidate fighting headwinds."

Another man chimed in – in his seventies, almost completely bald, with rodent-like features and darting eyes.

"What if his plane or helicopter went down? Wouldn't that stoke the sympathy fires?"

"Not nearly the same. In the first scenario, you have somebody else to blame – in this case, a group that many Americans have been coached to hate. Evil Mexicans. Satan's foot soldiers, killing our beloved leader as he heralded a message of peace and hope. With a domestic assassination, it's not so easy or clear, and you can't harness the fury factor. Let's learn from the whole war-on-terror gambit. Give the country someone with different cultural mores or skin color or language, and it's easy to characterize them as the enemy. But if it happens domestically, even by Muslims or whatever, it's not so clear-cut, especially after the last administration's flubs, invading other countries. For these things to really work, you need an undeniable, larger-than-life bad guy. That doesn't work so well if it's domestic." Kent paused to let the reality of the situation sink in. "This would have been perfect, but it's over and done with. We got close enough to kiss, but no sex. It happens. We just have to move on."

The Speaker of the House pondered his words. "All right. Kent's talking sense. We need to shift gears and get into campaign support mode. It would have been nice, but hey, we gave it our all and lost in overtime. Next time, maybe we win." The Speaker looked around, trying to collect a consensus. "Are you with me? And, Kent – you did a remarkable job. We just had some bad luck. We're not holding it against you, and I want you to know you're still a valued member of the team."

A chill ran up Kent's spine. "I'm glad to hear that. I've worked very hard to keep everyone's confidences, and I hope I get to continue doing so for a long time," he volleyed. Let them suck on that. There was no way he was going to wind up trying to swim with an engine block chained to his feet. If they had any bright ideas about taking him out, that would give them pause – that their confidences were in danger should anything happen to him.

The speaker held up his wine glass, toasting Kent.

"To another day."

⇛⇝

Cruz stood at the foot of Briones' bed, Dinah next to him, watching the monitor track the steady beating of his heart. It hadn't been too long ago that Cruz had been the one in this position. The view from the ambulatory side was better.

"The doctor says you'll be fine. A week living in the lap of luxury, waited on hand and foot by beautiful young nurses, enjoying the fine dining of the hospital commissary, and then you'll be playing tennis and cross-country skiing again in no time," Cruz assured him.

"You might want to get your skull checked while you're here. You sound delusional, *Capitan*," Briones warned.

"Seriously. How are you feeling?" Dinah asked.

"I've been better. But all things considered, this could be a lot worse. The blood loss was the main problem; the actual wound wasn't a big deal. If it hadn't hit an artery, I could have walked into the doctor under my own power," Briones assured her.

"Well, it seems you're going to get a commendation. And you managed to duck all the flack that came from you manhandling that poor innocent tomato-guy. It was hard for anyone in management to bitch when you'd taken a bullet keeping the presidents alive," Cruz reflected. He turned to Dinah. "Would you give us a few minutes? There are a few work things we need to discuss…"

"I still remember where the soda machine is." She appraised Briones, and then Cruz. "I'll see you in a few, *Capitan*," she said, before shimmying through the door. Both men watched the show admiringly.

"You're in real trouble there, *Capitan*," Briones warned.

"You may be right." Cruz pulled a chair to the side of the bed, and sat. "I'm sure you have a lot of questions, so I'll just tell you what I know and save you the trouble of drilling me. First, no, we didn't catch him. Second, no, we don't know where he is. Third, nothing we did stopped him. The truth is that the two presidents were saved by a hyperactive schoolboy amped up on too much sugar," Cruz explained.

"Come again?"

"Well, once you'd been stabilized at the local hospital in San José del Cabo, I went back over to the site, and we examined the *piñata* that the kids never got to break open. There was a reason. The whole thing was a bomb, with a carbon fiber shell. We found the transmitter trigger in *El Rey's* discarded uniform in the Humvee."

"I don't understand. So why didn't it explode? What happened?"

"The detonator was located in the bull's nose, concealed by the steel ring. The best our experts can tell, the wire from the battery had worked free – it was less than a millimeter out of place, but that millimeter was enough to render it useless. The battering from the kids slamming it must have jarred it loose. That's the only explanation," Cruz concluded.

"But I don't understand. They weren't hitting it yet when *El Rey* approached the stage. He must have been trying to detonate it then…"

Cruz nodded. "Correct. I didn't understand it either, so I went by and talked to the teachers as the kids were waiting to leave. One of them told me that a few of the boys had been bashing it like mad in the tent, and she had to fix it with a pen to cover up the evidence of the damage – most of it inflicted on the bull's head. So the kids' misbehavior saved everyone's life. Not our efforts. We actually failed miserably…"

"My mom used to say, it's better to be lucky than smart," Briones observed.

"Your mom was a sage woman. I have no argument," Cruz agreed. "Though whether she was lucky with her offspring…"

Dinah returned, and they made small talk for another few minutes before Briones began to visibly tire. For all the bravado, he'd come perilously close to dying – they'd actually lost him on the table for a minute in San José, though no one was about to tell him as much right now. Fortunately, he was young and strong, so they were able to revive him and get him stable enough to be air-ambulanced back to Mexico City, where the hospitals were considerably more advanced. He would make it and have a small puckered scar to show for his adventure, as well as honors from the force. But he still needed time to recover, so they said their goodbyes and left him to slumber.

Two armed *Federales* sat outside his door. Cruz experienced a sense of déjà vu. Nothing had changed. The bad guys still ran amok, they were still at war in their own country, and evil ruled the day more often than not.

Only on some days, they caught a break.

Maybe that was the story of the human condition.

For today it was enough.

Dinah nodded to the two stony-faced sentries and then took Cruz's arm.

"So, *Capitan*, can I convince you to have lunch with me? I recently came into some money, so I'll buy. It's the least I can do for a genuine, wounded hero," she offered, delivering a flash of teeth to sweeten the proposition.

Briones was right.

He was in trouble.

↋—↊

Mendoza was cold in late July – it had snowed two days earlier, typical of the Southern Hemisphere at that time of year. But today was one of those rare, crisp days when the sun warmed the sidewalks in the afternoon, making it practical to sit outside, admittedly with a sweater or jacket, and dine or sip coffee or wine at one of the myriad restaurants downtown. The area was quickly becoming one of his favorites, with a European architecture that was typical of the larger Argentine cities, but also with the particularly relaxed yet vibrant energy unique to South America. The population was attractive and well-educated, he'd found, mostly descended from Spanish or Italian stock; immigrants who had come to the region to escape the turmoil in Europe and make a new future, many in the hospitable valley's wine business. Mendoza had steadily grown into the largest wine production area in the country, with an area nine times that of Napa Valley, so whenever he tired of the bustle of the city, within ten minutes he could be out in rolling vineyards, the snow-topped Andes mountains towering in the background with picture-postcard perfection.

El Rey didn't drink alcohol, but he'd made an exception once he'd landed in Argentina, and he'd quickly incorporated a glass of wine with lunch and dinner – Malbec, of course. To drink anything else in Mendoza was close to sacrilegious. He still didn't like the small loss of control it brought, but he had to admit that the taste was an experience, so now that he wasn't on high alert at all times, perhaps he could relax a little.

He'd leased a flat two blocks from the Park Hyatt, near the expansive park that served as the central gathering place for the town's population on weekends and evenings, and had already settled into a pace after only a month in town. *El Rey* had found that Argentina was nothing like Mexico, and yet there were similarities; the language being the most obvious. The pace was faster but still suitably relaxed, and the locals also appreciated the *siesta*, brought across the Atlantic from Spain and a Latin American tradition. Every afternoon the shops all closed between two and four, and in some cases from two to five, so that the workers and proprietors could enjoy a leisurely lunch, followed by a snooze. It was a very civilized lifestyle, he had to admit.

The restaurants contrived fare fit for a gormandizer; he'd already found a few that rivaled the cream of Mexico and Europe, which he'd sampled while fulfilling contracts overseas. The beef was incredible, the Italian food superb, and new restaurants seemed to open daily even in the difficult financial times that seemed to be an inevitable part of the Argentine existence. He'd quickly come to appreciate that food was one of the most important things in the country's psyche, and the denizens took their time to savor the culinary bounty – everything else might be uncertain, but a good steak and a glass of wine was a constant in good times and bad. Currency crashes, purges, political upheaval and an economy in shambles might come and go, but a long lunch and a *siesta* were perennial.

He'd quickly tired of Rio, and had caught a television program on the wine country in Argentina, which had piqued his interest. Drawn by the picturesque footage he'd decided to trek south and spend several days roaming around the region, which had turned into a few weeks. Surprised that he wasn't anxious to keep traveling, he'd taken a flat on a month-to-month basis, reasoning that if he got tired of Argentina he could just move on.

The Los Cabos hit bothered him, but not so much that he was willing to return the money for the contract. Santiago was dead so he wasn't going to need it, and Mexico was too hot for him to operate in until any manhunt died down. He hadn't spotted anything online or in the newspapers about the summit or the cop he'd shot, so the Mexican authorities had obviously clamped a lid on it, pretending that nothing had happened. That was easier to do than one might think – no bombs had detonated, no audible shots had been fired. A military helicopter had crashed, which was regrettable, but helicopters bit the dust all the time. It was not unexpected, and the papers paid mere lip-service to it all, preferring to underscore how there had been none of the protests and civil unrest that had plagued the last few G-20 summits in Canada and France.

As far as the American and Mexican publics were concerned, nothing had happened except some boring meetings where a bunch of finance wonks had voiced the hackneyed tenet that the world was all screwed up, and getting worse. It had hardly rated a few column inches. The presidents waved at the cameras, vague assurances had been made, fake smiles had been dispensed like after dinner mints, and within a few days the entire affair was forgotten, other than a few amusing to *El Rey* side notes.

Ironically, the outrage over the Mexican federal policeman terrorizing the protestor had been the most memorable part of the G-20 summit coverage. Footage of the out of control officer, murderous intent etched deep into his features as he drew his weapon on the unarmed (save a tomato) peace advocate, received heavy network television and internet play, and the disheveled man in the Rastafarian cap had become somewhat of a minor celebrity, landing a few talk show appearances and even getting a book deal – though who would write it wasn't disclosed.

No news was forthcoming on the cop. *El Rey* figured he'd either survived, or the government had covered up the shooting. After all, Mexico got enough bad press without aggravating its image with reports of gun battles at the global financial summit.

The old shrimp trawler had gotten to him, right on time, and it had then taken forty-eight hours for it to make its way to Mazatlan, where he had disembarked and waved goodbye to a life at sea. Once on the mainland he'd taken a bus to Culiacan, where he had a condo with a safe containing half a million dollars in cash and gold. From there he'd driven one of his cars to Mexico City, where he'd sold it to a man he knew who could make things disappear, then boarded a flight to Santiago, Chile, using one of his four fake passports – this time, a Spanish one. In South America, a Spanish passport got you waved through customs without comment, a throwback to the times when Spain had been the conquering victors.

After a night in Chile's capital city he'd taken the recommendation of the hotel concierge and decided to start his explorations in Mendoza, which had gotten glowing reviews from the man, who had described it as a kind of paradise on earth. The rest was history. He'd settled in, found a few strip clubs with world-class talent, and cultivated an appreciation for fine wine and great food. He didn't know where he'd wind up settling permanently, but for now, Mendoza was as good as anywhere.

He swirled the deep purple liquid around the curve of the glass and savored the aroma as the waiter arrived with his entrée: a medium rare filet over a bed of grilled tomatoes and onions, drizzled with a balsamic glaze and accompanied by roasted vegetables and grilled potatoes. Heaven. He made a mental note to increase his time at the gym so he wouldn't pay the piper for his indulgences. It wouldn't do to get soft. One never knew what the future might bring.

Carefully setting his glass down, he sliced into the perfectly cooked filet and took a bite, admiring the way the beef flavor melded with the complements.

El Rey caught sight of his reflection in the restaurant window and saw a bohemian world traveler smiling back at him, enjoying the experience of being at peace with the world. He supposed he was, for once. For now.

He took another bite and leaned back in his chair, savoring his meal on the crisp, sunny day. His adventure as an assassin had come to an end and a new one as a *bon vivant* had started. He would miss the excitement and adrenaline of the chase, but there were always ways to keep himself stimulated. With the kind of money he had, that wouldn't be a problem.

He eyed the goblet of rich wine and took another sip, pausing to appreciate the aroma before filling his mouth with the intoxicating nectar.

A pair of chatting young women passed his table, the smaller one tossing him a flirtatious glance as they took a seat at a table at the café next door. He returned her look and smiled.

She smiled back.

Life was good.

ABOUT THE AUTHOR

Russell Blake lives full time on the Pacific coast of Mexico. He is the acclaimed author of the thrillers: *Fatal Exchange, The Geronimo Breach, Zero Sum, The Delphi Chronicle* trilogy (*The Manuscript, The Tortoise and the Hare,* and *Phoenix Rising*), *King of Swords, Night of the Assassin, The Voynich Cypher, Revenge of the Assassin, Return of the Assassin, Blood of the Assassin, Silver Justice, JET, JET II – Betrayal, JET III – Vengeance, JET IV – Reckoning, JET V - Legacy, Upon a Pale Horse, BLACK,* and *BLACK is Back.*

Non-fiction novels include the international bestseller *An Angel With Fur* (animal biography) and *How To Sell A Gazillion eBooks (while drunk, high or incarcerated)* – a joyfully vicious parody of all things writing and self-publishing related.

"Capt." Russell enjoys writing, fishing, playing with his dogs, collecting and sampling tequila, and waging an ongoing battle against world domination by clowns.

Sign up for e-mail updates about new Russell Blake releases

http://russellblake.com/contact/mailing-list

ABOUT NIGHT OF THE ASSASSIN

Night of the Assassin is best read as a companion piece after *King of Swords*. It can certainly be read first, but I suspect it will be more satisfying and resonate more if the reader digests *King* first, *Night* second, then the sequels. That's how I envisioned it, but you're free to do as you like. Even if read as a stand-alone or first, *Night* should entertain and satisfy. I'd just recommend it after *King*.

To grab a free copy for your Kindle or PC
or
purchase a quality hard copy from Amazon

visit RussellBlake.com for details

Made in the USA
Lexington, KY
19 April 2016